Hannah's
Gate

1994

Hannah's
Gate

Daoma Winston

Thorndike Press • Chivers Press
Thorndike, Maine USA   Bath, Avon, England

This Large Print edition is published by Thorndike Press, USA and by Chivers Press, England.

Published in 1994 in the U.S. by arrangement with Jay Garon-Brooke Associates, Inc.

Published in 1994 in the U.K. by arrangement with Piatkus Books.

U.S.   Hardcover   0-7862-0217-3 (Romance Series Edition)
U.K.   Hardcover   0-7451-2682-0 (Chivers Large Print)
U.K.   Softcover   0-7451-2683-9 (Camden Large Print)

The text of this Large Print edition is unabridged.
Other aspects of the book may vary from the original edition.

Set in 16 pt. News Plantin by Minnie B. Raven.

Printed in the United States on acid-free paper.

British Library Cataloguing in Publication Data available

Library of Congress Cataloging in Publication Data

Winston, Daoma, 1922–
    Hannah's gate / Daoma Winston.
        p.   cm.
    ISBN 0-7862-0217-3 (alk. paper : lg. print)
    1. Large type books. I. Title.
    [PS3545.I7612H36   1994]
    813'.54—dc20   94-20265

For Murray
who made all things possible

Chapter 1

All through that autumn's Indian summer lights had burned until dawn in the White House on Pennsylvania Avenue and in offices beneath the Capitol's glowing dome. Shining in long ribbons on the dark streets of Washington, they reflected the urgency of the times.

The depression decade was only recently ended. Then movie news reels had shown hungry people standing before soup kitchens. There had been other scenes too; Japanese soldiers marching into Manchuria, Mussolini saluting excited crowds in Rome, Hitler haranguing cheering mobs under swastika banners in Berlin.

German tanks blasted into Poland in September of 1939, and soon there were troops goose-stepping in Oslo, in Copenhagen, in Amsterdam and Brussels. Finally, by June of 1940, they were in Paris. Twelve months later they invaded Russia, pressing on toward Moscow.

While American radios broadcast word of the British withdrawal from Dunquerque, and Edward R. Murrow described the Nazis' rain of death from the skies over England, the Japanese allied themselves with Italy and Germany, and began to expand into Indochina.

Still, on this cold Saturday evening in the first week of December, few Americans foresaw what was to come, and most were busy with their own concerns.

Thus, Claire Loving, on a Capital Transit bus that lumbered north on Connecticut Avenue, was thinking about a man named Leigh Merrill. When the bus stopped, she climbed down.

The avenue at that point had wide sidewalks lined with small shops. Their windows shone with early Christmas decorations of poinsettias and holly wreaths.

Claire gave the happy displays a cursory glance, then turned expectantly to look at the parked cars.

Leigh had said he would meet her here if he could. Already she could feel the touch of his lips on hers, the strength of his arms drawing her close, the quick awakening of tiny pulses through her body.

But she didn't see him, nor his bright blue jalopy, old but lovingly re-painted every year. She hesitated. Should she wait, give him a few more minutes? A chill wet wind lifted her auburn curls and tugged at her dark green coat, ballooning her full skirt around her long rayon-claid legs. Her face was small, heart-shaped, nearly overwhelmed by her eyes. Large, slightly slanted, they sparkled with a mysterious gleam when she laughed. At other times they were dreamy. Often they were sombre. And now, for just a moment, they were sad.

She hated to miss Leigh. They didn't have enough time alone together. But she knew that no matter how much time they had, it would never be enough. She would always want more. That was how she felt about him.

But he wasn't here. Her disappointment became fatigue. She was suddenly aware that her feet ached. Her face hurt from straining for a constant smile while saying, "Hi! How can I help you?" or "Thank you. Come back again." And at the same time, contending with Lena, the other girl behind the handkerchief counter at Murphy's Five and Dime.

Claire decided that she'd better go home. Perhaps Leigh would call later on. Oh, she hoped so.

As she waited to cross the avenue Leigh pulled up. He opened the door, and she climbed into the car, laughing now, happy, no longer tired. "I thought you weren't going to make it," she told him.

A cigarette hung from the corner of his mouth. A lock of light brown hair fell across his forehead. He squinted long hazel eyes at her through a veil of smoke. "I almost didn't. My uncle kept finding things for me to do. But I finally got away from him."

His uncle, Jeremiah Merrill, was a successful attorney, a confidant of Harry Hopkins, who was President Roosevelt's right hand man. Jeremiah himself was at least an acquaintance of the president, and his clients were wealthy and important, men often mentioned in the pages of the Washington *Post* and the *Evening Star*. He was the younger brother of Leigh's father, and had cared for Leigh and his mother, Letty Merrill, since his brother Ralph died of a stroke immediately after losing his fortune in the stock market crash of 1929. Jeremiah made it possible for Leigh to graduate from the George Washington University Law School a year ago, and had given him his first job. Leigh never seemed particularly grateful for Jeremiah's help. And, although he hadn't said so, Claire suspected that he didn't like being a lawyer either. But she knew he was lucky to have a start in a profession at twenty-four.

"Want to go for a ride?" Leigh asked now.

"Whatever," she said, snuggling close to him, her thigh against his, the gear stick between their knees. "I told Mom I'd probably be late."

He drove out of Connecticut Avenue, turned toward Rock Creek Park. Soon they had left traffic and lights behind. He pulled into their favourite parking place.

It was sheltered by brush and tall bare-limbed trees, and they had discovered in previous visits that few cars passed by.

Their headlights flashed on several wooden tables with attached benches near an outdoor stone fireplace. The picnic area had been cleared and built by boys from the Civilian Conservation Corps several years earlier.

It was very dark in the car when Leigh cut the lights, and said, "You look like somebody bursting with news."

She was delighted that he could tell how she felt. "I quit Murphy's, Leigh!"

How she hated that job! Forty cents an hour. Half an hour for lunch. And a steady stream of invective from Lena Denton, who disliked her because she was a college graduate, disliked her because she was a native Washingtonian, disliked her because she was pretty and only twenty-one years old. Claire had realized all that after only days behind the counter with Lena. But understanding had made the woman no easier to take. She had told no one about it, except Leigh, to whom, for as long as she could remember, she had confided her secrets, because, for as long as

11

she could remember, she had loved him.

"And," she went on now, "when I told the manager I was leaving, he asked me to change my mind! He offered me a raise to fifty cents an hour!"

Leigh chuckled. "Tempted, weren't you?"

"Only until I remembered Lena," Claire said. "But I'll find something else." But she knew it wouldn't be easy. Jobs were hard to come by. She'd had applications out for teaching jobs since last June. She'd haunted the agencies, tried even the private schools. She had finally taken the clerk typists' test for a government job. Murphy's had only been a stopgap. A place to earn at least something while waiting for a better opportunity.

"Of course you'll find something else," he said.

She was going to tell him how good it was to know that the next time she passed 12th and F Streets, she could look down the block at Murphy's and laugh. But Leigh drew her into his arms, his cheek against hers, his warmth slowly spreading through her. She forgot what she'd been planning to say.

They both dated other people so their folks wouldn't know. Not that her parents would mind. And certainly, Leigh's mother, Claire's courtesy 'Aunt Letty', wouldn't either. Claire was certain they'd been taking for granted a

12

match between Leigh and Claire for years. But neither she, nor Leigh, was ready to share what they felt for each other.

He was her brother Ian's closest friend, even though Ian was two years younger. They'd known each other, lived as neighbours, all their lives. Until only a few months before, Leigh had been like a second brother to Claire. He'd helped teach her how to throw a ball. He'd picked her up when she'd fallen on her roller skates. He didn't seem to have noticed that she had grown up until just after she graduated from college, when, by accident, at the end of June, he saw her walking home from Connecticut Avenue, and stopped to pick her up.

Her mother, Dora Loving, had been the only daughter of Senator Jack Gowan of Mississippi. Dora never forgot that, nor allowed anyone else to. She didn't accept that her life had changed. The money they'd once had was gone. It pained her that Claire was content to shop at Lerner's instead of Garfinckle's, that Claire went to Wilson Teachers' College, a city supported school, where, she said, Claire would meet only shopkeepers' children. It hadn't mattered to Claire. Ian had already been enrolled at the George Washington University, the best the family could afford. So Claire went to Wilson.

Her cheek was soft to Leigh's lips. He whispered against it, "When you least expect it, something good will turn up." But as he reassured her, he felt impatience. The last thing on his mind was her job. He was so goddamn horny. And restless. And wishing something would happen to free him. From his mother. His uncle. To free him. But mostly he was horny for Claire, almost bursting with it.

She was saying, "I don't much care what I do. But you know my mom."

"I ought to. Mine's the same, isn't she?"

The two older women spent their time together speaking of their past lives, when they had belonged to the Sulgrave Club, and dined at the Occidental Restaurant, and watched the polo matches at Potomac Park.

He shrugged the subject away, and turned his face toward Claire's. They looked deep into each other's eyes. Slowly he ran his fingertips across her forehead, then down the silken length of her hair to the curled-under ends of her pageboy. Then, with his hand at the nape of her neck, he drew her closer. His lips, sweet-tasting and warm, pressed to hers, and his tongue was in her mouth, touching hers, and she felt his hand enclose her breast.

It had begun just this way, the dark enfolding them, a few stars glittering through broken clouds, an easy conversation.

But now, as she snuggled into his arms, she

felt some new intensity in him, in herself. They kissed so deeply and for so long that her breath was gone and her head swam.

It was wonderful and funny at the same time, the way he managed to hold her, the steering wheel thrusting into his ribs, the gear stick poking up beneath her right arm. She slid her hand under his jacket, his shirt. The skin of his back was silken, but with heat in it. His hand caressed her thighs, moved between them.

He whispered, "Claire, Claire . . ." against her mouth.

Soon, laughing breathlessly, without saying a word, they parted for just long enough to climb into the back seat. Cramped still, but with the sudden luxury of more space, they held each other, and he was saying, "Please, oh, please, Claire . . ."

Then they melted together in unspoken agreement, with his weight on her and her body receiving it with pulsing joy, while the few stars shining over the black limbs of the trees seemed to explode in glittering fragments.

She got out in front of the house, stood watching as his brake lights blinked at the corner, then disappeared as he turned. When she could no longer see his car, she went up the steps.

This section of the city, west of Connecticut Avenue, was known as Cleveland Park, named for President Grover Cleveland, who had once owned a country home there. It was a place full of ancient streams channelled into culverts, and hills and ravines, and was particularly notable for its old trees; oak, magnolia, dogwood, bamboo, mimosa, and honey locust.

The street on which Claire lived was called for the last of these, Honey Locust Lane. It was narrow and curving, and bordered by tall locust trees that were foamy with white blossoms in the spring, and in winter, cast lacy black shadows on the road.

Near the front path there was a titled wooden post with a discoloured brass sign saying 'Hannah's Gate'. It was an ostentatious name for the big old Victorian house that was Claire's home. There were three storeys, including what had once been an attic for servants. A huge front porch ran across its face. Two magnolia trees cast dark shadows on one side. A driveway ran along the other side, ending at an old shed, once used as a carriage house. Ian's car was in the driveway. He'd given her the keys to the 1937 Chevrolet when he went into the Army, telling her to use it until he came home.

Hannah's Gate had once been a luxurious

dwelling, well-cared for, and beautiful. But now it needed paint and carpentry to restore it.

The ridge on which the house sat sloped away from its back in a long broad yard enclosed by a six-foot wire mesh fence. Big Jack Gowan, Claire's grandfather, had a gate put in that fence because his wife Hannah often went to visit an older generation of Merrills, who lived in the house that stood just behind but much below the house on Honey Locust Lane. He always referred to the gate as Hannah's Gate, and over the years the name extended to the house itself.

Now Claire let herself in. As always, there seemed to be a weighty silence ready to engulf her. A held-breath sort of silence. She thought to herself that there was finally one more secret in this house of secrets. One more. This time her own.

She heard the radio playing in the study to the left of the staircase. She looked in. Her father, Casey, was sitting in the high-backed wing chair, his feet propped on a footstool. Both pieces of furniture were brown velvet, worn at the back, frayed at the arms, well-scuffed where his shoes rested.

She wondered briefly if she had remembered to smooth her hair, if he could see the marks of Leigh's love bites on her throat.

17

Casey glanced up. "Late getting in, aren't you?"

"I ran into Leigh." It was a relief to say his name. She wanted to repeat it. Sing it. Cry it. Leigh. Leigh. She belonged to him now. And he belonged to her. She said, "We took a ride."

Casey nodded. He was a tall man, lean, with dark hair and deep-set dark eyes. He looked at the portrait over the fireplace. It was of Big Jack Gowan, as he had been in his prime. It showed a man with a ruddy face, a faintly smiling mouth and a hard grey gaze. His hair was cut very short, frosted with white, but still had auburn streaks the same shade as Claire's. He looked like a powerful man, the man that Dora Loving always spoke of. But Claire remembered him only as old, shuffling about the house in worn bedroom slippers and a moth-eaten damask smoking jacket, muttering "Hannah's Gate," under his breath.

Casey was studying Big Jack Gowan with a mixture of dislike and interrogation. But now he let his head fall back on the chair, plainly paying no attention to the portrait or to Claire.

She decided to tell him later about leaving her job. She wanted to be alone now, to think about Leigh. She saw that Casey, too, wanted to be alone. He hardly seemed aware that she

18

had remained standing in the doorway.

It was always like that. As if there was some distance between Casey and everyone else, as if his mind, his feelings, were far away.

She turned to go, thinking what a strange man he was. Even now, when she was grown, she didn't understand him. She supposed she never would.

Casey listened as her footsteps receded. He knew he should have had more of a conversation with her. But what was there to say? To her. To anyone at Hannah's Gate. All he wanted was to be packed and gone. He'd been home for seven long months.

Once more he glanced at the portrait. A man shouldn't be expected to pay forever for a single mistake. What would Big Jack say to that? No matter. The old man was dead.

Casey got to his feet. This was what he never permitted himself. No brooding. No considering. That was why he had survived. While he was here he'd be Casey Loving.

Claire, crossing the hallway, heard from upstairs the sound of voices. Voices, but no words. Secrets, she thought. Hannah's Gate was full of them. It was swept by unnamable currents. Ever since she could remember, she had been aware of conversations between her parents that ended abruptly when she walked into a room. She had heard angry whispers during the night, and shivered at the unknown threat they posed. Now she wondered if Casey's so evident detachment was the cause of the menace she had so often sensed.

As she turned towards the centre staircase, she saw a partly-finished navy blue sweater, needles poking through a tangled skein. It was her mother's handiwork, undertaken when Dora heard that they were needed by the Free French, training now in England with the hope of regaining conquered France from the Germans. There were other misshapen and partly-finished sweaters scattered through the house. Beside this one, on the marble-topped foyer table, lay an Army cap. When Claire saw it, she cried, "Ian! Ian? Are you home?"

She raced up the stairs, thinking how like her father not to have told her.

Ian met her at the top of the steps. He hugged her. "I was wondering where you were."

His dark hair was cut short, shaven over the ears, flat on top. He was of medium height, and very thin. His trousers bagged at the knee, his jacket sagged over his chest. He had blue eyes, and a sensitive mouth.

"I didn't know you were coming," she said.

"I got a last minute two-day leave. I'm on my way to Massachusetts. To M.I.T." He saw her questioning look and explained, "Massachusetts Institute of Technology."

Soon after he'd graduated from college with a degree in chemistry, his number had come up in one of the earliest Selective Service drawings, part of the first peacetime draft in the nation's history. He'd done his basic training at Fort Benning in Georgia, then spent three months in Officers' Candidate School in North Carolina. Now he was what he laughingly called a ninety-day wonder, a second lieutenant, and ordered back to school for a special course.

"How are you?" he asked. "What's been happening since I was home last?"

What's been happening? she thought. Leigh's my lover. She gulped. She'd almost said it aloud. But she couldn't tell Ian. He wouldn't approve or understand. She said, "Oh, nothing much. I'm fine. But I quit my job. I'll start looking for something else on Monday." She paused. What else? But she had to say Leigh's name. She blurted, "I ran into Leigh tonight. We took a ride."

"I'll call him tomorrow."

She linked arms with Ian. "Come on down. I'll make coffee."

"I'm bushed, Claire. I stood all the way home on the train. It was packed, just like a holiday weekend, so I'd better get to bed.

We'll talk in the morning. Okay?"

It was a relief to go into her room. Another moment or two with Ian and she would have said too much. Ian was always teasing Leigh about being a wolf. They'd gone on dates together before Ian went into the Army.

Maybe next time Ian came home, she and Leigh could tell him what their plans were. Maybe by then they'd have plans.

She went to the window. An old wistaria vine, planted when the house was built in the 1890s, spread across part of it. Its main shoot was as wide as a tree trunk, its stems as thick as a man's arm, and its tendrils had grown across the whole back of the house, covering sections of the windows on that side. It was leafless now, but in summer it was crowded with green growth and heavy with purple blossoms. A sudden crackle vibrated through the vine, indicating that she had disturbed the squirrels that nested there.

As she looked down the sloping lawn to the Merrill house on Afton Place, she saw a light flash on. She waited. Perhaps Leigh would walk by. She would see him one more time before going to sleep. But he didn't appear. And soon the light went out.

She was in pyjamas, her face scrubbed, her pageboy hair brushed, when there was a familiar scratching at the door.

"Come in," she said, knowing who was there.

The door opened. Rea, her thirteen-year-old sister, sidled in. She was straddling the line between childhood and being grown up, and was having a hard time of it. She had round breasts that she tried to hide beneath loose sweaters, and her knees were still scabbed from playing kick the can in Cleveland Park alleys. She was tall for her age, thin, and had Casey's dark hair and eyes. Her skirt was wrinkled, her shoes scuffed. She slumped on the bed beside Claire, saying disgustedly, "Mom's on the warpath again. God, I wish she'd leave me alone."

"You wouldn't like it if she did."

"You don't know anything about it," Rea retorted. "You can do what you want. She doesn't pick on you."

Claire held back a laugh. "If you want to tell me about it, okay. If you want to fight with me, then I'm not available just now."

In spite of the eight years difference in their ages, Rea and Claire had been close. Rea had always tried to copy Claire, requisitioning Claire's outgrown clothes as her own, trying to do her hair in the same pageboy, even mimicking her speech. But in the past year Rea's style had become her own, and she was distant, as if echoing Casey's manner. But she was also combatative. She argued constantly. With Dora. With Casey. Even with Claire, when she could provoke her. Which happened sometimes, but not often.

Now she said gloomily, "Mom's so hypocritical."

"What's she being hypocritical about?"

"Me, for one thing. She says, 'If only you'd smile, you'd be pretty.' " Rea scowled. "For God's sake! Me! Pretty!"

"Look in the mirror," Claire told her, biting back mention of uncombed hair, hanging shirt tails, and grubby hands.

"You're as bad as Mama! Don't you understand? I don't want to be pretty. What does it get you? Mama used to be pretty. And where did it get her?"

Claire didn't answer. What was there to say? She was as aware of the tensions between Dora and Casey as Rea was. Both girls, and Ian too, had been affected by them.

Rea went to the door. "Hypocritical, and phoney too. Mom says we're important. Second generation Washington. Our grandfather was a senator. So what? Gowans and Lovings . . . all that stuff." She drew an angry breath. "We're nobodies."

"You know how Mom is," Claire said. "She can't help it."

It wasn't that Claire disagreed with Rea. But

24

Dora's pretensions were part of her. And they didn't hurt anyone.

"She ought to help it," Rea retorted as she went out.

Alone at last, Claire turned off the lamp, slid under the covers, and lay looking at the shadows on the ceiling, her thoughts going back to Leigh.

Claire always remembered that Sunday at the end of the first week of December in 1941.

For the others in her family it began like any other day. Under the dull winter sky, Honey Locust Lane was empty and silent. The Washington *Post* was on the front porch near the hemp mat, and by the time Casey had gone to look for it, Rea, up earlier, had dismantled it and was immersed in the funny papers. Casey, who liked his newspaper untouched by human hands until he was finished reading it, yelled at her. She responded with a pout that was partly a child's controlled defiance, and partly an adolescent's flirtatiousness. In the kitchen, Dora was beginning preparations for the ritual Sunday dinner that she insisted on, and in the driveway next to the house, Ian was polishing his car.

So, it always seemed to Claire, that it began for all of them as an ordinary Sunday.

For her it was different. Her first thought

on awakening was of Leigh. She felt a tingling in her breasts and a soft warm throb deep in her belly. Her own secret too. A little frightening, but wonderful. Leigh, whom she had known all her life. After so many years of loving him, wanting to belong to him, it had happened, and now she was his forever.

She threw the blankets back and jumped out of bed. In the mirror, she studied her face, wide brown eyes anxiously searching for signs that she was no longer the same, no longer a virgin. Did it show? Could anyone tell? If her family knew, they would be shocked, angry. But Claire didn't care. She loved Leigh. She was happy to belong to him. They would be married one day. What difference did a piece of paper make when they were so deeply linked to each other?

She saw no giveaway sign in the mirror, yet her mouth still felt hot and bruised from his kisses. Her breasts felt full, the nipples rising suddenly, as if his lips had just enclosed them. A sweet trembling spread through her thighs.

She laughed softly on the way to the window. She saw no sign of movement around the Merrill house. Was Leigh up yet? Was he thinking of her? Again she felt a spreading warmth inside her. When would she see him? She could hardly wait to hold him again.

★ ★ ★

Dora Loving glanced at her wrist watch. Two o'clock. Soon the roast would be ready. Sighing, she checked the dining-room table. Linen napkins and cloth. Silver knives and forks, old and lustrous, brought back from Ireland by her father. China plates from England. It was a chore to do a formal Sunday dinner, but Casey didn't care. Neither did the children.

She wrung her slender hands. If only . . .

She had turned forty a few months before, but she looked older. There was grey in her fading hair. She wore it in a braided bun that hung at the back of her thin neck like an ornament on a wilting Christmas tree. Her blue eyes were at times imperious, at times anxious. Her mouth was always petulant. She had the voice and bearing of a Southern belle, copied from her mother, Hannah Gowan, who had grown up in Mississippi before the turn of the century. Although her parents were long dead, Dora's dreams and hopes had been formed for her by them.

She was sure her life would have been different if Big Jack hadn't lost everything. Still, Casey had managed to make a living during the depression. Dora had been unhappy that his geologist's job with a large oil company made him spend long months away from home. She could have gone with him. At the beginning, he'd suggested it. But she'd been determined to keep Hannah's Gate. In the thirties she couldn't sell it for what it was worth, and couldn't imagine renting it to strangers. So she hadn't gone with Casey. After a year, he stopped suggesting it. Now he spent three or four months away at a time, then would return home for stays of varying lengths. She had become accustomed to the routine, but continued to resent it. He'd been home longer than usual this time. She expected him to announce soon that he'd be leaving again.

At two-thirty, she called, "Dinner's ready. Come to the table everybody."

Casey sat in his usual chair in the study, the radio on his left. Rea was curled up on the floor beside him, her face hidden by the veil of her hair. Claire was on the sofa, daydreaming about Leigh. And he was upstairs with Ian, listening to the radio broadcast from Griffith's Stadium of a Redskins' home game.

The New York Philharmonic was playing, Casey nodding to the cadence of the music. Suddenly a deep voice, throbbing with suppressed excitement, broke in. "Ladies and gentlemen, this is a special announcement. We interrupt this program to tell you that this morning Japanese kamikaze planes launched a surprise attack on American naval forces

28

at Pearl Harbor."

It seemed to Claire that time stopped, life stopped. There was an instant of absolute silence.

Then the announcer went on, "We have battleships sunk or in flames. Little information is available yet about casualties. We'll return with further bulletins as soon as possible."

Claire sat frozen, her eyes stinging with held-back tears. Casey muttered an oath. Then Ian and Leigh burst into the room, Ian calling ahead, "Did you hear it, Dad? Claire, were you listening?"

He was pale under his tan, his blue eyes ringed with sudden shadows. He went on, as if thinking aloud, "I'd better change. I'll have to go to Massachusetts as soon as I can."

Leigh's cheekbones were pink. His hair fell over his forehead, giving him the look of a small boy. "We should have known it would happen." A wave of excitement rose in him. This changed everything. At last he'd have an excuse to escape Jeremiah's clutches. The old bastard wouldn't try to stop him. Not with all the citations he had on his office walls. Citations for bravery in action in the 1918 war.

Casey leaned closer to the radio as the announcer cut in again with a repetition of the previous report.

Ian and Leigh ran upstairs, talking softly, while Claire and Rea and Casey sat silently, listening for more.

Japanese envoys had been in Washington for several weeks discussing compromises to resolve American objections to Japan's expansion in the Orient. Thus the attack on Pearl Harbor came as a stunning surprise that Sunday afternoon.

For the next few hours the Lovings followed the short radio bulletins. The announcer grew hoarse as he spoke of five battleships known to be sunk, 177 aircraft destroyed, and three cruisers lost. Only later did they learn that there were 2343 casualties, and 876 missing, with 1272 injured.

When, finally, the family gathered at the dinner table, it was without Leigh. He had gone. Claire wished that he had stayed.

Casey, she saw, was pensive as always, and Ian, too, looked abstracted. He was already in uniform, ready to leave for Boston by early evening.

Only Rea ate unconcernedly. But, Claire thought, one could make no assumptions about Rea. She often hid what she felt or thought, until suddenly she would explode, small grievances or large ones, small joys or large ones, erupting with the same force. At least *she* sometimes let go. Casey never did.

Claire saw him glance at Dora, who was saying, "It means that we'll go to war, doesn't it?" When no one answered, she went on, "I remember the World War. Oh, the town suddenly came alive then!"

Casey's look was a mixture of pity and contempt.

Claire felt a small lurch in her chest. She averted her gaze from his face. She'd seen that expression many times before, but had never known what it meant. Now, as if a blindfold had been taken from her eyes, she *did* know. And she didn't want to. Pity. Contempt. Dislike. She had no business seeing that. It concerned only her father and mother.

Soft words came from the radio in the other room. It was known now that while Japanese bombers were destroying the American fleet, their peace envoys had been preparing a message to be delivered to the State Department.

What would happen now? Claire asked herself. She couldn't even guess at what was to come. She knew only that none of them would ever be the same.

And Leigh! she thought. Oh, God, what would he do? He was the lowliest clerk in his uncle's law firm. Would his uncle try to have him deferred? Would Leigh allow that?

"It was exciting," Dora said, as she passed

31

the food. "Do you remember?" She smiled at Casey.

"No," he said. "I wasn't here until afterwards."

"That's right," she agreed. "And my father brought you home with him. And the minute I saw you. . . . so handsome in your boots, with that funny little cap tilted over your ear . . . the minute I saw you . . ."

"The kids have heard it before," Casey said.

"I haven't," Rea said. "Tell me, Mama."

But Dora, with a hurt look at Casey, began to clear the table. Helping her, Claire thought that Rea was just being contrary. Of course she'd heard how Dora and Casey had met. It was Dora's favorite topic of conversaton, and it led, inevitably, to whining bitterness and ended with long injured sighs.

Casey ignored Dora and asked Ian, "When are you leaving?"

"In a little while," he answered. But he was thinking of Claire, of the way her eyes had gone to Leigh when the two of them came down after hearing the news. She was getting too serious about Leigh. He wasn't yet grown up. Even though Ian was the younger, he saw his friend's immaturities. Leigh wasn't ready for real love. Maybe he'd never be. Ian didn't want Claire to be hurt. How could he phrase a warning to her?

Now he was aware that his parents and Rea and Claire were looking at him. He forced a smile. "It'll be okay. Don't worry."

Claire took the barely touched food into the kitchen. She put the dishes down and clung to the sink edge, tears burning her eyes. It was real. Not a terrible nightmare that would end. It was real.

The radio voice, uttering bulletins in the study, spoke of the choices President Roosevelt had.

"Oh, God," Claire said softly. "Ian." And then, silently: Leigh. What would happen to them?

That night crowds gathered to stand sombrely, silently, in Lafayette Park across the street from the White House, watching as automobiles glided between its tall iron gates.

For the first time that anyone could recall the big light under the north portico remained dark.

It was Monday, December 8th. President Roosevelt called an emergency session of Congress, and asked for a declaration of war against Japan.

On December 11th, four days after the attack on Pearl Harbor, Germany and Italy, in alliance with the Japanese, declared war against the United States.

And on Friday of that same week, Claire received a Western Union telegram from the War Department, informing her that she had been hired as a clerk typist at $1440 a year. It directed her to appear for her assignment at 8 A.M. December 16th, at a temporary building on 23rd Street N.W. in Washington.

Claire excitedly read the message. She had a job! And with the War Department! She would be doing something useful, even if it was only typing and filing. She dashed into the study to tell her mother.

Dora listened, frowned. "Oh, why did you try for a clerk-typist position? You have a B.S. in education. You can do better. And you'll never meet anybody worthwhile working in an office full of women."

"But I'm going to be needed," Claire said quickly.

"There's that," her mother agreed. She brightened. "What'll you wear? You want to make a good first impression." Suddenly there was a dreamy look on Dora's face. "First impressions . . . the first time I saw your father I fell in love with him. Papa wasn't too happy about it. Casey didn't come from a special family like us. They were just . . . people. And they didn't even have money. But I had my way. We got married." She looked up at the

34

portrait of Big Jack Gowan, whose arrogant blue eyes surveyed the room which had once been his, the walls still covered with shelves holding his books and papers.

Dora had loved him more deeply than she'd loved anyone, ever. And then there had been that awful business with Fergie — Betsy Ferguson, his secretary. She'd been a friend to Dora's mother, Hannah, and to Dora herself. Fergie was another Mississippian, included in all family dinners and parties, trusted and admired. Dora didn't know when Hannah realized what was going on. But suddenly Fergie no longer came to the house. Dora herself, sensing the estrangement between her parents, knew Fergie was to blame. It was Dora who cut from the family albums the pictures of Fergie, and Dora who told her father that Fergie shouldn't be working for him any more. He ignored her. But a few months later, Fergie was gone. Big Jack didn't explain her disappearance to Hannah or Dora. They learned about it from the new young man who had taken her place. Fergie had returned to Mississippi, he had said. And that was that.

Then, a year after Dora and Casey were married, those terrible rumours had begun to circulate. Rumours questioning Big Jack's honesty, claiming that he'd accepted bribes. In the beginning Big Jack had laughed at them.

35

But in the end he'd been forced to give up his seat in Congress. He stayed home, slowly becoming an ineffectual old man. Dora's mother died. Ian was born. And Casey . . . Dora sighed deeply. Then she looked back at Claire and said brightly, "That's how it was. Love at first sight."

Claire thought of Leigh. It must have been the same for her. Surely that was how it had happened. She'd fallen in love with Leigh at first sight, although she no longer remembered when that was. She had, it seemed to her, known him forever.

Chapter 2

Claire first met Margo Desales when she went to pick up her job assignment at an office in the temporary building on 23rd Street.

Margo, just ahead of her in the long line, was there for the same reason. She waited impatiently, shifting from one slim foot to the other, the high heels of her ankle strap sandals wobbling under her. She shook back her long wavy black hair, then smoothed it, her scarlet-tipped nails like flower petals gleaming against the dark, her ring reflecting the light like flashes of blue flame. She sighed, and coughed, and whistled softly. Then she lit a cigarette, and offered one to Claire.

Claire refused, smiling. Many girls were smoking now, but she hadn't been tempted to try it.

"It's taking so long," Margo complained, watching a young man pass by. He was tall, slim, blond. Moments later he returned, again passing near the girls.

Margo suddenly dropped her purse, exclaiming, "Oh, gee!" with faked distress.

The young soldier picked it up for her.

She thanked him, and laughing said, "It's been so long since I've said a word, I thought maybe I'd lost my voice for good."

Claire was amused at the girl's ploy. It was obvious, but it had worked.

The soldier told her she would probably get in soon, and went on.

"Not bad," Margo said.

Claire agreed. The soldier *was* nice-looking. But nothing like Leigh.

She and Margo exchanged names. Then Claire asked, as was usual in Washington, then and always, "Where are you from?"

"A town in Illinois you've never heard of. And boy, am I ever glad to be here! What about you?"

Claire explained that she was native to the city.

Margo's brows arched. "Are you? I didn't know anybody was born here. I thought people always came from somewhere else to work in the government. And when the job was finished they went back where they came from."

"It was my grandfather who came here," Claire said. She didn't explain that Big Jack had been a senator.

But Margo wasn't interested anyway. She didn't know a soul in the city. It would be good to have someone who knew the ropes to help her get settled. Usually she didn't care about girls. It was men that mattered to her. But right now, she knew that making a connection with Claire would do her some good. She said, "Oh, boy! Are you lucky! You don't have to find a place to live. I'm trying to figure out what to do. I don't want to spend too much on rent, but I've got to have a roof over my head. Would you believe I just got in this morning? My stuff's checked at the station. That's why I'm such a mess." Although she flicked her hands at her outfit, she didn't seem concerned that her slip showed from beneath her tight black skirt, and that a frayed cleaner's tag poked up from the collar of her sweater.

Claire noticed that, as Margo spoke, her eyes flicked here and there, studying the people going by.

She went on, "You must know your way around. Do you know where I could get a room?"

"I don't think so," Claire said doubtfully.

It was then that Margo reached the threshold and was waved through the double doors. She said, "I'll wait for you. Okay?"

Claire nodded. Soon she too was waved inside. The processing took only half an hour. When Claire returned to the hall with her assignment slip, Margo was there. She suggested that they have lunch together.

They went to the building's cafeteria. Over sandwiches and coffee, they compared notes. Both had been assigned to the mail room in the Office of Engineers at the War Department. They were to report the following morning.

"I'm glad you're going there too," Margo said, as the young soldier who had picked up her purse stopped at the table.

Margo's face brightened when she saw him. Her red lips looked lush. This was what she'd hoped for when she learned she had a job in Washington. Still, she'd wondered . . . now she knew. She could hardly wait to make her first Washington diary entry. Oh, this was going to be fun. She said to the soldier, "We're going to be in the Office of Engineers," and nodded at Claire. "This is my friend, Claire Loving." She made it sound as if they had known each other for years. Then she introduced herself.

The soldier's name was Jim Carsson. He sat down with them. Within moments he and Margo were exchanging biographies, and within a few more moments, they had collected several other men.

Claire followed the conversation, answered questions and asked them, but she thought only of Leigh. They'd seen each other only twice since that terrible Sunday night nine days before. Leigh had been moody, saying little. They hadn't managed even a moment alone. But she hoped to see him that evening.

Now she heard one of the men ask for Margo's phone number. Margo drooped. "I don't have a place to stay. Claire's going to give me some clues on how to go about finding a room. But we haven't gotten to that yet."

The man scrawled on a piece of paper. "Okay. Then you call me."

Jim Carsson did the same, and then asked Claire for her number, saying he'd like to call her, and besides, she'd know how he should reach Margo, wouldn't she?

After agreeing that they would all meet again, the men left, Margo's dark eyes following them until they disappeared beyond the cafeteria doors.

At last she turned to Claire, "Gosh, I'm tired."

An impulse led Claire to ask, "Why don't you come home with me? You can spend the day, get some rest, look over the newspapers. Maybe you can even go and see some places."

"Hey," Margo cried. "That's great. The minute I saw you I knew you'd be a good friend."

It was later the same evening.

Margo was studying the newspaper's 'rooms

41

for rent' columns, with Rea sitting beside her, saying 'no' to one neighbourhood, 'yes' to another.

Leigh telephoned Claire. "I have to see you," he said.

"Come over now."

"Meet me at the corner of Newark. Okay?"

"I'll be there," she told him.

When she hung up, her hands were shaking. She was filled with an awful foreboding. Leigh had sounded so grim, determined. She dreaded what was to come.

And from another room she heard her parents' angry whispers.

Leigh was at the corner, waiting. He swung the door open for Claire, and she slipped into the car. Silent, with only a single quick look at her, he drove away. She knew where he was going. They left the lights of Connecticut Avenue, descended into the park. Soon he stopped in their usual place, the shadowed lovers' lane that was a picnic area on summer days. Now it was cold, dark.

He sat with his hands clenching the wheel, staring straight ahead.

She waited. A small pulse ticked in her throat. Her eyes felt hot.

"I enlisted today," he said at last.

"Oh." The response was only a whispered

breath. But her heart seemed to swell in her chest, engorged with pain. Oh, no. No. They belonged together. They couldn't be separated now. Pictures she had seen in the news reels spun through her mind. Helmeted soldiers, exploding earth . . . flame arrowing down from the sky. "Oh, Leigh, why? Did you really have to?"

Now he turned to look at her, his hazel eyes shining. "Of course I do. There wasn't any use in waiting. I'd be called up right away anyhow."

"And besides . . ." His voice became fierce. "I *want* to go. Don't you understand? I want to!"

The heat in her eyes became tears. She fought them back. She wouldn't cry! If he had to go, and she knew he did, she wouldn't make it harder for him. Remembering her foreboding, she said, "I knew you'd volunteer." She put her hand on his. "I'm proud of you."

"We don't know what'll happen . . . how long it'll be." He paused, thinking how much he needed to feel free, to leave without the burden of connection to her, to anyone. He said slowly, "I don't want you to feel you owe me anything. I want you to go out, have fun. Maybe somebody else will come along. Whatever happens, do what you want. Okay?"

She pressed close to him. "No, no, it's not

okay! And no! I'm not going to go out. I'm not going to have fun. I'm going to be waiting for you! No matter what you say. No matter how long it takes. I'll be here, waiting for you, until you come back."

"We'll see when the time comes," he told her.

It was a relief that Margo was already settled in the guest room when Claire came home. There was no need to talk to her.

It was a relief to close the door against the rest of the world, to be able, finally, to allow long held back tears to overflow her eyes and run down her cheeks.

Claire sank down on her bed, stifling her sobs in her pillow. Leigh was going away to the war. God, God . . . how could it have happened? Just when they'd found love he was going away. She might never see him again. Suppose he was killed? She couldn't imagine her life without him. How would she go on?

The door opened softly, closed with a faint click. Bare feet whispered on the rug. A small warm hand touched Claire's arm.

Rea breathed, "What's the matter, Claire?"

"Leigh's enlisted in the army."

Rea said nothing, but she remained there, her hand on Claire's arm, while her sister cried herself into exhaustion and then into sleep.

44

A cold morning rain tapped at the window and whispered through the bare limbs of the wisteria.

Claire awakened to the soft sounds. Her first thought was of Leigh. She wanted to burrow under the blankets, to hide once again from her anguish in sleep. But this was the day she was to start on her new job. She rose and doggedly forced herself through her usual morning routine.

When she went downstairs, she found Margo already there.

Margo smiled. "Oh, what a night's sleep I had!" And then, turning to Dora, who was pouring coffee, "This is a wonderful house, Mrs Loving."

She stretched her shapely body, breasts rising high as she swept her dark hair back. At that moment Casey came in. She batted her lashes at him. "Honestly, I never felt so at home so fast any place in my life." She went on wistfully as Casey sat at the table, "I wish I never had to leave here. I mean, it would be just perfect. A real home to live in. A real family." She paused, as if thinking about the home she had left behind. "And Connecticut Avenue is so close to the bus stop. Claire and I . . ." she beamed at Claire ". . . both of us working in the same place."

45

Neither Dora nor Casey responded to that.

Claire remembered their angry whispers the night before. Now Dora's eyes seemed red. Casey had his usual detached look.

"We'll have to leave in ten minutes," Claire told Margo.

"Ready when you are," Margo answered. Then, as if struck by a sudden thought, she cried, her face alight, "Oh, listen, I've just gotten the best idea! Why didn't we think of it before? The room I had last night, next to Claire's . . . you don't usually use it, do you?"

"It's Ian's room," Claire said. "My brother. Since he's away, I guess it'll be the guest room."

"That's what I was hoping. Oh, do let me be the guest. Paying, of course. Whatever the going rate is. I won't be any trouble. Honestly," she looked pleadingly from Dora to Casey, "I promise I won't. You'll never regret doing me a favour."

Later Claire was to remember those words, and ruefully ask herself why she had brought Margo home with her. Why she had let herself be carried away by a good-natured whim.

But then, seeing Margo's anxiety and hope, and sympathetic to her need to be settled, Claire said, "It's not a bad idea, Mom. Rooms are awfully hard to come by now."

"I never did such a thing before," Dora said.

"Renting out rooms. In Daddy's house? He'd turn in his grave." She paused. But maybe it wasn't a bad idea. Times had changed. You never knew what was going to happen. You'd better get what money you could, and not pass up a chance to put a little something by. She'd learned that much in the past ten years. Finally she turned to Casey. "What do you think?"

He shoved back his chair, rose. "Do what you want. I've got to get to the office."

So Margo took the room next to Claire. The wistaria spread across her window too, and through its tendrils, she too could look down the sloping yard, and beyond it to the house where the Merrills lived.

The two girls went to work together.

The new War Department building filled a huge corner lot at 21st Street and Virginia Avenue, looming over a row of old redstone houses, the end one converted into a grocery store, that still remained on the other side of the road.

Inside, past the armed sentries at its entrance, there was a double height marble lobby.

Claire and Margo were directed to the mail room of the Office of Engineers. It was a large windowless place, its ceiling covered with fluorescent lights. It was filled with desks set in small groupings, and with what seemed miles of green metal filing cabinets.

The girls completed a variety of forms. Then they were photographed for their identification passes. At last, Claire was taken to one section, Margo to another. They would soon discover that although they worked in nearby areas they would rarely see each other during the day.

At first the job seemed interesting to Claire. Every piece of mail that went out or came in to the Office of Engineers was abbreviated and recorded for the files. Claire's task was to assign a file number for such correspondence according to subject, and to reduce the contents of each letter to a single sentence.

After several weeks it became tedious.

Margo said the same about her work as a cross-reference typist.

By then she was completely settled in her room at Hannah's Gate. She had hung her clothes in the closet, set two small fat teddy bears on the chair, covered her dresser with bottles of lotion, perfume and eye make-up, and a tray with an array of lipsticks and rouges.

She never received any mail, never spoke of her home or family. She made friends quickly, and soon the phone calls for her began early in the morning and ended late in the evening. Some of those calls were from Jimmy

Carsson, with whom she had several dates before refusing to talk to him any more. He was, she told Claire, boring. Still, there were other men. She went out frequently on dates, and sometimes alone. A few times she talked Claire into going to the movies with her. Otherwise, except for going to work together each morning, they tended to go their separate paths.

Claire watched for letters from Leigh, but there was only one — a brief note, saying he was okay, and would write later. Aunt Letty too said that she'd heard only once, and just a few words then.

So Claire determined to wait, be patient, to think ahead to when he would be home again. But at night, when she lay alone in her bed, she would think of him. She would stir restlessly, driven by faint hungers. Her skin would prickle, her nipples rise. Her lips would burn with remembered kisses, and her arms would ache with the need to hold him close, to hold him and love him. And when sleep finally enwrapped her, the need would linger on in her dreams, so that when day came, she would remember and hunger all the more.

Chapter 3

Christmas had come and gone. There had been only small attempts to capture the usual joy of the holiday season. The Lovings had decorated a tiny tree, exchanged presents, and had a family meal.

Now, at the end of January, a bit of tinsel still glittered on the carpet near Casey's foot. He sat in the easy chair, eyes fixed on the portrait of his father-in-law. You damned old fool, he said silently to the arrogant face. You didn't have the guts to carry it off, did you?

Dora watched him, wishing she knew what was in his mind. Finally she said, "You don't need to volunteer. You're too old."

He didn't look forty-three years old. The few white strands in his hair only seemed distinguished. He was as lean now as when she'd first seen him in 1918, tall, handsome in his uniform. She didn't want to see him in a uniform again.

"I have experience," Casey told her.

"But what about us?"

"You'll manage, Dora."

Her mouth trembled. "You've been home

eight months. And that's too long, isn't it? You hate me. You just want to get away."

"Dora," he said wearily, "don't start that. If I hadn't travelled for Geostat all these years, I'd have been out of work."

"It's because of my father. Not Geostat. And it isn't the war. You just want to get away. You thought you'd be married to a senator's daughter."

"Dora, for Christ's sake, stop being an idiot! I can't watch Ian go, and Leigh, and everyone else I know, and stay home myself. I have to enlist."

"You just want an excuse for leaving me," she said miserably.

"Okay," he said. "Then have it your own way."

He left the room. She stood at the window, shivering. It had been like this for so long. All through the 30s, when he'd taken the job with Geostat, she'd been frightened. He went away. Always, at the back of her mind, there was the conviction that he'd married her because of her father's prestige and power. Always at the bottom of her heart was the feeling that he'd never forgiven her when her father had to leave the Senate in 1923. Of course he hadn't accepted a bribe to support and present a bill, but he hadn't been able to prove the allegations false either. The disgrace had ruined him, and when he'd died in 1930 he'd left nothing but the house called Hannah's Gate.

But it was after Casey took the job with Geostat that she saw the difference in him. She knew he no longer loved her the way she loved him. He came home from a sense of duty, remaining only as long as he was needed in the home office on K Street. She suspected that he asked for out of town work to get away from her.

But now he wanted to enlist. This was different. Anything could happen if he went to the war. And there was no need. He wouldn't be drafted. It occurred to her then that he most likely wouldn't be able to get a commission. She told herself that everything would be all right. They'd go on just as they were.

But unease still plagued her, and that afternoon she decided to visit Letty Merrill.

Sitting in the kitchen, as the two women often did, Dora told Letty that it seemed as if Casey was once again afflicted with itching feet, and sighed, "I ought to get used to it, I guess. But I don't."

"Men!" Letty said. She was small and plump, with very pink cheeks.

"If only things were the way they used to be," Dora answered, mourning the days when she had been Senator Jack Gowan's daughter.

Letty agreed. Then, changing the subject, she asked how Dora's new roomer was working out.

"Margo? She's fine."

"I thought about renting a room too," Letty told Dora. "The daughter of a friend of mine will be moving to Washington. I don't know when exactly. Her name is Linda Grant. I don't know her, but her mother is a lovely person." Letty sighed. "It would have been nice to have company. But when I mentioned it to Jeremiah he got very upset, so I shall have to let it go." She paused. "What about you, Dora? Would you have space for one more?"

"I suppose I would."

"I'll write and tell her not to worry." Letty smiled. "It'll be good to have her close by."

Dora thought it would do no harm to take in a few more dollars every month. She wouldn't count on it, however. When Linda Grant arrived, Dora could decide what to do.

Soon Dora and Letty were talking about the past, their good times, their beaux, the parties they had gone to.

After an hour of that, and two cups of sweetened tea, Dora went home, feeling much better.

Soon, though, reality assailed her again.

Rea came home from school, disappeared upstairs, and in a little while, came down to the kitchen.

Dora squealed with horror. "Rea! What have you done?"

The girl's lips were a scalded red, her brows a black slash, her cheekbones burned by rouge. She wore a sweater so tight that Dora could see the outline of her belly button. "Don't I look a little bit like Margo?" she asked. "I mean, if my hair were blacker, and I could get the pompadour right?"

"You look like a clown. Wash that garbage off your face this instant."

"Oh, Mama," Rea wailed, "you just want to keep me a baby. I'm thirteen now. It's time you realized that."

"Do what I say," Dora answered.

Rea stamped out. Footsteps echoed like curses from the stairway. A door banged.

Dora sank into a chair, folded her trembling hands together, and asked herself why things never went right.

It was late March. Golden forsythia glistened in the sunlight. A faint mist of green had appeared on the honey locust trees.

At dinner one night Claire and Dora were discussing the relocation of the Nisei, second and third generation Americans, of Japanese descent. They were being forced to leave their California homes, to live in guarded camps, because they were considered threats to the nation's security.

Casey interrupted the conversation to announce that Geostat was sending him on a six-month exploration survey, operating out of a base in southern New Mexico.

He didn't say anything about the many attempts he'd made to join any of the services; nor that, once he'd found a berth, he'd been turned down because of a heart murmur. As soon as he'd learned that, he talked to his boss at Geostat. He didn't mention that either.

It had been so long since Casey spoke of enlisting that Dora had stopped thinking about it. And he had been home for so long a stretch that she'd convinced herself he was home for good, or at least for the duration of the war.

So his words struck her with the force of a blow. She cried, "No! You can't! Not now, when we don't know what's going to happen. You're leaving because you don't love me any more. And you're never coming back."

"Get hold of yourself, Dora," Casey said quietly.

Claire, thankful that Margo was out for the evening, pushed back her chair, and reached for Rea's hand.

Dora screamed, "Wait! I want you girls to hear this!"

Claire froze. Rea's eyes were wide and fearful, Claire saw. Her heart pounded in a slow roll within her chest. Oh, if only they'd remember that Rea was still a child. If only they'd realize and care, how hard it was for Rea, for Claire too, to hear this.

Casey said, "Stop it, Dora. I have to do this. It has nothing to do with you. None of the services will have me, but the company has gotten a government contract. I can at least do my share that way."

With that he rose and left the room, and Dora, with a piteous look at the girls, covered her face with her hands and wept.

The end of that week, Claire heard him whistling joyfully as he packed. The next day, with a light kiss and a jaunty smile, he was gone.

Dora was inconsolable. "Oh, it doesn't make sense," she moaned. "Ian gone. Now Casey. It was so different in the other war. I was young then, and it was exciting. And Papa was there to take care of me."

Claire listened, but didn't answer. She was thinking of Leigh.

He was home for the first time after his basic training. She expected to see him that night and was determined to make him understand how she felt. She planned the words in her mind all through Dora's complaints.

But that evening, instead of calling her to meet him, he came through the back and knocked at the kitchen door.

Dora and Rea were there, and Margo too.

Margo brightened when she saw him. A smile flashed across her face. Even her hair seemed to acquire sudden life in his presence.

Claire noted those symptoms with some amusement. By now she knew that Margo had more than an ordinary affinity for men. In uniform or out. Tall and dark or short and fair — if they wore pants, Margo was interested. But she went through them quickly. Just as she had gone through Jim Carsson. After three or four dates, he had disappeared. They all did. One week she would say she was madly in love with so and so. The next week she'd say he was dull. Soon after she'd have forgotten his name.

Leigh said hello to her, kissed Dora, Rea and Claire, in that order, and sat down to make small conversation, talking about pack drills and forced marches.

He was thinner, browner, and very relaxed in his olive drab uniform.

Claire watched the way his hazel eyes narrowed when he smiled, the play of muscles in his arms when he moved them. She waited for some signal from him to tell her when, how, they would finally be alone. But none came. So, when he rose to leave, she said, "I'll walk you down the yard," and went to get her coat.

He was waiting outside when she returned.

She took his arm, and they walked to the gate. When he didn't speak, she asked softly, "Is something wrong, Leigh?"

"No." It was crisp, almost harsh, although he didn't mean to sound that way. He went on more gently, "Really. Nothing's wrong." He didn't know how to explain the way he felt. He didn't even want to think about it. The future was uncertain. He couldn't guess what would happen. He couldn't take on any new burden, didn't want to either. He needed to be free, ready for whatever came along.

She said uncertainly, "I keep thinking about you . . ."

His big hand folded around her wrist, fingers tight. "I worry about you, Claire. What if something happens to me? Then where'll you be?"

"If you still want me, I'll take my chances. Oh, Leigh, if only you knew how much I miss you." She rose on her toes, put her arms around him, her cheek against his jaw. "Leigh."

"And I miss you. But you've got to consider. We don't know how long it'll be. You're young. I want you to go out, have fun. I don't want you sitting at home, waiting. You, and what's her name? Margo? The two of you can team up . . . go places . . ."

Claire's voice was a hot whisper, "Stop it! Don't you understand? I only want you, want to belong to you." She paused, and then, without thinking, blurted out, "Leigh, listen, we can get married. Let's do it tomorrow. Go to a justice of the peace in Maryland. Then I'll be your wife, and waiting for you to come back."

"Claire." Now his voice was husky. He had thought about that too. But he knew it would be a mistake. He wasn't ready. It was himself he was thinking about. He knew she was taking their relationship too seriously. He didn't want to be tied to her, to feel he owed her anything. Sure he was horny for her now. But he was horny for any woman he could get. He'd hardly said hello to Margo Desales, and he'd been ready to get into her pants. He knew from one look that she was easy to lay, easy to forget. Claire was different. She was a one man girl. If she said she'd wait, then she would. And he didn't know how he'd feel when the war was over. How he'd feel when he came back. If he came back.

"It's what I want more than anything," she said.

He seemed wrapped in stillness, rigid as she pressed against him. At last he said, "I want it too, Claire. But I know we shouldn't marry. We don't know what's going to happen. I might be killed. I might come home a wreck."

"I'm willing to risk it."

"I can't, Claire. I know it would be wrong." But now, holding her, he looked around. He wanted her so much that his whole body ached with it. "Damn!"

"The car," she said softly.

They hurried through the yard, around his house, and into the driveway where his blue jalopy was parked.

Before he turned the ignition key, he gave her a long look. "Where shall we go?"

She twined her fingers together to keep them from trembling. "Wherever you want." Just so they could be close. So they could lie in each other's arms. So she could show him how much she loved him. So he'd know once and for all that nothing else mattered to her.

He cut across the park instead of stopping there, and headed north and east to pick up Route 1, which was lined with hamburger joints, truck stops, and a few not very pleasant motels.

He stopped at one, quickly returned to the car. "Full."

They drove on. A few minutes later he stopped again. That time he rented a room. As he drove into the parking place, he said, "It's not the Mayflower, Claire."

"It doesn't matter."

Arms linked, hips pressing close together, they went in. The light bulb hung from the ceiling on a frayed wire, unshaded and glaring. The double bed was plainly as old as the building, sagging in the middle, curling up at head and foot. The spread was threadbare, washed colourless.

Leigh switched off the ugly light. They undressed each other, clothes dropping discarded around them onto the uncarpeted floor. They fell on the bed, entwined as they had never before been able to. His love-making was different. Tenderness mixed with desperation. His lips touched hers lightly, and then seemed to devour them, so that later she would taste the saltiness of blood in her mouth. His hands caressed her breasts, and then tightened until she cried out. It was the same when his weight covered her. Gentleness becoming desperation again. She, feeling the same deep driving force, clung to him.

Later they slept together, and when they awakened, they made love again. That time there was a slowness, a savouring about it. There was leisure to delight in every sensation, and when they were both spent, they lay holding each other, awake but silent, each thinking their separate thoughts.

Leigh was thinking ahead now to the trip back to the base where he would receive his new orders. Would he go to Officers' Candidate School for three months, and get his bars? Or would he be shipped to a port on the east or west coast and end up on a transporter moving closer to the war zone with every mile?

Claire stared wide-eyed into the dark and wondered how she could say goodbye, and when she would see him again.

Before midnight, he drove her home.

The goodbye she dreaded was never spoken. He held her tightly. They kissed long and hard, and smiled at each other, and then she tip-toed inside. As she locked the front door behind her, she heard the car pull away.

In the morning, Leigh was gone.

Chapter 4

In April, sixteen B-25 bombers made the first American offensive strike by bombing Tokyo, flying in from the aircraft carrier *Hornet*, 800 miles from Japan.

Claire read about it in the newspapers, and later, in her room, studied the map of the Pacific war area that she had hung on the wall next to the map of Europe.

Twice weekly, she wrote to Leigh. She had an occasional note in response, one telling her that he was going to Officers' Candidate School. She went to work, came home, spoke to Dora, to Rea, to Margo, but always through a veil of pain. Still, as the weeks passed, the ever-present ache of missing Leigh was dulled.

She noticed that Dora was even more haggard than usual, often pacing the house through the night.

Finally, one day, her mother told her, "We could rent two more rooms, Claire, and still be comfortable. There's an awful lot of nice young women looking for places to live in."

Claire realized that Dora no longer thought about what her parents would say if they knew. There had to be a reason. She asked, "Is it the money, Mom?"

Dora flushed. "I *do* get cheques from your father. They just don't go very far any more. He doesn't realize . . . or maybe he doesn't care . . ."

Aloud Claire told her mother to go ahead and rent the two rooms. Privately she wondered if she could squeeze another five dollars out of her salary. She was already contributing ten dollars weekly to household expenses.

Dora seemed relieved at Claire's reaction. She said, "I'll ask Letty if she's heard any more about the girl she mentioned to me. If she hasn't, then I'll see about placing an ad."

That same afternoon she went to see Letty. Her friend was tired, her attention wandering. She didn't seem interested in Dora's plans, but she had heard that Linda Grant would be coming to Washington within the month. When Dora tried to make conversation, Letty plainly didn't want to talk about the wonderful life she had had before she was widowed.

Worried about Letty, Dora returned home. She mentioned her concern to Claire that evening, and after dinner, Claire walked down to the Merrill house.

She found Letty sitting in the darkened kitchen, her usually busy plump hands lying slackly in her lap.

Claire asked if there had been a letter from Leigh.

Letty slowly shook her head, then said, "Something's going to happen. I have the worst feeling, Claire. Something bad's coming. But I don't know what it is." Her round cheeks were pale. Her eyes seemed without light.

Claire's thoughts were full of Leigh. Something terrible was going to happen. It felt as if her heart had stopped beating. As if all life were draining out of her. She sat very still, fighting panic. Finally, she managed to say, "You must try not to worry. Everything's going to be all right." She spoke to herself as well as Letty Merrill.

When she left, she knew she hadn't been able to comfort Letty any more than she'd been able to comfort herself.

Then, some time past midnight several evenings later, she was awakened by the sound of wailing sirens. She rushed to her window, and saw the spinning red lights of an ambulance in front of the Merrill house on Afton Place.

She threw on her robe, and raced into the yard and down to the Merrill house. Dora and Margo rushed after her, followed by Rea.

But there was nothing anyone could do. The

ambulance men had found Letty on the floor of the foyer. It was too late. Only moments before, they believed, she had died of a heart attack. The telephone dangled from its stand near where she lay. It was decided that she'd felt ill, placed the call for help, and then fallen dead.

Claire called Jeremiah Merrill, and he was able to get in touch with Leigh, who returned home for three days of compassionate leave. He looked stricken, red-eyed and pale. Except for his uncle, he was alone in the world.

Claire had only moments with him, none when they could really talk. If only she could tell him he had her, her love. He wasn't alone. He never would be. Not as long as she lived. That was what was in her mind. But she wasn't able to tell him. The opportunity never arose.

Jeremiah handled the funeral arrangements, and after Leigh had returned to camp, he had Letty's personal belongings, tearfully packed up by Dora, picked up by the Salvation Army. The house, Jeremiah told her, would be sold. Until then it would be rented. This, he said, had been what Leigh wanted him to do.

"But the Merrills have always lived there," Dora protested.

It had been Leigh's decision, Jeremiah repeated.

That news was one more shock to Claire. If he was planning to come back here, why decide to sell the house? Why not keep it to return to? She felt that Leigh had deliberately broken a bond between them. Why? What had happened? Still, he must have some good reason. And later, in her room, she looked at his photograph on her dresser. She touched it gently and whispered, "I love you, Leigh."

It was a hot Sunday morning in June. Claire leaned on a hoe, brushed perspiration from her upper lip, and surveyed the plot she had readied for the victory garden she intended to plant. She ought to have put the seed in earlier, but preparing the soil had taken longer than she'd thought it would.

A door slammed nearby. She looked up.

A man came down the back steps of the Merrill house. He scattered peanuts around him, then looked up into the trees. Sunlight glinted on his blond hair. He was tall and wide-shouldered. He smiled as he came toward her. Behind him, a grey squirrel snagged a peanut, then scampered away. He leaned on the fence. "Good morning. I'm your new neighbour. I want to introduce myself — Logan Jessup."

Claire told him her name, coolly and politely. But she was thinking, so this is who has taken Leigh's place. He walks around Leigh's room, uses Leigh's chair. A bitter taste rose in her mouth. Oh, if only it was Leigh standing here now.

Logan said, "I see you're doing a garden." But he wasn't looking at the plot of hoed earth. He was staring at her. Her long slender legs. Her white shorts. The deep V at the throat of her shirt. She was a very pretty girl. But not his type. The other one . . . the dark-haired one — with big breasts . . . she was more his style.

Claire answered, "I think I've taken on more garden than I should have."

"But you've finished the difficult part," he assured her.

Soon Rea came out. She and Logan greeted each other like old friends. They had, he explained to Claire, spoken together several times before.

Now Rea asked, "Do you live by yourself?"

"I do now. But I expect a friend to join me when he's transferred to Washington."

"Are you in the Army?" Rea asked.

Claire wished her sister wouldn't ask so many questions. But Logan didn't seem to mind. He answered, "No, I'm not in the Army. Not exactly, that is." He paused, then added, "But I *do* work for the government."

His voice had dropped suggestively, Claire

thought. And his words had been evasive. Yet he had the right to speak in generalities, if he wanted to.

Rea wasn't satisfied. She asked, "What department?"

His smile widened. He shrugged. "Oh, we don't talk about that," he said genially.

He was in his thirties, Claire supposed. His face was weathered, but still quite young. He looked strong, competent. She guessed that he was with one of the secret groups, like the Office of Strategic Services, maybe even Army Intelligence, and was so proud of it that hints escaped him even when he was being careful about what he said. *We don't talk about that.* The phrase was even more suggestive than silence would have been.

Claire and Logan exchanged a few more words, then he went into the house.

He stood at the back window, hidden by a curtain, watching the girls, hoping that the dark one, the one who *was* his style, would come out too. He thought how his luck always held. This was going to be exactly the place he needed. And he would have the diversion he wanted at the same time.

A faint smile touched his lips. Once, and not so long ago either, he had felt lost, alien, alone, with no one to turn to, and nothing to live for. He hadn't been Logan Jessup then.

His name had been Walter Braun. But in these five years past he had become part of the most important movement in the world. A part of, and builder of, the new order that would shape the future.

His parents had emigrated from Germany to America before the First World War. In 1918 his father had died in the 'flu epidemic. Six months later, his mother had been killed by a runaway horse in front of the tenement where they lived. He was taken in by upstairs neighbours, the Greenbergs, also German immigrants, but Jews. He could still remember sitting on Mrs Greenberg's lap, his face pressed into her full bosom, weeping a seven year old's tears of terror and loss. The Greenbergs had a daughter his age named Esta. They treated him like the son they had never had. All through his childhood and young manhood, he felt safe, loved. He loved the Greenbergs in return, but he felt more than a brother's feelings for Esta. She had thick dark curly hair, sparkling dark eyes, and, in her teens, a voluptuous body. He always wanted her, but never touched her, except in his dreams.

And then, suddenly, something happened. Hitler became chancellor of Germany. The Nuremberg laws were passed, disenfranchising the Jews. The Greenbergs spoke worriedly of relatives left behind. Letters arrived from Germany, and soon a young man came, a nephew. Later, his brother, then their father, arrived. The room that had once belonged to Walter was his no longer. He shared it with the others. They looked at him with wounded eyes. They said little. But with every passing day Walter sensed that he was an outsider, that the Greenbergs wanted him to leave, that they blamed *him* for everything that had happened. What had been his home for so long, was his home no more. The family had turned against him. Against him, who had done nothing to them. Nothing but love them. Gradually that love became hatred. He left the Greenbergs, and Esta, and never saw any of them again.

One day in the park he heard a man speaking to a small crowd. He stopped to listen. Germany would no longer be ground underfoot by the European powers, the man said. The Fatherland needed space. It would take back the earth that was its history and its life blood. The Aryan race was destined to rule the world. Walter's heart beat quicker as he absorbed that message. He found himself nodding when the man said the Jews of Germany were responsible for the plight in which the nation now found itself. Soon he made friends with another young man in the crowd, and went with him to a meeting. In time, he became Logan Jessup, a man with an important mission to perform.

Now he heard the sound of the door knocker. He turned from the window, ran down the steps to open the door.

The man on the porch was short and red-faced. He said, "Charles told me you'd be home."

"Good morning, John," Logan said.

John made a movement of his right hand.

"No!" Logan said sharply. "Not here. Not ever. Remember that." Too many people could recognize the Nazi salute.

"Sorry," John said.

They talked for a little while. Then, as John was leaving, Logan said, "You'll remember? Drive past every day. But don't stop. Don't park. Drive past. When I want you, the flower pot will be on the right. As long as it's on the left, keep going. Come back the next day."

"I'll remember," John assured him. "On the right, you want me. On the left, come back the next day."

One evening during that week, Dora said to Rea, "I saw you talking to our new neighbour. When is his wife moving in?"

"He's not married," Claire said.

"Then what does he need that big house

72

for? And why isn't he in the Army? He's certainly in good health. And just the right age too."

"It's his job," Rea said. "He does something secret he can't talk about."

Dora didn't like the sound of that. "I don't want you bothering that man, Rea. We don't know him, or anything about him."

"I know he's from Chicago. But he's worked all over. He doesn't know a lot of people in Washington yet, but he thinks he will one of these days. He says he's lucky to have found the house on Afton Place because we have such a nice back yard to look at, and he likes good scenery of all kinds."

At that, Margo choked. She and Claire exchanged amused glances. They didn't explain that Logan Jessup had been talking over Rea's head when he said that.

But they both knew what he was implying.

The day after Margo saw him talking with Claire and Rea in the yard, she had taken to sunbathing as soon as she returned from work, and on Sunday mornings too. Often, when Claire weeded the garden plot, Margo settled herself near the fence, her red two-piece bathing suit as tight as it could be, her long hair shining in the sunlight. That was the scenery both girls were certain that Logan had been referring to.

It wasn't long before Logan and Margo spent hours in bantering conversation. From that they progressed to dating. But, as always with Margo, that stage didn't last long. After going out with him a few times, Margo stopped seeing him. She shrugged away Dora's questions. "He's okay," she said. "Only not for me."

But there was a lot that neither Dora nor Claire knew.

On the first date Margo had with Logan, he took her to a supper club called the Russian Troika. It was a dimly-lit room with walls of shining mirrors. Margo was glad she had dressed so carefully that evening.

He ordered a bottle of champagne, and pâté served with triangles of toast. They sat side by side on a narrow banquette, his big shoulders crowding her, his thigh pressed tightly to hers. When they danced to the music of the three piece combo, they melted together, a beguiling reflection in the mirrored walls. The tall blond man, his head bent slightly, the curvaceous dark-haired girl, floating in his arms, her red skirt swirling around them both.

She didn't pretend, didn't want to. This man was very different. She already knew that. She hungered for him as she had never hungered for a man before.

Later he parked in front of the Merrill

house, led her to the porch. It was dark, bare, except for a single large flower pot at the left of the steps. There was an odd lack of furniture inside, only a sofa in the living room, a chest holding a telephone and small lamp.

When he had turned the lamp on, he stood looking at her, a slanted smile on his lips. Then he pulled her into his arms. "I've been wanting this since I first saw you," he said gruffly.

His kiss was hard and hot and deep. With his mouth pressed to hers, he undressed her. Then his weight brought her down to the sofa.

Their love-making was intense. He was concentrated, in control. Afterwards she knew that it would always be that way. For the first time she had met a man who didn't respond to her flirtatiousness nor to her laughter. He just took what he wanted, and the wanting depended on him, not on her. The knowledge excited her. She was determined to see him again.

She knew that she would when he told her, "I don't like people knowing my business, Margo. I'm a very private person. Don't talk to those women at Hannah's Gate about tonight, nor about me. This is just between us. Do you understand?"

"Of course I do," she said, laughing. "Do you think I'm going to gossip about myself?"

He grasped her chin in his hand. "I mean

it. Seriously." His blue eyes were suddenly hot, fiery.

"Okay," she said, "Okay."

But that night, much later, before she went to sleep at Hannah's Gate, she sat down with her diary and described her first date with Logan in minute detail.

Chapter 5

At summer's end, a few weeks after Churchill and Harriman met with Stalin to discuss a possible second front in Europe, one of Claire's neighbours on Honey Locust Lane stopped to ask how Ian was, and what he was doing. Claire said he seemed well, that he was still stationed in Massachusetts, but expected a transfer soon.

"Two F.B.I. agents were at my house questioning me about him," the neighbour said. "They've been to everyone else on the street." She smiled. "I told them everything I know about him. All good."

Claire smiled back, but as she went on, wondered why Ian was being investigated. It was unlikely that every man in the Army could be checked.

Soon after that, Ian came home for a weekend. He took Claire's room, and she moved in with Rea, because Dora had completed cleaning the third floor attic space as well as the vacant room on the second floor, and she didn't want either one occupied before showing them to prospective renters.

Ian looked well. It was hard to talk to him however. When she mentioned the F.B.I. agents' visits to the neighbourhood, his face went blank. Dora asked him about his living conditions, and if he had made any suitable friends. He snapped at her, saying he wasn't in the Army to further her social ambitions. He did say he'd soon be joining a special engineering detachment, but didn't say where.

Margo pretended to be taken with him, thinking of it as a diversion, although she was certain no one suspected the relationship between her and Logan.

Ian was, she told Claire, a real stud. She spent as much time with him as she could manage, a situation Ian enjoyed, not knowing that when she left him, and everyone was asleep, she slipped out to be with Logan for a few hours, returning to her own bed before dawn.

Ian was glad when the weekend came to a close. He was anxious to get to Oak Ridge, a tiny town in Tennessee.

Within a day there, he was settled, and at work. Even though information about what he was doing was highly compartmentalized, he soon had an idea of why he was studying an element called tube alloy, from the code the British had given it.

Soon it became apparent to him that while he could be useful in Oak Ridge, he could do even more in New Mexico, and he decided to get himself transferred there as quickly as he could.

A few weeks after Ian left, Linda Grant called Dora. She had just arrived in Washington, and was phoning because Letty Merrill had suggested to her mother, months before, that the Lovings might have a room for her. Dora told her to come right over.

Linda was a small girl, thin-faced, and narrow in the shoulders. Her eyes were pale blue, and wide. Her mouth was tiny, thin-lipped, pursed. She was twenty-nine, but looked like a prim twelve year old, with nearly invisible breasts and flat hips. She was soon moved in. On her dresser, she placed silver-framed pictures of her parents. On her bedside table, she put her Bible, with another picture of her mother as a bookmark. She worked at a law office on Fifteen Street. She was quiet, kept to herself, and was plainly religious. It became apparent almost immediately that she didn't like, or approve of, Margo, who felt the same about her.

It came into the open one morning over coffee. Margo was telling Claire, "You're making a mistake. You could be having fun." She grinned at Linda. "Don't you think I'm right?"

"I don't," Linda said. "I couldn't advise Claire to live like you."

Margo raised her brows. "What's wrong with how I live?"

"Men. That's all you think about," Linda said, her lips narrowed.

"Now don't be jealous," Margo laughed. "If you wore some make-up, you wouldn't be a bad-looking girl. You could have a good time too."

Small red circles appeared on Linda's cheekbones. "You don't understand. I'm not interested."

"Then have it your way," Margo snapped.

That was only the beginning. Linda and Margo exchanged words about how much time Margo spent in the bathroom each morning. They had small spats over who stayed too long on the telephone.

Margo told Claire, "That girl's a real old maid type."

Linda told Claire, "Margo's a tramp."

But, very soon, Linda became obsessed by Margo, her comings and goings, her telephone calls and clothes, and above all, what she did with the men she went out with.

At night, after reading in her Bible and kissing the photograph of her mother, Linda would turn out the lamp, and listen as Margo, humming or whistling, readied herself for bed. Creamed her face, put her hair into pink rollers, perfumed her throat . . . Listening to Margo, or else listening *for* her, waiting for her to return home. Meanwhile, fantasizing, imagining, dreaming: Margo, leaning across a table, the tops of her breasts showing, to smile into a shadowed face. Margo, raising her face for a kiss, her arms going around broad shoulders. After awhile, it would be Linda raising her face for a deep smouldering kiss, *her* arms wrapped tight against hard shoulders. By night, she dreamed of Margo. By day she had only pursed lips and disapproving stares for her.

Dora ignored the friction, and prepared to advertise, hoping to fill the third-floor attic room. But she hesitated, uneasy about it. Margo had been Claire's friend. Linda had come recommended by Letty Merrill. But how did Dora know who she'd be getting this time? Maybe inviting a stranger in wasn't a good idea.

It was while she was trying to decide what to do that Carrie Day appeared. She knocked at the door one evening, smiled when Claire opened it. "I'm Carrie Day. I hear you have a room available." Her voice was softly slow, the accent familiar. Hearing it, Claire knew that Carrie would soon be moving into Hannah's Gate. She asked her in, and called Dora.

Carrie Day took off her gloves and said, "How do you do? I'm very pleased to meet you, ma'am."

Dora's face instantly brightened. "You're from Mississippi!"

"Oh, yes, I am. That is, I was," Carrie said. "Until a few years ago. I work in Washington now. Last week I heard that you might have a room, and I'm looking for a new place. It's too noisy where I live at present. It's hard to read, or even to think." She looked around the study, her eyes lingering on the portrait of Big Jack Gowan. "This is so nice." She took a deep breath. "It reminds me of home, Miz Loving. It truly does."

She was a tall woman, buxom, with big round breasts and wide hips, and broad curving thighs that showed under her straight skirt. Her eyes were deep-set, and blue, her mouth wide and soft. Although thirty-two, she seemed older, set in her ways, and very serious. She told Dora that she was a research assistant at the Library of Congress, but added that what she really wanted was to be a freelance writer of magazine articles and maybe even short stories.

Dora asked where she had heard about the

room, thinking that she and Carrie might end up having friends in common. But Carrie was vague, saying, "We were a big group. Someone mentioned it." She smiled faintly. "I guess I wasn't paying that much attention at the time. But your name stuck in my mind — Loving. It's not very common. So then I looked you up in the phone book." She paused, looked again at the painting of Jack Gowan. "Forgive me, Miz Loving, but that man looks so familiar to me. I do wonder if . . ."

"My father, Jack Gowan," Dora said proudly. "The senator."

"Oh, my! Senator Gowan!" Carrie's blue eyes glowed. Inside, she was singing. All her life she'd heard about this man. Now, for the first time, she knew what he looked like. But she said only, "My goodness, imagine my being here! Why, everybody at home knew the senator."

The room, Claire knew, was Carrie's. Dora could never resist that. Within moments Dora led Carrie up to the top floor, showed off the tiny room. Claire could hear the two voices blending softly together.

When they returned downstairs, Carrie drew on her black gloves, settled her small black hat on her tightly curled sand-coloured hair. "I'll come at the end of the week, if I may." She knew it would be all right. She'd played her part to perfection. At long last she was inside Hannah's Gate.

Dora said warmly, "Of course. Move in any time you want to."

In mid-November Casey came home. He said the job was going well. He would be in Washington only a few days, just long enough to report to Geostat. He planned to leave just before Thanksgiving.

Dora said nothing then. But that night Claire heard the angry whispers again.

Three days later, her father went down the path, whistling, a suitcase in one hand, the morning newspaper folded under his arm.

He took a train to Chicago, went to the Dearborn Station by taxi, and late that afternoon, boarded the Santa Fe Chief for Albuquerque. The following day he caught a bus for Hobbs in the eastern part of New Mexico, not far from the Texas state line.

It was snowing when he left the terminal and started out along the main street. The town was small, only a few blocks of shops, a post office, two gasoline stations. In the distance, across bare fields, tall windmills stood out against lowering clouds.

A car pulled up beside him. A young woman leaned out. "Casey!"

He went toward her, waving. "Maria! I could have walked it."

She swung the door open. "I thought you'd be tired maybe. And I couldn't wait to see you."

He climbed in, leaned close to kiss her. Instantly her hand went inside his jacket, his shirt. Her fingers caressed the hair on his chest. When he drew away, he said, "It was a long time for me too." Then: "How's Carlos?"

"Excited. Because his daddy's coming home today."

Maria was twenty-one. The same age as Claire, Casey sometimes remembered. The similarity ended there. Maria had black eyes, dark tousled hair, and plump dimpled cheeks. One day she would be fat, but now she was pleasingly full, soft as fresh bread. She had been a waitress in a diner when Casey first met her. She considered him the most wonderful man she'd ever known. And showed it. He loved her fiercely, grateful for the accepting warmth in which she wrapped him.

"Everything okay in Washington?" she asked, as she drove on.

He nodded. He didn't like to talk about that, but if she asked, he'd answer her.

"Good," she said.

"Don't worry about Washington," he told

her. "I'm finished with that."

It was in that oblique way that his family, Dora, Claire, Rea, and Ian, were mentioned. His other family, that is. The Lovings. This family, the Hobbs one, was different, even had a different name. He had done what Big Jack Gowan had never been able to accomplish. Casey had what he wanted. Here, in Hobbs, he was called Casey Utah. Geostat's mail, Dora's letters, went to a post office box seventy miles away. He emptied it a few times a month. He and Maria had been married under the Utah name, making Carlos legitimate, at least as long as nothing was known of the Lovings. When they'd taken their vows, Maria hadn't known about his other family. But it wouldn't have mattered to her anyway. Washington, D.C. was another world. It wasn't real to her. The Lovings weren't real either. She, and Carlos, were what Casey wanted. And what he would have, she was determined. For as long as he felt that way. She didn't worry about what might come after.

She parked in front of a small house. There were window boxes at the windows, empty now, though they'd be bright with red geraniums by summer, and a cactus garden near the steps. The light snow danced like blown feathers along the hard red ground.

"I've made up my mind," Casey said. "I

don't care what happens, I'm not going back."

"Do what you have to, Casey. Whatever you want, it's all right with me."

They went up the path to the house holding hands. The door swung open. A small boy stood there, joy in his big brown eyes. He shouted, "Daddy!"

"I'm home, Carlos," Casey said, and swung the boy off the steps and into his arms.

At Hannah's Gate, the talk was of Thanksgiving dinner.

Carrie had offered Dora her ration stamps, saying, "I won't need them. Use whatever you want."

Linda announced that she had a ride, and would be going home. Her office would close for the whole holiday weekend.

"Lucky you," Margo told her. "Our office never closes." She meant hers and Claire's.

Carrie said in her soft slow voice, "But Linda doesn't work for the government."

Margo made a face, but Dora said quickly, "I'll make a turkey, and the fixings, and pumpkin pie."

"We should ask Logan," Rea said.

There was a silence. Then Dora asked, "And why should we?"

"He doesn't have any place to go. That's why," Rea answered.

"How do you know?" Dora demanded.

"He told me," Rea said.

"It's not a bad idea," Margo put in. "I mean, it's a neighbourly thing to do. I'll put in my ration stamps too, if it'll help."

Dora considered. Then: "No, I don't think so." If Casey wasn't going to be home . . . if Ian wasn't . . . Then she wouldn't have Logan Jessup, the only man at the table, acting as if he belonged there. "No," she repeated when Rea pressed her. She went on, discussing the menu, but her eyes kept going back to Rea. How come the girl knew so much about Logan Jessup and his plans? Dora didn't like the man, but she didn't know why. She'd hardly spoken more than a good morning and good evening to him. It was just . . . well, she didn't know. There was something about him. And Rea was almost fourteen now . . .

That Thursday, Claire was setting the table. She went into the study to get a lacquered tray for a dried flower arrangement she planned to use as a centerpiece for the Thanksgiving dinner table.

She found the tray, but as she started to leave, noticed something peculiar about the bookcase. The row of books looked different, somehow disturbed. There was a collection of histories of the Civil War, called by her grandfather the War Between the States. The titles of his books referred to it both ways. Now they were out of their usual order. Two stuck out, as if they'd been hastily replaced. Claire put them where they belonged, and returned to her preparations. But she wondered who had been looking at those old books.

She thought about it through the evening. After dinner, Margo went out. Dora and Carrie settled in the study with some old albums of Dora's.

Claire heard their conversation as she went to look at the books again, troubled without knowing why.

The following week, Claire was in the kitchen writing to Ian. As she described the Thanksgiving dinner, she thought of her father. The strangely final look he'd had as he'd walked away from Hannah's Gate. Now a chill rippled down her back. He'd seemed the same as always during the visit, but still, at that moment, when he'd turned away, whistling . . .

Claire shook her head as if shaking the memory away. She didn't mention her uneasiness to Ian, but she couldn't forget it.

She remembered, long before, when she'd been a child, her mother weeping, saying, "I'd have gone with him, if I could. But what could I do when I had three children to think of?"

Now Claire told herself it didn't matter any

more. She sealed the letter to Ian, put it aside to mail the next morning.

Linda came in. A week before, when she'd returned from her trip home, she'd been joyful, smiling. Now, though, her eyes burned with fury. "Where's Margo?" she demanded in a shaking voice.

"Out for the evening," Claire said, wondering what was wrong now. Linda and Margo always seemed to grate on each other.

"Out as usual. Of course. What else? But I've got to talk to her. I want her to stay out of my room. It's my private place, and I don't want her in there."

Claire said quietly, "Now, Linda, why should Margo go into your room?"

"I don't know why. But she has. And I don't like it."

"What makes you think so? Maybe my mom . . ."

"It couldn't have been your mother. It was Margo. Who else would go through everything?"

"You're probably imagining that," Claire said gently.

Linda sat down, hands folded in her lap, her knees together.

In the brief silence, the sound of Carrie's typewriter could be heard faintly from the top floor.

"I'm not imagining it," Linda said. "You know the feeling as well as I do. You leave things just so. And when you come back they're not just so any more. And the only person it could be is Margo. Look at her! You can see she doesn't care what she does!"

That was when Margo appeared in the doorway. "I hear you, Linda Grant! Talking about me! Just say to my face what you've got to say! Don't whisper behind my back!" Her voice was shrill, her face flushed.

"Okay," Linda said. "I'll say it to your face. You were looking around in my room. What do you want? What were you after?"

"In *your* room?" Margo looked astounded. "Who says I was ever in your room? Why would I be, for God's sake?"

"You were!" Linda's blue eyes filled with tears now. "My closet. My drawers. My books. You even touched my Bible. And you moved my mother's picture too."

Claire interrupted. "Listen, you two . . . there's been some mistake, I'm sure. It doesn't make sense . . ."

"I've never been in your room, Linda," Margo said tartly.

"Well, somebody's been looking through my things," Linda said stubbornly.

Carrie came in, her eyes moving quickly from Linda to Margo to Claire, her soft mouth quivering. She stood there for a moment, then turned and left without saying a word.

"Oh, shit," Margo muttered, and then with a shrug of disgust, "Grow up, Linda." She flipped her hand at Claire, and went upstairs.

She closed the door to her room with a quick hard bang. Then she went to the window to look out, wondering how long it would be before Logan raised the shade in his bedroom. She wanted to see him.

But the shade remained down. Sighing, she pulled the hat box from the closet, took out her diary, and sat down to write. She put in the details of Linda's accusations, her own reactions. Once in a while she glanced out to see if Logan had signalled her. The shade remained lowered. When she finished writing, she closed the diary.

If somebody had searched Linda's room, then maybe the same somebody would search hers. She sat at the table, looking carefully around the room for a long time. Finally, with a sudden grin, she rose. She knew exactly what to do. Nobody snooping in her drawers would lay hands on her diary, read what she'd been writing. Nobody, ever, would find it where she'd decided to hide it.

Several days went by. Linda and Margo didn't speak.

Then, one morning at breakfast, Margo said, "You don't have to play games, Linda. We're quits now. I told you I hadn't searched your room, and I hadn't. You didn't believe me, I guess, and went to see what you could find in *my* room. We're even. Let's stop."

Linda's narrow shoulders went rigid. "I haven't. I wouldn't. I'm not the kind of person . . ."

"You deny it?" Margo demanded. She knew somebody had been in her closet. She could tell. She didn't really care. The diary was safe. But she wasn't going to let Linda get away with it.

Carrie got up. "I've got to go," she told Dora. She left the kitchen quickly, moving fast for so large a woman.

"I don't care what you think," Linda went on. "You're nothing but a tramp!"

Dora intervened. She said, "Girls, you're upsetting all of us with your feuding. Let's not have any more."

Margo and Linda looked daggers at each other, but dropped the subject.

Soon the argument forgotten. But it weighed on Claire. She sensed that something was happening, something she didn't understand. It was as if a distant threat had suddenly moved closer.

Why had both Linda and Margo thought

someone had searched their rooms! They blamed each other, but perhaps they were both wrong. Perhaps someone else was responsible. Could it be Rea? Or Carrie? But why? What could either of them be looking for?

Then, one evening, when she and Margo returned from work, Dora said, "The most peculiar thing happened. The lock on the storage shed door is broken. As if somebody tried to get in. But nothing's missing as far as I can tell. And what could be? There's only old junk in there."

It was a small thing, but it became one more on the list of unexplainable happenings.

Soon there was another question to which Claire had no answer.

She had gone to bed early. Hours later she was awakened from a sound sleep. She sat up in bed, listening. Something had disturbed her. She didn't know what.

She waited, straining to hear. The house's night noises were familiar. A squeak. A window rattling. Then she heard a thud. It wasn't a familiar night noise. It came again. Now there was a small scratching sound. And once more, a thud.

Heart beating hard, a prickle of fear running along her spine, she climbed from bed, and stood listening. Momentarily something seemed to stir at the window. She went toward it. But now there was silence. An ominous silence. She drew a breath, another. There was a faint rustle. She peered into the darkness. Nothing.

Shadows lay across the yard, a blanket of black. A silver glint of light marked the corner of what had been Leigh's house. A wave of loneliness swept her. Oh, if only he were there now. If only . . . But it was no use to wish that. Logan Jessup lived in the house on Afton Place, and Leigh was far away.

Claire slowly returned to bed. She told herself that she might have imagined the sound. She might have dreamed it, and risen from sleep believing it to be real.

The next night, however, she once again awakened suddenly, not knowing why. She sat up, listened. Had there been a movement in the hall? Had she dreamed the sound of footsteps? She tried to go back to sleep, but couldn't. She turned one way, then another. She sat up and fluffed her pillow and snuggled down once more. But it was no use. All her senses were alerted. At last she rose. She went into the corridor. It was dark, empty. All the bedroom doors were closed.

Slowly she went down the stairs. A cold wind touched her cheeks. She paused. Where was it coming from? There was a sound now.

A thud. A rattle.

She gave a start of recognition, relief flooding through her. She knew what had happened. She hurried into the kitchen. The door stood open on the black night. She crossed the dark room. The refrigerator hummed. A hiss of steam came from the radiator. Her legs trembled, her weakness a reaction to her earlier fright. She smiled at her imagination. She knew that the door latch had been unreliable for years. If the key wasn't turned all the way in the lock, the wind could easily swing the door open until it bumped against the cupboard. Now she turned the key carefully. There. This time it would hold for sure.

She returned to the staircase. But then, as she started up, she froze. A shadow. Black. Unmoving. A breath that became a gasp. She turned back. "Who's there?" she whispered.

"Me." Rea giggled softly. "You scared me, Claire."

"What are you doing?"

"I heard a noise."

"The kitchen door blew open, Rea."

"So that's what it was."

"Yes. Go back to bed."

Rea yawned. She went up the steps before Claire, tiptoeing on stockinged feet.

Claire saw her into her room, then went to her own. But as she climbed into bed, she remembered Rea's stockinged feet. Did she sleep in them? It seemed an odd thing to do. And then, as she fell asleep, Claire wondered if Rea had just come downstairs when Claire saw her. Or had she been on the way up when Claire returned from locking the kitchen door?

Margo had turned back when she heard the door swing open behind her. But she'd seen Claire's silhouette in time, and frozen in the shadows. After a long second, the door slammed shut. The lock clicked. Margo grinned, fingers tightening around the key she carried in her pocket. Just in case. She'd never needed it before, but she did now. Still, if she really had to, she could use the wistaria as a ladder, something she'd done when she couldn't get out because somebody was wandering around downstairs.

She glided swiftly down the long yard. Frost crackled faintly under her feet. There was a mild smell of wood smoke in the air. A few distant stars glittered in the black canopy of the sky.

She'd waited all evening for Logan's signal, but then, finally despairing, decided she'd wait no longer. She *had* to see him. She *had* to tell him. He would have to help her. There was no one to turn to, only Logan.

She saw a tiny streak of light at the side

window. The drapes were drawn, so she couldn't see into the room. She felt tears burn her eyes. Damn, damn! She stood there, determined to wait until his visitor was gone, trembling with cold in spite of her coat. She *had* to talk to him tonight.

Then, suddenly, she forgot the cold. The staccato rumble of the voices she heard became sharper, the words clear. Gradually, as she listened, her eyes widened. Her teeth chattered. She listened for a few moments longer, then backed away to creep up to Hannah's Gate through inky shadows.

Chapter 6

The holiday season was over. Both Christmas and New Year had been quiet in the Loving household.

At the end of January 1943, Claire read that there had thus far been 60,000 casualties of the war.

By then she had received a note from Leigh written on thin blue paper. A V-letter, which meant that he had been shipped overseas. The return address was an Army post office box number. He said he'd been lucky. He'd been sent to his most favourite city. So Claire was sure he was in London. It had been the place he'd spoken of as the one city abroad he really wanted to see.

She smoothed the letter and put it away with other notes of his. She tried to imagine that he was walking on Baker Street, looking for Sherlock Holmes' house. She pictured him at Piccadilly Circus. But it was impossible to believe he was seeing the London he'd dreamed of. The war had turned that old London into no more than a dream. She looked at her maps, at the English Channel. There was talk that one day soon there would be an invasion of the continent. There'd have to be. If only it was over, she thought. So Leigh could come home again.

Time dragged although her days were full. Still, when she looked back on them, she wondered what she had done. She had an occasional date with an old friend from school, or someone from the office. But the hours seemed wasted. She preferred to hurry home each evening. Maybe there'd be a letter from Leigh awaiting her.

A warm end of April breeze filled the room with the scent of plum and apple blossoms from trees that Letty Merrill had once lovingly tended. She was gone, but the trees continued to flower.

In the house where Letty had lived, Margo lay close to Logan Jessup, her hip and thigh hot where they touched him, her lips stinging from his kisses.

She had been as eager for him as he had been for her, so she'd gone immediately into his arms, and then to bed, even though she'd thought, on the way over, that she wouldn't let him anywhere near her until she'd told him.

She'd planned her words many times, but somehow she hadn't been able to bring herself to it. Now, finally, she admitted to herself that she was scared. But she had no choice. She had to tell him. She took a deep breath and said, "Logan, I have to talk to you about something."

He turned his head on the pillow. She saw the glimmer of his smile. "Yes? What?"

"I'm pregnant, Logan." She blurted it out on a single breath.

The glimmer of his smile faded. He pulled away from her. Her lip and thigh, so hot before from his touch, were suddenly chilled. Reaching for his clothes, he said distantly, "Are you sure?"

"Of course," she said.

"Then so what? Why are you telling me?"

"Why am I . . ." She sat up, flung back her hair. "What do you mean? I'm going to have your baby."

"My baby?" he said nastily. "*My* baby? And how do you know? How many men have you been with besides me?"

"Logan! I haven't! Those dates were nothing. You wanted me to go out with other guys. Don't you remember how you told me to? To keep from giving anybody at Hannah's Gate ideas about us?"

"Get rid of it," he said.

"But why? We love each other. We can get married." It was what she wanted, had hoped for. She'd never felt about a man the way she felt about him.

"I don't remember saying I love you. I don't remember asking you to marry me either." He stood over her, his eyes hooded.

"Wait a minute," she said.

"Get up, Margo. Get dressed, and get out of here."

"Just like that? 'Get out of here.' You think you can treat me that way? Well, you're wrong. I'm pregnant with your child. And I'm not going to have a bastard and raise him all alone."

"You silly bitch," he said evenly. "I don't care what you do. You let yourself get caught. Maybe you did it on purpose. Either way, it's your problem."

Suddenly she was so angry she could no longer contain herself. Eyes as dark as tar pits, voice harsh, she yelled words she had never before allowed herself to think. "You damned spy! I know all about you and your friend. And how you meet at night, and make your plans. And don't think I won't tell. Because I will. I'll yell it from the rooftops! They'll stick you in jail for the rest of your life. If they don't hang you, that is."

She got up, went to the chair where she had left her skirt and sweater.

In a single stride, he was close, looming over

her. His face was white. "What are you talking about?"

"I heard you," she told him. "I came over one night, hoping to surprise you. He was here. The two of you were talking."

Logan's hands clenched around her shoulders. "And so?"

"So we're going to get married," she said.

"Stupid," he muttered. "One day I'll control this country for the Führer. Do you think I'll risk that?"

Now, suddenly, she was frightened. But it was too late for her to scream, to break away. "My diary," she said. "It's all in my diary."

But he smashed his fist into her face. Long after her head lolled, and her legs gave way, he held her on her feet, and hit her again and again.

Her face was bloody, her eyes wide open and cloudy, when, finally, he let her drop to the floor.

It was the next morning. A Friday. Claire came down to breakfast at the usual time. She was dressed, ready to leave for the office.

Dora said, "You'd better wake Margo up. I haven't heard a sound out of her room."

Claire went up to tap at the door. There was no answer. She called, "Margo? Are you up? It's late. We have to go." When there

103

was no response, she tried the door. It opened, and she went in. The room was dark, the shades drawn. Margo's bed was empty. It hadn't been slept in.

Claire hesitated, thinking. Margo had come home the night before. Claire had spoken to her before going to sleep. Margo must have gone out again. And decided to stay out. That was unusual for her. She always came home to sleep. But perhaps . . . Claire thought of herself and Leigh. Perhaps Margo had found someone she really cared about. Claire hadn't known her to be serious about any man she'd gone out with. But maybe this time it was different.

In spite of what Linda thought, Margo wasn't promiscuous. She was flighty, and man crazy. But that was all. So she must have found a man that mattered deeply to her.

Claire closed the door behind her. She'd see Margo at work.

She told Dora that Margo must have left very early that morning, and got a doubtful look. Linda grinned knowingly, "Oh, I'll bet." Carrie appeared not to be paying attention to the conversation, which seemed often to be the case. Mostly when Carrie was home, she disappeared into her attic room, to peck away at her typewriter. When she remained downstairs, it was only to talk to Dora.

Claire said, "Margo probably had a special job at the office this morning," hoping she was right.

But Margo wasn't at work, and the supervisor said she hadn't called in, and when Claire returned home that evening, she realized that Margo still wasn't there either.

Dora asked, "Did you see Margo? What happened?"

"She's probably run away from home with a man," Rea said.

"She doesn't have to run away," Claire retorted, exasperated at Rea's suggestion. "She's a grown woman. She can do what she wants."

"And she does," Rea answered, eyes sparkling.

"You mind your own business," Dora put in. "What Margo does is nothing to you."

Claire looked at her watch. It was after seven. Margo ought to be back, ought to have phoned. Claire was worried now. Why hadn't Margo said she was going to be away? Why hadn't she at least left a note?

She went upstairs, and into Margo's room. She felt uncomfortable, remembering how annoyed Margo had been when she'd thought Linda had been looking at her things. She would be even more annoyed this time, Claire thought. But still . . . she wasn't here. She had to be somewhere. Maybe she'd gone off for a few days.

Claire looked in the closet. Margo's two suitcases were on the floor, where she always stored them.

And then Claire's eyes widened. She caught her breath, worry turning to fear. On the back of the closet door, on a hook, hung Margo's handbag. Her purse! She wouldn't have gone out without it. It was impossible. She'd have taken money, house keys, her bus pass. She had to have her bag with her.

Quickly Claire checked and found three bags in all: a red one, and a white one, and a black one. The white was wrapped in tissue paper, for storage until summer came. The red was full, containing Margo's wallet, her compact and lipstick and a small mascara container. And her house keys. Everything. And there, right in front of Claire, she suddenly realized, was Margo's spring coat. And her winter coat, just back from the cleaner's, hung at the end of the bar.

Breathless now, alarmed pulses pounding in her throat, Claire made a swift search. One pair of shoes was gone, a blue skirt, a blue rayon blouse, a lightweight blue sweater.

Claire knew what she had to do, but stood rooted to the spot. What could have happened? After talking to Claire, when everyone was asleep, Margo, wearing the same outfit that she'd had on all day, had left the house.

And she hadn't come back.

Claire started down the steps. Midway, she stopped. But wait — how did she know Margo had gone out? Perhaps she was here, somewhere in the house. The basement. The storage shed. In an unused attic room.

They would have to look. First within. Then in the yard. Perhaps she had fallen, hurt herself. Perhaps she was somewhere close by.

The doorbell rang. She hurried to answer it. It was dark by then, but the porch light glinted on shiny metal buttons, on a leather belt. A policeman stood there.

He asked quietly, "Can you tell me if Margo Desales lives here?"

"She does," Claire said. "What is it? What's the matter?"

"Is she . . . by any chance, is she at home?" he asked.

"No." Now Claire's voice shook. "She's not. And I'm awfully worried about her."

Claire realized that Linda had come into the hall, stood listening. Carrie was at the top of the stairs, leaning over the banister. Dora was in the living room close by. Claire could almost feel their held breaths. She said softly, "I've just been upstairs to her room. You see, she didn't come home to sleep last night. And I . . . I've found her purse. Her coat. I'm afraid something has happened. I was about to call . . ."

The policeman said, "I see." He paused, then went on, "I'm sorry to have to tell you this. A woman was found this morning near the C & O canal at Fletcher's Landing. She was dead. Murdered. She had no bag with her, no driver's licence. But there was a cleaner's tag on her sweater. We've traced it. The sweater belonged to a woman named Margo Desales, who lived at this address."

"Margo," Claire breathed.

"You understand that anybody could be wearing that sweater, so we're not certain. Her prints are being checked against F.B.I. files, but that'll take some time of course. And we'd like a positive identification as quickly as possible."

Linda moaned.

"No, no," Carrie said, while Dora burst into tears.

Rea was suddenly there, pressed close to Claire, her fingers tightening around her hand, as Claire asked quietly, "What do you want me to do?"

Chapter 7

The sky burned crimson with the fading spring sunset but the street was grim, the few trees still leafless. The building was soot-blackened, with peeling window frames and doors.

Although Claire had offered to drive herself down to the morgue in Southeast, a distant area of the city, the policeman had insisted that she go with him. Now she was glad he had. He had told her, on the way, that a homicide detective would meet them, and as he led her inside, a man detached himself from the shadows along the wall.

He was whistling 'The White Cliffs of Dover'. When he reached her, he stopped, smiled faintly. The policeman turned her over to him as if disposing of a package he hadn't wanted, said, "Take it easy," and left.

The homicide detective introduced himself as William Eagan. He was tall, no longer young, with a full paunch above his belt. He had tired-looking blue eyes and a small piece of white tape covered a shaving cut on his long narrow chin.

"This isn't going to be pleasant," he said. "But it'll only take a minute."

Unable to answer him, she nodded.

They walked down a dimly lit hall. The air was sour with a scent she didn't recognize. A door opened, and she moved into blinding light.

The detective murmured to an attendant. She was aware of movement, a squeal of metal rollers. Dizziness swept her.

"Miss Loving?" the detective said, his fingers pressing into her elbow.

Inside her head, she heard her own voice whispering, Oh, please, please, no . . .

The attendant drew back the sheet.

The girl who lay there had a mass of tangled black hair. The lashes that lay on her swollen cheeks were long and black. Her face was misshapen, the bones beneath the flesh crumpled, the lips torn. Her throat was black and blue. Her hands were folded together on her bare breast. A familiar blue stone winked at Claire.

Claire turned away. She was suddenly covered with perspiration. She felt the dampness in her auburn hair burning with heat. Her cheeks, her hands, were hot and wet.

"You identify the body as that of Margo Desales?"

"Yes. It's Margo." The answering voice was a croak. A stranger's speaking from far away.

"For the record," the detective said.

"I heard," the attendant confirmed. Then: "You claim this body?"

"Yes — I don't know. Her family . . ." Claire shivered. Now she was cold. It seemed as if her brain were encased in ice. Margo's family had to be notified. But how would Claire do it? She didn't know Margo's relations, where they lived even. Margo had never spoken of them. But then Claire thought of the office. Oh, yes, the office would have a record. Someone would know.

Detective Eagan guided her to the door. She walked down the hall again. It was a terrible nightmare, she told herself. She would awaken and wonder why she had had such an awful dream. She would awaken, and she and Margo would go to work on Monday morning just as they always did.

Then the detective said, "I'll drive you home. I want to have a look at your friend's belongings. And you and I need to talk."

So she knew that she hadn't been dreaming. She couldn't have imagined the man's matter-of-fact monotone. His calm questioning as they headed across town, about the others who lived at Hannah's Gate. Margo was dead. She would never laugh again, nor dance, nor look with an interested gaze at a man. She'd never

111

wear a skirt with a torn hem, nor forget to take out the cleaner's label. She'd never strut across a room in her high-heeled sandals. Margo was dead.

It didn't make sense. There was no reason for anyone to kill Margo. She'd never hurt anyone. But now, suddenly, Claire thought of Linda Grant. Sweet, religious Linda, who had a temper, who disliked Margo. But the thought was ludicrous. It couldn't be. If for no other reason than Linda hadn't the strength to do what had been done to Margo.

The detective had told Claire, and she'd seen for herself — only a man, a man's fists, could have struck those terrible blows.

At Hannah's Gate, Detective Eagan asked everyone to come into the living room so that he could discuss what had happened.

Rea went to get Carrie and Linda. When they joined Claire and Dora, the detective took out his notebook.

But Dora said quickly, "Just a minute." And to Rea: "You don't have to stay."

"Why not?" Rea demanded. "I want to hear about it too."

"You don't know anything about Margo," Dora retorted. She looked pleadingly at the detective. "This is so sordid. And she's just a child."

"I'm not a baby," Rea yelled. Her lower

lip jutted out. Suddenly she looked even younger than her fourteen years.

The detective waved her away. "Okay. I don't need you, I guess. At least not for now."

Rea gave him a hard haughty stare, but Dora took her by the hand, and pushed her from the room, closing the door firmly behind her.

All right, Rea said to herself. Treat me like a baby if you want to. But you'll be sorry. A small smile crossed her face. Her eyes lit with glee. One of these days, she'd show them. But not just now. No, after what they'd done to her, they could damn well stew for a while.

In the living room, Dora was saying, "She was a nice enough girl, I suppose. But . . ." She fluttered her hands helplessly.

"Tell me about her men friends," the detective said.

Linda grimaced. "There were so many of them. We'd never know where to begin. At least, I wouldn't. I just didn't pay attention. I didn't care who she went out with." She believed what she was saying. The men she'd imagined with Margo had always been faceless. They were *men,* not individuals.

Carrie made a soft sad sound. "But she was such a generous girl, Linda." Carrie wondered how this would affect her. She asked herself if maybe she should move, but she knew she wouldn't. She wouldn't move until she'd accomplished what she'd come to do. She knew it would happen. She just needed time.

"I need names," Detective Eagan said. He looked at Claire, waiting patiently for her answer.

After a moment's hesitation, she mentioned Jimmy Carsson then a number of others, some from the office, some not. She also spoke of Logan Jessup. But she explained that Margo never had prolonged relationships. She seemed, very quickly, to tire of the men she knew, to go to others.

Margo wasn't like Claire herself. She, having fallen in love with Leigh, didn't want anyone else. But then, Margo hadn't fallen in love. Perhaps that was why she'd become so quickly bored.

But the detective, having written down each name as Claire spoke it, seemed dissatisfied. He glanced at Linda, then at Carrie. "What about it? Any names to add? Anything at all?"

Carrie shook her head slowly from side to side.

Linda shrugged.

"And you?" he asked Dora.

"She seemed a respectable girl," Dora told him earnestly. "High-spirited, but respectable. And she needed a place to stay."

He said then that he wanted to see Margo's room.

When Claire took him upstairs, he asked, "What about her address book? Any papers around! Anything you think will help?"

"It's all just as Margo left it," Claire told him. "The policeman said leave everything alone. So before I went with him, I locked the door."

Now she put the key in the lock, turned it. The door swung open. The room was dark. She fumbled for the wall switch. When the light came on, the detective stood still, slowly looking around. Finally he asked, "Do you know if she had any special problems? Was she worried about anything?"

"No," Claire said. "She didn't seem to be. But she never confided in me. We weren't that close. I don't think she was close to anybody."

"You don't think that's funny?"

"Not particularly. Some people are like that. And we lived together more by accident than anything else. That goes for the other girls too. It's the roof over their heads that keeps them here."

"Did you like Margo?"

"We got along. I didn't expect too much of her, I suppose." Claire took a deep breath. "She had a sense of excitement, and I admired that. I didn't realize it until now maybe. But I *did* admire it."

"I understand," the detective said. Without saying any more, he set about searching the room. He went through the drawers in Margo's dresser, delicately sifting through her underclothes, examining each pair of silk stockings. "Couple of nice hose here," he muttered. "I wonder where she got them."

"At a small shop on G Street. She happened to pass by at the time a new shipment came in."

"Did she have any other hard to get items?"

"No. But you'll see when you get to her closet."

He soon understood what Claire meant. Margo's clothing had been flashy, but not new, not well made nor expensive. She certainly had nothing of any black market value.

He was more interested in what he found in her purse. There was a matchbook advertising the Domino Club. He asked if she had gone there. Claire said she'd mentioned it once. He also found an address book, and pasted inside, a name and address to be notified in case of emergency. The name was Frederick Desales. The address a town in Ohio.

"Her father?" the detective asked. "Or brother?"

"I don't know."

"You really *didn't* know much about her, did you?"

"I told you."

"And that didn't seem peculiar to you?"

"No. But it does now."

"The twenty-twenty vision of hindsight." He examined the tubes, jars, and eyebrow pencils on the tray on the dresser. "Easy to see when it's too late," he sighed.

They stood there silently. From somewhere within the house, there came the faint sound of music. Rea must have turned on the radio. Outside there was the rustle of a squirrel darting along a thick wistaria vine, and further away there was the grinding of gears, as a truck labored up the hill.

Detective Eagan said finally, "I guess there's nothing more for us to do here."

"Will you find out who killed Margo?" Claire asked tremulously.

"Maybe. There'll be an autopsy, of course. Maybe that'll tell us something more. And we'll check out the guys she dated, now or earlier. From the list you gave us, as well as from her address book. Then we'll see where we stand."

"You'll let me know?"

"Sure." Then, "Are you going to call Frederick Desales?"

"Yes. Right away."

117

The detective scrawled a number on a card. "Tell him to phone the morgue about the arrangements."

Her hands trembled as she took the card.

He went on, "And my number's there too. I'll want to talk to him. Maybe he'll know something."

Claire didn't reply. But she didn't think Margo's father — or was it brother — would know anything about what had happened to Margo in Washington. Margo had received no mail from anywhere in Ohio. She had never had a phone call from there, nor made one either.

Even so, after the detective left and she spoke to Frederick Desales, who she learned was Margo's father, she was taken aback. He reacted to news of Margo's death only with resignation. "I always feared she'd come to a bad end," he said regretfully and asked for no details. He accepted without comment the information that Claire gave him, and when she asked what she should do with Margo's belongings, said, "Dispose of them. Give them away. I don't want them."

During Detective Eagan's visit to Hannah's Gate, and while Claire spoke on the phone to Margo's father, Logan Jessup had stood at his bedroom window, concealed by a thin curtain, and watched the house at the top of the slope.

But now he knew that Margo's body had been found. There had been a news flash on the radio about it. He supposed that it had been identified, or would be soon. That's why he was watching.

He was certain, or almost certain, that Margo's wild threat about her diary was only that. A wild threat to stop him. But almost certain wasn't good enough. Yet there was nothing he could do at the moment. He couldn't get into Hannah's Gate now. He could only wait.

Still, late the next afternoon, after the radio spread news of the identity of the dead girl found at the C & O canal, Logan was among several other neighbours who dropped by Hannah's Gate to commiserate with Dora and Claire, and to ask in whispers what had happened.

He shook his head sadly. "She was such a nice girl. It's really too bad. She didn't deserve to end up that way," he told Claire.

She murmured her agreement. Dora wrung her hands.

"I suppose there's been no news about what happened?"

"None," Claire said.

"I wish I could help. We went out a few times, you know. But then she seemed to

119

get tired of me." His voice deepened. "One of those things."

He was sure now, having made the visit, that if there was a diary, Claire didn't know about it, hadn't read it. Or else that Margo hadn't written about him in it. Claire couldn't be so good at acting. Nobody could be, he was sure. Except him, of course. He was. Still, there remained a small niggling doubt in his mind. Maybe Claire hadn't examined Margo's belongings. Maybe the police had overlooked the diary, or hadn't recognized it for what it was. It meant taking a small chance. But he would have to wait.

That night Dora wrote a frantic letter to Casey, telling him about Margo's murder, begging him to return home.

For weeks afterwards, she watched the mail, but there was no response from Casey, until finally she had a brief note. "It's impossible," he told her. "I can't leave my job now. I'm needed here, and the war effort comes first. Let me know what the police find out."

In mid-May, a full month after Margo was murdered, Claire called Detective Eagan to ask if he had any news.

He said briskly, "Sorry, there's nothing. And I might as well tell you. I'm beginning to think there's not going to be anything. It looks as if your friend picked up the wrong man in a bar somewhere. Somebody she didn't know, somebody you never heard of. We've talked to every man we know she dated, and we have no reason to suspect any of them. So it's got to be somebody you didn't know about."

"Are you going to pretend it never happened?" she asked bitterly.

"We won't do that, but try to understand. After a while, a case like this goes on the back burner. There's a lot going on. Things keep happening. If we don't get a lead right away, the chances get slimmer all the time. Girls, taking up with strangers, lonely, away from home, wanting a good time . . . It's common these days in Washington."

It had been while the detective was questioning him that Logan realized there was a good way to make sure the police continued to believe that Margo had died as a result of a casual pickup.

He had delayed for a while. There was no use in being too anxious. But now, at the end of May, he parked his car. It was almost eight o'clock in the evening. A thick purple twilight hung over the city.

He walked slowly along the street, eyeing the women he passed. One was too stout, a

W.A.C. with big hips wearing flat shoes. Another was thin, with shoulders like a wire coat hanger. A third had a wrinkle under her chin, a fourth had dark hair on her upper lip. Finally, he saw what he wanted. A young woman, of perhaps twenty-three. Her hair was red, her complexion fresh. She had a prancing walk that reminded him of Margo. He had almost caught up with her, was ready to make his move, when he remembered that he'd been to the Neptune Bar and Grill with Margo. No, it wouldn't do. He couldn't go back there. Someone might remember him, remember Margo. It wasn't likely, but why take a chance?

He went on, cut up Thirteenth Street, then turned left at F Street. There were other bars, other girls. For a moment he thought regretfully of the girl with red hair. How lucky she had been. And she'd never know it.

He began his search again. Ahead he saw Old Ebbitt's. At the same time, his eyes narrowed. There she was. Just what he wanted. A tall girl, her shoulders bare, the deep V at the back of her dress exposing smooth tanned flesh. Her long legs scissored smoothly, giving her a roll as she walked. He wet his lips. He could feel her slender arms closing around him.

He took a long step, then another. Suddenly

he was on her, stumbling, his weight sagging into her so that she staggered and went to her knees.

With a cry, he caught her by the shoulder, raised her up, "Oh, my dear, I'm so sorry. I didn't see you . . . rubbernecking . . . what a hick I am. Do forgive me. Are you all right?"

"I'm fine," she said breathlessly.

He flapped supposedly incompetent hands at her skirt, her arms. "God! I can't think how I . . . are you sure you're okay? Your dress? Your shoes? Perhaps you'd better take a good look. I'll be glad to pay for any damage."

"No damage," she said, smiling. "It's perfectly all right. I realize it was an accident."

"You *are* kind." He put a hand under her elbow. "My dear, you must let me buy you a drink at least. Some small recompense for nearly trampling you into the sidewalk."

She was saying that it wasn't necessary even as he urged her, led her, thrust her, over the threshold and into the dim front room of the bar, and sat her down at a corner table. She was still saying that when he ordered two gin and tonics. She smiled her thanks when the drinks arrived, and stopped saying it wasn't necessary at the same time.

From then on, as Logan thought, it was a simple piece of cake. The girl's name was Harriet Raynolds. She was from Oyster Bay, Long Island. She was a typist at the Labour Department. For two years she'd been in Washington, and she was lonely for her home, her folks, and most of all, for her boyfriend, who was somewhere in the Pacific. Pulling out a snapshot of a smiling boy in uniform, she said, "And if I don't hear from him pretty soon, I think I'm going to go crazy. After reading about the Aleutians, I'm scared for him."

Logan made soothing noises. "It's hard," he said. "I know how you feel." He looked at his watch, ordered another round of drinks.

Soon her eyes were glazed; her lips seemed numbed. She sagged closer to the mahogany-topped table.

Sneaking a glance at the waiter who had served them, Logan decided that the man was too busy to notice her, or Logan. He hoped he hadn't gone too far with the liquor. She still had to walk to the car.

Somehow, she managed, with his help. His arm under hers, his soothing laughing voice steadying her, answering her plaintive questions. "What's happening? Where are we going?" And she giggled, "I guess I've had too much to drink, haven't I?"

Once they were in the car, he drove out of town, picking up MacArthur Boulevard in Georgetown, and following it beyond the District Line into Maryland. There the house lights became further apart. The tree-covered lots grew larger. Logan took a right on to a dirt road. There were no fences here, no buildings, no electric wires crossing the dark fields.

He stopped the car, cut the lights.

She raised her head, murmured, when he pulled her to him, clenching his big hands around her breasts.

He squeezed hard. With a gasp, she opened her eyes, cried, "Hey! Where am I? What's happening?" And then, alarmed by the look on his face, suddenly sobered and whispered, "Oh, no, no, please . . ." and began to struggle, so that her black hair flowed across her face, and as he took her she could have been Margo, or she could have been another girl, a girl from long before called Esta, whom he had yearned for, yearned for secretly, and never had, and hated her for making him want her, and hated her even more because she'd never been his.

He didn't know exactly when she died. It was after he was through using her, and had begun to hit her. In a short time he realized he had finished the task. He carried her to the boot of his car, and put her down on the newspapers he had laid out earlier.

Soon he was on the way back to the city.

* * *

Claire saw the small item in the Washington *Post* that first reported the discovery of the unidentified body of a young woman near Fletcher's Landing on the C & O canal. The following day there was a recap of Margo Desales' unsolved murder, linking it to this new death. Both women had been in their twenties, both had had sexual relations shortly before being beaten to death, both were found in the same area.

When she had read through the second article twice, Claire called Detective Eagan. He wasn't in, but returned her call late that evening. He said, answering her first question, "I don't know if there's a connection. Not yet. There might be. But you've got to understand — just because two girls get killed doesn't mean they were killed by the same man."

"No," Claire agreed, "But the place where the bodies were found is the same."

"I know." The detective sighed. "Neither one of them was murdered there, however. It was the dumping ground, that's all. A good isolated spot. Maybe, after we get an I.D. on this new one, we'll be able to get started. But it won't be easy. Related or not. If, as I think, both your friend, and this girl, just met some guy in a bar . . ."

Claire sighed as she put down the phone. It

126

hadn't helped to call. If only she knew what had happened to Margo. Then she could put it behind her. Now she couldn't stop thinking about it. Wondering. Suspecting. Yes, that was the trouble. She kept suspecting Linda Grant, Carrie Day. What, after all, did she know about either of them? Yet neither could be implicated in Margo's death, surely. How could they be? It had taken a man to strike those blows, to have had sex with the girls. Then what of Jim Carsson? Logan? The other men Margo had known. Claire went over it again and again. Although she was unable to resolve her questions, she couldn't put them aside either.

Then, on a hot Saturday evening at the end of July, Rea came into the back yard where Claire was sitting with Dora. Fireflies glittered in the tall trees. The sound of Carrie's typewriter floated down from her room.

Rea said, looking pleased, "Somebody to see you, Claire."

"Me?"

"You. And it's nobody I know. Although I'd like to."

"Rea!" Dora said. "You *are* forward!"

Rea groaned.

Claire went inside, with Rea following her.

Brett Devlin was looking at the portrait of Big Jack Gowan. He turned at Claire's greeting.

He introduced himself, then went on, "Excuse me for intruding. Let me tell you right away that you might not want to talk to me. I'm Margo Desales' cousin. We were close. We grew up together."

Claire waited, not knowing what to say. What was Margo's cousin doing here? Her father had seemed so uncaring, so unsurprised by Margo's death.

Brett went on, "I was given your name by the police. I've been talking to them. They said you were friendly with her, worked with her since she came to Washington."

Claire nodded.

Rea said, "I was too. Margo used to lend me her clothes." Unconsciously Rea smoothed the sweater she was wearing. It had belonged to Margo, and after her death, Rea had appropriated it, over Dora's hysterical objections that Margo's clothes were bad luck and had to be given away immediately.

Brett said, "Maybe you can tell me about her life here?"

He was a nice-looking man, probably about thirty, Claire thought. He had a solid build, and short dark hair and level brown eyes.

He was explaining that he'd come to Washington very recently, and worked as an aide in a congressman's office. Claire listened, wondering why he wasn't in one of the services.

As he looked at her, he was swept by a wave of embarrassment which brought colour to his cheeks. It wasn't right to come here, to her home, like this. Under false pretences. Lying. He already knew she didn't deserve that treatment. But then he thought of his reason for being here and made up his mind that he had to accomplish what he'd set out to do.

He asked, "Did you find her diary?"

"Diary?" Claire echoed.

Rea sat down on the floor near Brett, and fixed her eyes on the points of his shoes.

Brett said, "She always kept one."

"We didn't find one," Claire told him.

He looked unconvinced. "All the time she was growing up, she kept one. And later, too. I know that for sure. It was a complete record of everything she did. The people she knew. Where she went. What she thought. Everything about her life." And that was what he wanted to see. The diary. Because it could tell him what he had to know. What had happened before. As well as what had happened since she came to Washington.

Claire was shaking her head. "I don't know about a diary. She never spoke of it to me. I'm sorry."

He sat very still. There was no doubt that

she had once kept a diary, although he himself had never seen it. Others had seen it years before. Others had known she began writing in it when she was twelve years old. Her father was certain she'd never stopped writing in it. So there had to have been a diary. And if there was, then it was there that he would find out what Margo had done . . .

"You're sure it's not hidden away somewhere in her room?" he asked.

"It's not likely," Claire told him.

"We could look again," Rea said. "Maybe we missed it. Not knowing what we were looking for."

Brett smiled at her. "You're very kind." Then he looked at Claire. "Would you mind . . ."

"The police did a thorough search of the room."

"Just the same . . ."

"All right," Claire told him. "You can see for yourself."

She led the way upstairs, Rea trailing behind.

Margo's room no longer looked as if it had ever belonged to her. The dresser was bare, dusted and polished. The bed was made up with fluffy pillows and spread. The teddy bears were gone, the closet empty.

It took only a little while for Brett to ex-

130

amine the room, to check the closet shelf, to search under the mattress, and feel the backs of the furniture.

It took only a little while, but to Claire, watching him, the time seemed endless. Why had she allowed him to question her? Why had she brought him up to the room?

When he had finished, stood looking around, his hands jammed in his pockets. "I guess nothing's here." But he sounded doubtful.

"It didn't hurt to try," Rea said, wishing that he would look at her instead of Claire. He was the best-looking man to come to Hannah's Gate in a long while.

Claire said nothing.

As the three of them went down the steps, he said apologetically, "Sorry I've been a bother to you. It's just that . . . if only I knew . . ."

"I feel the same. If I could help you, I would," Claire told him.

He thanked her, saying that he understood her feeling. But, even as he left, he knew he'd be back. He still believed that Margo had kept a diary. Plainly Claire Loving hadn't known about it. But just the same, it was somewhere. And he had to find it. The answer to his questions would be in it. Maybe the answer to her murder would be in it too, but besides that, he was determined to see Claire again.

Claire slowly rolled the pen between her fingers. She had always been careful about what she wrote to Leigh. She didn't want to worry him. She didn't want to alarm him. He surely had enough on his mind as it was. But still . . . she had to say that Margo had died. Now she had to write that the crime remained unsolved, and that there had been another murder much like it. She wrote a few words, paused, wrote a few more. Finally she put the pen aside, dropped her head on her folded arms.

Leigh, my dear love, Leigh. She was almost certain that he was in England. What was it like to be in London now? Every evening when she listened to the war news, she shivered.

Chapter 8

Jeri Marcher eyed the thin blue sheet in Leigh's hand. "Bad letter from home?" She had seen his face change as he read it, a frown creasing his forehead, his mouth tightening.

"In a way." He flipped the letter away. He'd answer Claire some time. But not now. He grinned at Jeri, opened his arms.

The room was dark except for the one corner where the lamp spilled pale light. The blackout curtains were closely drawn. The chill thin rain of late August whispered at the window.

Jeri paused to put out the lamp before she stumbled to the bed and into Leigh's embrace.

He'd met her soon after his arrival. He was assigned first to Ruislip, the big American airbase north of London. Not long after, he'd been transferred to London itself, where he worked deep underground in an office complex beneath the streets of the city.

Leigh wanted her the moment he saw her.

She was a W.R.E.N. Small, with tiny hands and feet, and slanted grey eyes. Her warm smile gave the lie to her crisp casual manner.

When he was moved to London, he was billeted in what had been a private home but had now been taken over to house both English and American soldiers. He was on the second floor in a back room. The first evening after he moved in, he met Jeri on the stairs. She had the attic room at the front of the house.

That night she ended up in his bed, and the night thereafter too. And every other night when they were both free. Sometimes he had to report for duty when she was off. Sometimes it was the other way around. But always, somehow, they managed to have some little while together, at dawn, at dusk, occasionally even at tea time.

It didn't matter to him. He loved her. Any time was the right time to be with her. He'd never felt that way before in his life. He hardly understood what had hit him. Washington, Claire, both were far away, unreal.

He held Jeri tightly. "After the war, we'll go home together."

"We'll see," she said.

"You'll love America."

"Maybe. I hope so, Leigh."

"And if not, we'll stay here. You know how I feel about London."

The big old city, where bits of the ancient

Roman wall still remained. The Thames. The tower. St Paul's. Even the bombed out blocks, debris-covered, fascinated him.

"We'll be together," she said. "That's what matters. Not where we are, but that we're together."

Months passed. One day when he came back to his room, he found her sitting in the dark, wrapped in a blanket. He lit the gas, began to prepare tea.

"I must tell you, Leigh . . . I did it for us. For us. So we could be together." Her voice was a dry raspy whisper.

He set aside the tea kettle and went to her. "What is it, Jeri? What did you do?"

She bit her lip, held tightly to the blanket, staring into a dark corner.

The chill of the room seemed to penetrate into his bones. He asked again, "What did you do, Jeri?"

"I've had an abortion," she whispered. "It seemed the only way."

It took long moments for the words to sink in. He felt hollow, an empty man. It was as if he had been sentenced to death. "But you didn't tell me," he said. "You just went and did it . . . You just . . ."

"It seemed the only way," she repeated.

"Damn you!" he cried. "You didn't have the right. It was ours, made between the two

135

of us. You should have told me first."

She made a soft pleading sound, but he didn't listen. He left her. He got drunk, and stayed out all night. The next morning he went to the underground office for a sixteen-hour shift.

It was late, dark, when he returned to the street, ready to pretend to be sorry. To say that whatever she did was all right with him. There was plenty of time. They'd have a child one day. Once the war was over, he planned to promise her, they'd have a child.

There had been activity in the sky over London that evening. Planes had come through the air defences. Search lights had strewn great white paths in the sky, and the anti-aircraft guns had sent trails of fire through them. But it was over now, although traffic was moving very slowly. There were no lights. The blackout was nearly total. But, at the end of the street, Leigh could see a group of people. He walked toward them.

He knew there was something peculiar about the street. It seemed much too long. Too wide. A cloudy sky stretched overhead. He didn't understand.

The group stood near a mass of rubble. There had plainly been a fire. He could still smell it. A pall of smoke drifted on the damp air. Glass shards glistened from roiled earth.

"What is it?" he demanded. "What's happened?"

"The house," someone said, and pointed to where steaming boards and bricks and charred wood lay in disordered humps. That was when Leigh understood. There was too much sky because a house was gone. His house. The place where he and Jeri lived.

"Casualties?" he asked thickly.

"The W.R.E.N." someone said. "They got her body out a couple of hours ago."

Her body.

Leigh nodded, walked away. He stepped over the fallen fence, shuffled through the humps of debris. The street slowly emptied. The dark slowly lightened to silver as the August moon broke through the clouds.

Leigh walked through the area, kicked boards aside, thrust away a coal scuttle he recognized, picked up the remains of a green pillow, knowing it had been one on which Jeri had rested her head.

Then, close by, he saw a small shoe. A small plain black shoe. His eyes filled with tears. He picked it up, stroked it, fondled it, brushing dirt from its tip. Jeri's shoe. Without knowing why, he slipped his hand into it. There was something inside. Cold. Damp. Soft. Something . . . something . . .

He pulled his hand out. His fingers were

dark brown, smeared. He knew what was in the shoe. Jeri's foot. Her foot. Mangled, torn. He flung it away from him, and ran from the place, screaming.

Chapter 9

Once again Claire was in the back yard when Brett Devlin came to Hannah's Gate.

He said, "I'm sorry to bother you. I guess I should have called first." He hadn't called because he'd thought Claire might refuse him permission to come. And he had to talk to her about Margo. Besides, he'd wanted to see her again.

Today her auburn hair was swept back and pinned up. She wore white shorts and a white shirt. There was a smudge of dirt on her cheek as she rose from the garden where she was working. He was struck anew by how attractive she was. It was nearly a month since he'd last seen her, and he'd thought about her every day. Now, although he'd planned this meeting carefully, he didn't know how to begin.

She dropped some green beans into a bowl, and asked, "It's about Margo, isn't it?"

He nodded. He knew he would have to tell her what he'd learned only a few days ago. But he was finding it hard just to jump in, to put it into words.

Before he could start, Rea came out. She

139

greeted him as if they were old friends. Seizing his hand, she said, "Come up to the house. We've got iced tea."

"Okay. That sounds good." He grinned at her. "We'll be there in a minute."

Rea sauntered away, looking back over her shoulder.

When she was out of ear shot, Claire said, "I told you I couldn't help out."

"I've just found out that Margo was pregnant."

Claire's brown eyes widened. "Pregnant? No one told me. How do you know?"

"The police."

"You mean Detective Eagan knew? And he never said?"

Brett nodded. "They decided to keep it quiet." He went on, "You really didn't know?"

"No." Claire was quiet for a moment. Then: "Poor girl, she must have been terribly frightened."

"It means that the police idea that she was murdered by a stranger is less likely than we thought."

"Maybe," Claire agreed. "But even if she was pregnant, she could have met someone . . . Perhaps she didn't know it yet herself."

"Perhaps." Brett didn't think that reasonable. But he said, "It suggests other possibilities, doesn't it? Suppose the man involved didn't want to help her?"

Claire picked up the thought. "Didn't want to. Or couldn't. Because he was married. Because he couldn't afford to have it known that he'd had an affair with Margo." Claire stopped. She thought of Margo, how she'd have felt on learning she was pregnant. What would she have done? Who would she turn to? Claire was certain Margo would never have gone home, nor asked her father for help. At last she said, "You're right, Brett. I don't think she could have been killed by a casual pickup."

"We're guessing, aren't we?"

"Yes. And I think our guessing is at least more than the police are doing."

Brett looked up at the wistaria vine that covered so much of the back of the house. "That's old, isn't it?"

"It was planted when the house was built, before the turn of the century."

"It looks like a tree almost, with those thick ropy limbs."

He kept his eyes on the vine as he again mentioned Margo's diary.

Claire said, "She might have stopped keeping it when she grew up. Or, if she did keep writing in it, she may have burned it some time or other. Who knows?"

"I don't think she stopped," Brett said. "People don't change that much. And since she didn't know she was going to be murdered, I can't see why she'd have destroyed it."

He'd never been able to figure out what compelled Margo to put into writing her intimate ideas, motives, feelings, confessions. But whatever had made her do it, he was sure that 'whatever' wouldn't have disappeared. Although he'd never read any of it himself, he'd heard about it from those who had. And he knew how clearly, honestly, she could tell what she had done. As if she enjoyed living through the experience once more. Perhaps that's what she did. Wrote in her diary, and then, re-reading it, lived through the excitement, the pleasure or the pain, a second time. It was why the diary was important to him. In it, he was certain he'd find the explanation for what had happened long ago.

Now Rea called, "Come on. Iced tea's ready."

Claire and Brett walked up to the house together. For the first time, then, she realized that he walked with a slight limp, as if his leg didn't bend at the knee. She had wondered, asking herself why an able-bodied man wasn't in the Army. It was something everyone thought of those days. Now she understood.

They went to the side porch. Dora was seated in a rocking chair, presiding over a tray that held tea in a pitcher topped with mint, and a plate of sandwiches.

Carrie Day was beside her, an old photograph album on her broad lap.

Linda was perched on the railing, an embroidery hoop in her hands.

Dora passed the tea, served the cucumber sandwiches.

"Like England," Brett said.

Instantly Claire thought of Leigh. Why hadn't she heard from him? She'd been expecting a letter for days. Surely he'd write when he read about Margo. That's what Claire had thought. But so far there had been nothing.

"Miz Loving can make a party out of anything," Carrie Day said in her soft voice.

"I like to do what I can," Dora said. "Though I don't know what the English would say to iced tea."

Claire stopped listening. She wished Leigh was sitting with her. Leigh, instead of Brett. What did the man want of her? Why had he returned? She wanted to forget Margo's death. Not to be reminded of it. Not to dwell on it. Not to spend nightmare hours dreaming of it. She wished he would leave, and never come back.

But he stayed on, uncomfortably aware of her feelings, yet unable to pull himself away. He had to find out about Margo. And he had to extend his time with Claire a little longer. So he made small talk. He mentioned that he had done only a little sight-seeing since he'd come to Washington. One day, he said, when he had time, he would do more. He knew the Capitol well enough, but there was so much beyond that. It was too bad that so many places were closed to the public now, because of the war. But he imagined he could still see a great deal. A congressman's aide had some clout, he explained. And grinned. "Not a lot, but some." Then, more soberly, he went on, in an aside to Claire, "I'm sure that's why the police have been so forthcoming with me."

"I wondered," she said.

To prolong his stay, he took another sandwich, another glass of tea. He supposed she had noticed his limp. It was always worse when he was tense. But, of course, it was never completely gone. Still, he'd been lucky. He knew of others who had died of polio, and several who had been paralyzed and never recovered. He'd had a mild case, as such things went, and had been able to overcome the paralysis that had afflicted his left leg for several years. Now he wondered if Claire was bothered by his disability. Some people were. He hoped she wasn't one of them.

Still, in a little while, he got up to go. There didn't seem to be any more to say.

"If you hear anything, you'll let me know, won't you?" Claire asked.

He assured her that he would, and asked that she do the same, leaving his phone number and address so that she could get in touch with him.

After he'd gone, she asked herself why the police had given him information that hadn't been given to her. Maybe it was because a congressman's aide had clout. But maybe that had nothing to do with it. Was there some reason she couldn't imagine? What, after all, did she know of Brett Devlin? Only what he had told her. Today, when he spoke of Margo's diary, Claire had heard bitterness in his voice. He'd said they'd been close as children, that he was determined to learn what had happened to her because they'd once been fond of each other. Or had he said that? She wasn't sure. She wasn't sure about anything any more.

Now Dora said, "You know, Claire, I find it hard to believe that boy was Margo Desales' cousin. There's not the slightest family resemblance. I mean, usually, there's a little something that shows up."

145

"Why, Miz Loving," Carrie Day said, "you know, you're absolutely right. There's always some little something, isn't there?"

"Just the same," Dora went on, "I don't see a sign that those two could have been related."

Claire found those words coming back again and again. Was Brett really Margo's cousin? If not, why had he pretended he was? If so, and they had been close, what explained what Claire sensed was his bitterness toward Margo now? Had he loved her once? Had she harmed him?

After thinking for days about Dora's comment, Claire decided to resolve at least that one question. She called Frederick Desales. He said, "What's this about? I've never heard of a Brett Devlin. We don't have any relatives by that name."

She thanked Margo's father, and put down the phone.

Now she knew one thing: Brett had lied to her. He wasn't Margo's cousin. Then he had some other reason than the one he'd given her for being interested in Margo's death. The thought chilled her. He seemed nice, straightforward. But still . . .

She went up to her room, and held Leigh's picture. He seemed to smile at her. A wave of longing swept her. Oh, when would the war end? When would Leigh come home?

It was the following week, just after Labour Day. Logan stood at the side of his bedroom window, studying the yard at Hannah's Gate.

It was empty now. He expected, though, that pretty soon Rea would come out. He wanted to talk to her.

Claire had had a visitor the week before. Logan wondered who he was. Another policeman maybe?

No one had come back to question him. There'd been nothing more in the newspapers. He was sure he was in the clear. Margo had lied about the diary. She must have. Still, there was a faint uncertainty in his mind. He wanted to be sure.

Yes, he needed to talk to Rea. But it must look right. He didn't want her to realize that he was pursuing her. It must appear that they had met by accident. If only she'd come out now . . .

A little later, she walked down to the garden and stood staring at the neat furrows.

Logan hurried outside, got the lawn mower from the garage, and pushed it around to the back of the house, acting busy and preoccupied until he reached the fence. Then, as if seeing her for the first time, he said, "Hi, Rea. How're you doing?"

She shrugged, flashed him a look.

"Doldrums?" he asked.

"I guess."

"I'll tell you what, wait until I finish here and I'll stand you to an ice cream sundae on the avenue." He paused then added, "Ask your mother if it's okay."

She said her mother and Claire had gone to the movies, one she'd already seen.

No need then to get her away from the house. Logan wondered how to deal with that. He finally told Rea that he didn't know if her mother would approve of her going down to the avenue with him, without asking permission.

"What do you mean?" she cried. "I'm not a baby. I can do what I want."

"Of course," he said smoothly. "But it's good manners to ask her."

"I'll leave her a note," Rea said, all dignity and youthful sweetness. "So she won't wonder where I am."

Logan agreed that was a good idea, mowed for fifteen minutes, then put the mower away. It wouldn't take long, he decided. They'd have their ice cream, and probably be back long before Dora Loving returned. And if she returned before, well, it couldn't be helped. He had to talk to Rea.

When they got to the drug store, and had

ordered sundaes with everything on them, as Rea put it, he tried to think of how to begin, but she spoke first, a thin rim of chocolate syrup on her upper lip. She asked, "Say, Logan, whatever happened to that friend of yours?"

"Friend?" Logan's heart suddenly pounded. What the hell was she talking about? Had she seen John? Had she figured out that John came and went, sometimes stopping, sometimes passing by, depending on where the flower pot stood on the porch?

"Your friend?" she repeated. "The one that was coming to Washington to live with you."

"Oh, him," Logan said. "He took a job in Dallas instead."

"So you ended up by yourself," she went on. "You ought to rent a couple of rooms, the way we do. But, of course, you do take a chance." She stopped suddenly.

Logan relaxed. Now they were where he wanted to be. He said gently, "Like with Margo? That's what you mean. You don't know what'll happen."

"Like with Margo," Rea said.

"But it's all over, isn't it? I mean . . . the police . . . they don't come any more, do they?"

"They don't. But it's not over." She put down her spoon then.

"We want to forget about it. I do, and my mother. And Claire too. Just when we think we can, something happens."

"What do you mean?"

"It comes up all over again. Like Brett Devlin asking about Margo's diary."

A hot place within Logan's chest seemed to expand in waves. Diary? So Margo hadn't been trying to bluff. There'd really been a diary after all. Then where was it? Why hadn't it surfaced until now!

He asked quietly, "Brett Devlin? Is he a policeman?"

Rea told him what she knew about Brett Devlin. That he was a cousin of Margo's. He wanted to know who had killed her. Logan asked what the point was. The police were doing all they could, weren't they? What made this man think he could do better?

"It's because of the diary," she explained. "I don't know why he thinks it's still around. We've never found it. And the police didn't either when they searched Margo's things." Rea pushed her emptied dish aside, and smiled sweetly at Logan. "We can hurry back now, and my mother won't even know I've left the house if I get rid of the note I left her."

"Of course we'll tell her," Logan said, pretending to be shocked. "It would be very dishonest . . ."

"It's up to you," Rea said. "I'll do whatever you want."

Logan said he'd walk her back to Hannah's Gate, and together they'd tell Dora where Rea had been.

As she went up the steps before him, she strutted happily. Logan saw, and laughed to himself. The little devil was imitating Margo's ass-swinging walk.

Later that night Dora said furiously, "Stay away from that man, Rea. I don't care what he says, or you either."

"I'm not a baby," Rea screamed. "I can take care of myself. All I did was have a sundae. Nobody else does anything for me. Nobody else pays any attention to me. So if Logan Jessup wants to be nice, what's wrong with that?"

"Stay away from him," Dora said. "You hear me? If you don't, I'll have a talk with him myself."

When Logan returned home that evening, he watered the flower pot on his front porch and moved it to the right side of the steps. Then he went inside.

Much later, when all the lights had gone out at Hannah's Gate, and all the houses on Afton Place were dark, he heard a tap at his door.

He let John in and asked, "You brought the consignment?"

"I have it."

The two men worked swiftly, carrying the boxes into the house, then up the stairs, where, at the top, they shoved them into the crawl space under the roof.

When they had finished, John mopped sweat off his face and asked, "Anything else?"

"No," Logan said. "Not until I'm ready. Watch for the signal."

John nodded, and let himself out.

It was a hot evening. Dora touched powder to her flushed cheeks, tugged at her braided chignon. She had promised an old friend, Anna Taylor, that she would join a group for supper at Anna's Georgetown mansion.

Now Rea came in excitedly. "The limousine's here. And you should see the chauffeur!"

Dora was sorry now that she'd accepted the invitation. She hadn't been to such an affair for a long time. And she hated going anywhere without Casey. But, as Claire had pointed out to her, Anna Taylor would be offended if Dora were to change her mind.

Finally she left.

Rea and Claire waved her away, then Rea said, "I thought for sure she would come down with a sick headache and back out."

Claire said she'd been expecting the same thing, and suggested a game of Chinese chequers. But Rea wanted to get back to reading *Gone With the Wind*. This was her third time around, and she still thought it was a wonderful book.

Claire went to her own room. The house seemed unaccountably quiet. Dora was to stay overnight with Anna Taylor. Carrie was off in Philadelphia, and Linda Grant had taken a week's vacation to visit her family.

Claire moved the pins on her map of Europe. The allies had landed in Sicily, and defeated the Italian Army. Now they had crossed the Strait of Messina to the mainland. She had heard nothing from Leigh yet, so she assumed that he was still in England.

Later, in bed, she tossed and turned. It had been so long since she'd heard from him. Was he okay? When would he write? She wondered if his uncle had heard anything from him. She could call Jeremiah Merrill, but he was a busy man. Perhaps it would be an intrusion. Time seemed to drag, while she achingly missed Leigh. And remembered Margo . . .

At last she fell asleep, but even then her dreams were full of Leigh. His head bent to hers, his smiling hazel eyes . . .

She awakened with a start. Had she been

sleeping? Her heart was thumping against her ribs. Something . . . something . . . but what?

An odd dragging sound . . . Paper rustling? Scratching? Was it a squirrel outside her window?

She sat up slowly, listening. The bed creaked as she swung her legs to the floor. The floor creaked when she stood up. Silence. Nothingness. Only her heart pounding. Her blood drumming in her ears.

She moved quietly across the room. The sky showed black in the rectangle of her window. The hall was dark too. She walked cautiously into the shadows.

A single step down at the staircase. Suddenly she froze, sensing a presence before she touched a warm shoulder. There was a yelp. "Claire!"

"Rea, what are you doing?" she cried.

"Oh, how you scared me!"

"And *you* scared *me*. What are you doing here?"

Clutching each other, the two girls swayed together.

"I thought I would die. I thought I would fall over from fright, right here, on these steps," Rea said, and then she chuckled.

"Why are you walking around in the middle of the night?" Claire demanded. She was remembering that it had happened before. The kitchen door had blown open. She'd heard the noise and come down. And run into Rea, in stockinged feet, tiptoeing on the stairs.

"What about you?" her sister was asking now.

"I heard something."

"So did I."

They were both whispering, clinging to each other still.

"I suppose I heard you," Claire said.

"Or maybe I heard you," Rea answered, laughing softly again.

"It's not funny," Claire told her. "Next time stay put. Don't get up and look around."

"What about you?"

"Rea! Listen . . ." Claire stopped.

There had been another sound. A strange crackle and thump. And it hadn't come from the floor below. It wasn't the sound of the kitchen door banging against the cupboard. It came from the end of the hall. From the room that Margo had lived in.

Claire and Rea exchanged glances, and then, without speaking, hurried down the corridor to Margo's room.

The door was closed. Now there was an ominous silence.

Claire turned the knob, pushed gently. As the door swung back a warm breeze touched their hot cheeks. The white curtain billowed out. The window was wide open. And it should have been shut. It had been closed since Margo's death.

Claire turned on the light. Long shadows fell across the carpet, darkened the dresser mirror. The mattress had been pulled from the bed and lay on the floor. The drawers were half-open. The closet . . .

Claire stiffened, stared. The door was ajar. Was someone hiding there? What should she do?

"Run down and call the police," she told Rea.

For once Rea didn't argue. She raced from the room.

For a moment longer Claire stared at the partly open closet door. Then she pulled it back. The closet was empty. No one was hiding there.

Her gaze reached the open window. The curtain billowed out again. The wind rustled in the wistaria. She went to look out. The yard was shrouded in darkness. The house below, on Afton Place, was dark too.

In moments she heard the low whine of a patrol car. Rea came up, leading two officers.

Claire told them what had happened.

They looked around the room, then searched the house. They found no one. Neither the doors nor windows appeared to be tampered with.

They assumed that one of the doors had been left unlocked, and a cat burglar had found his way in. It was happening sometimes now, they said. Even here, in Cleveland Park.

Claire couldn't accept that explanation. She was certain that no doors had been left unlocked. With everyone gone except Rea and herself, she had been careful about checking the two doors.

And, of course, as soon as she realized that someone had been in the house, she had thought of Margo and her murder. She told the two policemen about it now. But they dismissed any possible connection. They assured her that she'd been awakened by a burglar, and that nothing was missing because she and Rea had interrupted him. Soon after, they left, promising to keep an eye on the block, just in case the man was still around.

When the police had gone, Claire persuaded Rea to go back to bed.

She herself walked slowly through the house, going from room to room once again. She remembered some while back thinking that the books in the study had been disarranged. She remembered the tray that had been moved. Now, more than ever, she was certain she hadn't imagined the occasional slight re-positioning of objects that had been in the same place for years. Someone was going through the house, surreptitiously, searching the bookcases and cupboards, looking into drawers.

Someone was looking for something.

But what could be the object of such a search?

When had it begun? It seemed to Claire that she had first noticed it after Margo's death, but she was no longer sure of that. Still, it made more sense than anything else. Brett said that Margo always kept a diary. He'd tried to find it in Margo's room, saying it might have in it clues that could lead to the discovery of Margo's murderer . . . Margo's diary . . .

Claire sat on the edge of her bed, waiting for dawn to break, eager for the sun of the day.

If the searcher had been looking for Margo's diary, then some time, not this morning, perhaps, not that night, but some time, he would surely come back.

There was a piece of tape on Detective Eagan's chin, the sign of a new razor cut. His blue eyes looked just as tired as when Claire had last seen him. He said, "You might be right. But it's only a might be, Miss Loving."

"It's more than that," she argued. "Can't

you see it's too much of a coincidence to accept? First Margo is murdered. Then someone breaks into our house."

"Lots of houses are getting broken into these days," he observed, closing his notebook and rising. "But don't worry your pretty head about it. We'll look into it. I'm sure it won't happen again."

"You can't be sure," she said, wishing he wouldn't talk to her as if she were a child, or an idiot, who could accept empty reassurances as if they meant something when they didn't.

He blinked at her sharp tone. "Well, I'm pretty sure anyhow."

"You'll let me know if you learn anything?"

"When we have news, you'll hear it."

But Claire knew he was dismissing her. She could tell by his voice, by the way he had closed his notebook. When he drove away from Hannah's Gate, he'd forget Margo's murder. He'd forget the break-in.

For the next few days she fidgeted and fumed. She tried to be matter of fact about the break-in when she told Dora about it. Dora hardly listened. She was too busy describing her visit to Anna Taylor's. The food, the decor of the house, the company . . . Carrie Day, returning from her trip, accepted the news with a faint cry, but said little. Only

Linda Grant took it seriously, saying, "It's scary, isn't it, Claire?"

When Brett Devlin called to ask Claire out to dinner, she accepted. She wanted to tell him what had happened. And she hoped he might have learned something new.

They went to the Roma, an Italian restaurant on Connecticut Avenue not far from Honey Locust Lane. They sat facing each other across a black-topped table in a booth. Over Chianti served from a straw-covered bottle, and huge platters of spaghetti and meatballs, she told Brett about the break-in, and what the police had said. She also reported her conversation with Detective Eagan, and his reaction.

Brett said, "I guess I understand how they think. They've never seen the diary. They don't know anyone who saw Margo write in it, or who admits to hearing Margo speak of it. So they aren't sure it exists, or ever did."

"You know about it, Brett," she said.

"Indirectly. I never saw it myself."

She searched his brown eyes. He seemed honest. But she knew he'd lied to her. He'd said he was Margo's cousin, and the Desales had no relatives named Devlin. Why had he said that?

"You *did* tell the police you'd heard about it?" she asked finally.

160

"Sure. But I had to explain that I knew about it only second hand." He was silent, wishing now that he hadn't presented himself to her under false pretenses. At the time, he'd thought it best. But because he'd started out with that lie there was a wall between them. He didn't want that. Here, now, was the chance to tear it down. He said, "I haven't told the police everything. And I haven't told you everything either."

She had a forkful of spaghetti halfway to her mouth. She put it on her plate, and stared at him.

He said quickly, "The first thing is, I am not Margo's cousin. I said that so you'd accept my being concerned about what happened. I shouldn't have done that, and I'm sorry now. But it was the only excuse I could offer for asking you questions about her."

"But why are you so interested?" Claire asked.

"It has to do with something in the past that Margo did. It might not be connected with what happened here, but still . . . there's just a chance . . ." He let the words fade away.

"What *did* happen?"

He went on slowly, as if choosing his phrases carefully. "There was a scandal a good number of years ago. Margo was sixteen then, in high school. She was a good student. Pretty, wilful and wild." He smiled. "That was the word they used then — wild."

"You mean everybody thought she was wild?" Claire said.

"Yes, I suppose. She had matured earlier than the rest of the girls. She was boy crazy. She gave her folks constant problems. Her father and aunt who raised her. Her mother had died when she was an infant. She ran with a tough crowd, kids that had left school and gone to work, and hung around the beer parlours and pool halls. Then, one night, she came home very late. She was messed up. Her father gave her what for, as you can imagine. And, finally, she burst into tears. She said . . ." Here Brett paused to swallow before he continued, "She said that her high school music teacher had picked her up in his car, and driven her into the country, and raped her. His name was Angelo Nira. He was young, married, with a pregnant wife. Margo's father called the police. They charged Angelo. He denied it. We were next-door neighbours. I'd known him all the time he was growing up. When he said he had had nothing to do with Margo, I knew he was telling the truth. He claimed the whole thing was a fantasy Margo had dreamed up. She had flirted with him, he'd noticed that. She'd tried to get him to pay attention to her. He'd always avoided her.

But he couldn't prove his innocence. He didn't have anyone to testify that they'd seen him the evening Margo said he'd taken her into the country. He'd been home, practising the violin. His wife was at work. Anyway, he was fired from his job immediately. His wife had a miscarriage."

"But, Brett," Claire said, "why would Margo lie about your friend?"

"I'm not sure. I've always thought it was just an excuse to get her father to stop yelling at her for staying out late. Maybe to avoid saying who she'd really been with." He took a deep breath. "I tried to help Angelo, but I couldn't. He was released on bond. When he was due to be tried, with Margo ready to testify against him, he couldn't take any more. He hanged himself."

"And Margo?"

"We never knew the truth. But the scandal didn't die down. Somehow talk got around about the diary she kept. It was said she'd written the whole truth down. That she always kept a record of the men she'd been with, what took place between them and her. So, when I heard she'd been murdered, I thought . . . well, I thought if I could get hold of her diary, maybe I'd find out about Angelo. Maybe she still had it all with her."

"I see," Claire said softly. Now she understood why Margo had never spoken of her hometown, her family, her past.

Brett wanted to go on, to explain the rest of it. To tell her about Angelo's wife Rose, and how she lived now, still shamed for Angelo, lonely, with not even the memories of love to sustain her. It was for Rose, for his old friendship with Angelo, that Brett wanted the truth. But, even though he felt Claire's questioning gaze on him, he held back. He couldn't talk about that part of it. Not yet.

Chapter 10

Claire dreamed of a Hallowe'en long past. She had been seven or eight, wearing a gypsy costume put together by her mother out of old clothes. The skirt was purple, the blouse red silk. She wore a bandana over her auburn curls, and golden hoop earrings. There was a knock at the door. She ran to open it, and Leigh stood there, tall, slim, a devil's mask concealing his twelve-year-old face. His voice demanding, "Trick or treat!" gave him away. Suddenly the red of the mask became blood. Her joyful excitement turned into horror. She awakened with a scream on her lips.

Leigh's face, covered with blood . . . Had something happened to him! She was shivering, icy sweat on her face. She knew it had been a dream, but it still seemed real to her.

And then there was a whisper of sound in the hall.

Now she was fully awake. She understood, Hallowe'en had been two weeks before. Some youngsters had come for tricks or treats. And of course, ever present in her mind there was the fear that something would happen to Leigh. That explained the dream. But what had she heard? Had that been part of the dream too? She strained to listen, waiting. Silence had returned. She pictured the empty hall. The staircase.

Finally she tiptoed to the door and eased it open. The hall was dark with shadows, but a bar of silver moonlight lay across the floor. Then, even as Claire stared at it, it narrowed. Slowly it became a ribbon, then a thread. At last it was gone.

She stepped into the hall. The door to Margo's room was closed as it usually was. But she knew it had been open when she first looked out. The moonlight had come through the window into the room, then into the hall. It had disappeared as the door was soundlessly eased shut while she watched. Someone had gone into Margo's room.

Who? Why? It had been empty since Margo's death. Claire pressed her ear to the door. From within, there was the sound of cautious movement.

She pushed the door open. The room was in darkness except for the moon-lit window. In its opening, poised on the sill, stood Rea.

Mindful of her mother sleeping near by, and of Linda across the hall, Claire whispered angrily, "Rea, what are you doing?"

Rea stepped down. She squinted at Claire. "Nothing," she said. She was dressed in jeans, a dark jacket, and tennis shoes.

"You were going out, weren't you?" Claire demanded, looking her up and down.

"Leave me alone." Rea's lower lip stuck out. She looked ready to burst into tears.

"But what were you doing?"

"I couldn't sleep," Rea said. "So I was going out for a while."

"You could have used the front door."

"I used to. Before Margo got killed. But it's handier to go down the wistaria . . ."

"Rea! What are you talking about?"

"It was handier, I said. Sometimes Mama is downstairs. And I never know when Carrie's going to be ducking into the study. So . . . after I got the idea from Margo . . ."

"Why do you go out so late? What do you do?"

"I just walk around," Rea said.

"You can't! That's terribly dangerous." Then, struck by what the younger girl had said, "You got the idea from *Margo?*"

"She used to climb down the wistaria. Not always, but once in a while. I figured if she could do it, so could I."

Claire said, "You can't wander around the neighbourhood so late. Promise me you won't do it any more?"

Rea agreed grudgingly, "Okay, okay. But you're as bad as Mom."

After the younger girl had returned to her room, Claire went back to bed. She didn't know if Rea could be trusted. She didn't understand what Rea had been doing. Was it true that she'd seen Margo leave the house through the window in her bedroom? Why would Margo do that? She could come and go as she pleased. It didn't make sense. Nothing did any more.

Margo's room had been empty for several months before it occurred to Linda that she could now occupy it herself. Once she thought of it, she could concentrate on nothing else. That room would be perfect for her. It had a nice view of the yard. She was determined to make the move. But it was months more before she could bring herself to mention it to Dora Loving.

Then, the weekend after Claire caught Rea sneaking out in the middle of the night, Linda finally brought the subject up. She said timidly, "I've been wondering if you'd care if I took the room Margo used to have? I mean . . . it's just sitting there. Empty. And it's bigger than mine." Linda's small face was flushed, her eyes anxious. "And I think the view . . ."

"I don't see why not," Dora said. "If you want it."

"Then it's all right?"

"Of course," Dora told her. It would be good to have the place occupied. Linda's being there would make it Linda's room, and no longer Margo's. It would help them to forget what had happened. And then, soon, Dora would find another person to rent Linda's room to.

Claire too was relieved. With Linda there she could be sure Rea would no longer be able to use the room as an exit. She still wasn't certain she could trust Rea to give up her night-time wanderings. She said to Linda, "It's a good idea."

So it was settled, and later Claire helped Linda carry her belongings down the hall.

That night, in nightgown and robe, Linda surveyed the room with satisfaction. It was larger and the closet more roomy, although she didn't have the clothes to fill it. Its window looked out to the back, down the sloping lawn. And there, outlined against the dark by a street lamp on Afton Place was Logan's house.

Logan's house . . . She leaned against the misted glass pane. She saw a light in an upstairs window. She waited, mesmerized. She could see into the room. He had a picture on one wall. She couldn't see any furniture, and wasn't able to tell if he slept

169

in that room or another one.

Then, as she watched, he moved into view. She drew in her breath sharply. His shoulders and arms were bare. The muscles were smooth, but well-developed. There was a triangle of shadow on his chest that suggested curly hair, but she couldn't be sure. Suddenly her fingers tingled. Of course it was hair, golden, silken. She sensed the feel of it. Her body seemed to melt. Her legs weakened. She began to breathe quickly. What a narrow, flat waist he had . . . and a beautiful line from his jaw down his throat to his collar bone. Her lips stung. There was a flood of saliva in her mouth. If only she could . . .

The light suddenly went out. Logan was gone. She waited a moment. But he was gone. The light was gone.

Her breath had left a white beady cloud on the cold glass. She wiped it away before she climbed into bed, suddenly tired, but already looking ahead to the next night.

But that time, when night finally came, although she retired to her room early, the Jessup house remained dark. She stood at the window for hours. She didn't have a glimpse of Logan.

Later, weary, she got into bed. As she lay curled in her pillows, waiting for sleep, she told herself a story. Logan leaned over the back fence, talking to her. His hair glistened in the cold winter sunlight. He wore a dark blue jacket. His smile was warm and gentle. In a little while, he invited her into his house. And then . . .

There were small faint pricklings in her flesh. Tiny arrows of sensation darted through her. Swift currents of cold, then quick currents of heat. The nipples on her breasts itched swelled, burned.

Logan leaned over her, whispering, "I love you, Linda. I love you. I want you."

In the morning, the alarm clock went off. It was a dim cloudy day. The imaginings of the night before were gone. It was as if nothing had happened.

She rose, gathered her clothes and went into the bathroom to ready herself to go to work. She brushed her hair, lightly powdered her face. She had breakfast with Dora and Claire. It was her usual routine. No one could have guessed what her fantasies had been in the dark of the night. They seemed, even to her, no more than a distant dream.

But that evening, as dark fell, she grew restless. She excused herself early. She didn't turn on the light in her room. She stood at the window. A light snow had fallen. Two long trails of squirrel tracks led to the house where Logan lived.

After a time, her patience was rewarded. Lights went on. First in the downstairs room. Then upstairs. At last she saw Logan. Tonight he was wearing a pale blue shirt. His shirt collar was open. She could see the wonderful line of his throat. She could see his blond hair, always so neatly combed. How wide his shoulders were. How strong his thighs looked in those dark blue trousers. And his arms . . .

Logan held her tightly. His voice was hoarse as he said, "I need you, Linda. I want you."

He swept her up into his arms, held her tightly to his chest, and carried her to the bed.

Slowly, he unbuttoned her blouse, drew it off her body. He unhooked her bra. He slid her skirt from her hips, and raised her to pull away her panties.

Breathlessly she turned her face up to his. He bent his head, pressed his lips to hers. They were sweet, warm. She felt his tongue . . .

Gasping, Linda stumbled away from the window, and flung herself on her bed.

Logan turned off the light. He stretched, yawned. He was bored. He needed a good time. By which he meant sex. He needed something to relax him. Again, he meant sex. His body was strung too tightly. He was aware of it in every waking moment. Even his sleep was uneasy. Because of loose ends. Loose ends he hadn't intended or expected. He knew that he was in the clear. The police had never come back to question him again. The two cases had faded from the newspapers. It was as if the two murders were completely erased. Still, since he'd heard about damned Margo's damned diary he'd been wondering. He hadn't been able to let it go.

He'd learned from Rea the comings and goings of those at Hannah's Gate, and he'd safely been there twice, searching. Just to convince himself that Margo's diary wasn't around. It was a dangerous loose end. It if existed, where could it be? He'd tried to figure it out by logic. That hadn't worked. Nothing had. He wasn't sure. He couldn't forget it.

And he had a schedule. Nothing could interfere with that. So he continued to make his short trips out of town as usual. But always, at the back of his mind, the questions remained. Did Margo's diary exist? If so, what was in it? It didn't help that he had developed a permanent hard on.

Suddenly he grinned into the dark. He could do something about that, couldn't he? And after that . . .

They were all at home. He knew because he'd watched the house, seeing the lights come on as early twilight faded into early dark.

It was sleeting when he went out to his car.

He drove the short distance to a florist's shop, then cut back to Honey Locust Lane, turned up the hill and parked in front of Hannah's Gate.

The two magnolia trees stood tall and dark beside the house.

Dora opened the door at his knock. "Yes, Mr Jessup?" she said.

He didn't actually bow, but the small movement of his head made it seem as if he had. He smiled, "Good evening, Mrs Loving." When she didn't step back in welcome, nor speak, he went on, "I hope you don't mind? I stopped by for a minute." He held out the six long stemmed roses wrapped in green tissue. "For you."

She had thought the flowers must be for Claire. She had also decided she didn't want Claire pursued by Logan Jessup. So his words flustered her. She looked at the roses, at him. Finally she said, "Why, thank you," and suddenly there was a flirtatious note in her voice. "They're truly beautiful." She accepted the flowers, threw back the door, and stepped aside.

He accepted the unspoken invitation. "Only for a minute, Mrs Loving."

She led him into the front room. He heard the sound of the radio from somewhere down the hall, and voices: Rea's and Claire's. Another that he assumed must belong to the big girl, Carrie, whatever her last name was.

"I came over for two reasons," he said. "First I wondered how things are going for you these days?" He was sure she wouldn't realize that through Rea he was completely up to date on what was happening at Hannah's Gate, including the moods, fears, even the plans, of women living there. Rea was, he had found, substantially more forthcoming than she knew when questioned by someone experienced in the technique. And he was experienced, having practised it for years. "Second," he went on, "winter's coming, and it occurred to me that there may be some chores you'd like me to do for you? With your son in the Army, and your husband away . . ."

Colour flooded Dora's face. "Casey's a geologist," she said defensively. "He's searching for oil. Very important to the war."

"I understand," Logan said smoothly. "We all do what we must."

As he himself was doing, he thought.

"He can't get home as often as he likes," Dora said.

"He must worry about you. A house full of women. And at this time too."

Dora said nothing. She'd written so many times, pleading with Casey, telling him she was frightened, she couldn't manage, she didn't know what to do. Mostly he ignored her letters. But once in a while she received a note from him. It would say the same thing each time but in a slightly different words. He was busy, he'd write. The work was important. She must do the best she could, the way all women left alone were doing.

She had tried to call him at the emergency number he had given her, but she must have somehow gotten it wrong. The call never went through, even when, after many tries, she was finally able to get a long distance line. Either there was no answer, or whoever responded had never heard of Casey Loving.

Briefly, pain, fear and loneliness showed on her face. Then, re-gaining her composure, she said in her company voice, "I'll make some tea, Mr Jessup."

"I don't want to be any trouble," he said.

As she rose, Rea appeared in the doorway.

The young girl smiled happily at Logan. "I thought I heard you."

Dora said she'd get the other girls, then bring in the refreshments. When she had gone, Rea perched on the sofa, studying Logan but saying nothing.

After a moment Claire and Carrie came in.

Logan leaned back, a pleasant look on his face. But his hard on was worse than ever. He looked at Claire's legs. He looked at her breasts under her pale green sweater. He looked at the smooth auburn waves that fell over her forehead. Suddenly there was sweat in his hands. He'd never before really noticed how desirable a woman Claire was. Margo had been his type. Margo's big ass, big breasts, sparkling black eyes. But now he was aware that Claire's cool level gaze was challenging. Her slim body was supple, strong. It was interesting to think of ways to lower the proud angle of her chin, to imagine her polite disinterest turned into gasping pleading hunger.

Aloud, he said genially, "I came to ask if there were any heavy chores I could do for you?"

"It's nice of you to offer," she said, "but we can manage." It was dismissive, as she meant it to be. She was amenable to exchanging pleasantries with him over the fence occasionally, but she saw no reason to be beyond that. She felt that Rea spent more time talking to him, and about him, than was good for her, considering the difference in their ages.

Carrie was wondering what the blond man wanted. She thought he had to be after something. She had spoken no more than two or three words to him, yet she didn't see him as a man who willingly undertook somebody else's chores. It was out of character. That's what made her curious about what he wanted.

But it didn't matter to her. She was at Hannah's Gate for her own reasons. And although she hadn't been successful thus far, she was sure that ultimately she would be. She didn't intend to be diverted from her own interest. So she said nothing. She sat quietly, her hands in her lap, blinking behind her wire-rimmed glasses.

"It must be hard not to know what happened to Margo," Logan said, directing the conversation to where he wanted it to go.

"Yes," Claire agreed. Her tone was uninflected. But her dimple was gone, and her lips tightened. She believed that the less said on that subject the better. It was impossible not to think about it, brood on it, continually ask silent questions. Talking about it only made it worse.

Carrie said, "But life goes on. After all, it's nearly seven months since Margo was killed. We have to accept that the police probably will never find the truth."

"They will," Rea said. "One of these days they'll arrest somebody."

Dora had returned, carrying a tray of cups and a platter of cookies. She paused at the threshold, looking from Rea to Logan. She came in, set the tray down with a thump, and said sharply to Rea, "You don't know what you're talking about." And to Logan, "We're trying to forget what happened." Her voice became shrill. "Rea knows nothing. We know nothing. Margo Desales moved here by accident. She died elsewhere. It has nothing to do with us, with Hannah's Gate."

"I'm sure you're right," Logan said uncomfortably. "I'm sorry I spoke of it."

Rea ambled across the room to the window. She gave Logan a long stare from beneath her lashes. She saw that no one noticed her looking at him, no one wondered about him. They were all crazy. They didn't realize that she had eyes and ears and a brain. They didn't know that a person could know a lot and not be able to tell, because if she told she'd have to say how she knew, and that might get her into trouble. Besides, what did she really know? Just that she'd seen Margo climb down the wistaria vine, and go down the slope to the fence to disappear in the dark. So what? That didn't mean anything. Just that maybe she had gone to visit Logan. Well, she, Rea, had walked over to Logan's house too, although Logan didn't know that.

She listened as Logan went to speak of the news, that evening largely about the Marines' capture of Tarawa in the Gilbert Islands.

Claire listened too, but with half her attention only. She had turned towards her mother,

179

watching the ceremonious pouring of the tea. Actually she was studying Logan from the corner of her eyes. She was thinking of secrets, the strange undercurrents that she'd always felt in Hannah's Gate. There was a prickling inside her. She felt some danger drawing closer. What was Logan really doing here? He seemed pleasant, considerate. But what, after all, did she know about him? Almost nothing. He lived on Afton Place, alone in what had been the Merrills' house. His job took him on frequent but short trips. Margo had seemed to enjoy talking to him, had gone out with him once, and then said he was dull. What did that mean? Claire wished she knew. And a part of her wished that she'd never met Margo Desales, never brought her home to Hannah's Gate.

Meanwhile Linda crept to the top of the stairs, drawn there as if hypnotized by the sound of Logan's deep voice. She hid, listening for a little while. Then she went down to the living room.

He was still speaking, smiling at Claire. He leaned forward. Linda quivered inside. He stopped speaking, turned to nod at her, then turned back to Claire. With that, he seemed to forget Linda's presence.

But she stayed, listening, watching, sucking in his looks, his movements, his voice, drawing

180

them into her mind to cherish later, alone, in the dark, when she would imagine him making love to her. Whispering that he wanted her, touching his tongue to her lips, to her nipples. Touching her all over her body, even those moist and secret places that no one except she herself had ever touched. Touching her all over, before he fell on her and punished her shivering flesh.

After a three-hour stop with a girl he had picked up at Dupont Circle, Logan returned home, his hard on temporarily relieved, feeling very satisfied with himself. This time he hadn't had to depend on catching Rea when she was alone to pump her to find out what he needed to know. He had learned for himself that Carrie was going to Philadelphia the following weekend, that Linda was going home for a visit, and that Rea, Dora, and Claire would be attending a dinner and staying over at Anna Taylor's home that Saturday night.
He made his plans accordingly.

Linda's small bag was packed. It was nearly time for her to leave if she was to make the ten-thirty bus. She pulled her soft knitted hat down over her hair, tied her scarf around her throat. She paced the room, back and forth, a few times. Sighing deeply, she picked up the bag and turned off the light. Then, in the dark, she went to look out. The window on the second floor of Logan's house was aglow. She stood there, waiting. Maybe she could see him one more time before she left. Maybe this would be the night . . . She didn't want to go. If she went away now, she might miss him. But her plans were made. Her father would be there to pick her up when she arrived. He and her mother would ask her a thousand questions about her job, and what she did when she wasn't working. They'd have a big family meal, with all the uncles and aunts and cousins. They would warn her about the bad things that could happen if she weren't careful, and question her about Dora Loving and Claire. They wouldn't mention Margo directly. But she, her death, and what she had done to deserve it, would be in their minds.

Still, Linda would regret it if she didn't go. She'd feel guilty. It would be silly to give up her weekend for nothing. She hesitated, shifting her slight weight from one small foot to the other. Why go if she didn't want to? But why stay?

Because, maybe, tonight, Logan would . . .

She imagined him as she had seen him last Sunday, sitting in the big chair in the living room, relaxed, his teeth flashing in a smile, long legs spread out, blond hair glistening, surrounded by a sweet masculine scent.

She jerked off her hat, untied her scarf. She unpacked her small bag. Soon she went to look out, and saw that Logan's window had gone dark.

She made a brief telephone call home to tell her parents that she had changed her plans, and cut off their anxious questions by pretending the line was bad and she couldn't hear them.

Afterwards she went back to the window. She watched the shadows sway in the yard, and pictured Logan coming through the gate, through Hannah's Gate, to her.

When she first heard the sound from below, she thought she had dreamed it. When it came again, she was startled into reality. Her imaginings faded swiftly.

Someone was moving around downstairs. But everyone had gone away. She was supposed to be alone in the house.

Her heart began to beat quickly. She tiptoed to the door, peered into the hall. Now there was silence. A dull drumming silence. Except for a single lamp burning on the hall table, the house was in complete darkness.

She started down the steps. When she was midway, a tall figure came soundlessly from the study. A strange featureless face, tipped up to stare at her. But those strong thighs, the thick shoulders, the muscled arms, were all familiar to her. She didn't know the face masked in a woman's stocking, but she knew the body. She had dreamed of it, yearned for it. Her fear disappeared. Instead of fear, there was hunger. Swift, hot, overpowering hunger.

She whispered, "Logan, I knew you'd come. I've been waiting for you."

There was an instant of absolute silence.

The faceless man stood frozen.

She too stood frozen.

Then, with an oath, he bounded up the few steps between them. She opened her arms to him, was murmuring his name, her eyes closed, her lips parted.

For an instant, he loomed over her, staring. Then he was on her.

Chapter 11

There was a thin pebbly layer of ice on the pavement. Claire felt her heel skid, and clutched empty air, trying to keep from falling. She managed to stay on her feet, but her heart was beating quickly when she gained the shelter of the front porch. As she fished for her keys in her purse, she heard her mother say, "You could have had a good time, if you wanted to, Rea."

"I hate those people," she retorted.

It was only a few miles between Anna Taylor's house in Georgetown and Hannah's Gate in Cleveland Park, but Claire felt as if she had moved from one world to another when she drove away from the Taylor mansion and turned into the cracked driveway on Honey Locust Lane.

In the one, there were servants, fresh flowers on polished marble-topped tables, newly upholstered sofas, thick rugs. Solid and luxurious comfort. In the other . . .

She turned the key in the lock, and pushed the door open. It mattered more to her mother than to her, but even she was aware of the difference. The lamp on the hall table was out. She noticed that, and thought that Linda must have absent-mindedly switched it off before she left. They had decided to leave it burning, through the night and the following day. In case someone was watching the house, Claire had said. The light was off now. Claire supposed it didn't matter.

The stillness of the house reached out to enfold her. She could hear the faint hiss of sleet falling out of doors.

Dora was still talking. Rea followed her in, and punctuated her mother's comments by closing the door with a bang.

The stillness receded as Dora asked querulously, "What's the matter, Claire? Why are you just standing there?"

But she didn't reply.

Beyond the dark spokes of the banister, between pale light and shadow, she saw a shoe. A shoe turned on its side. She saw a heaped sweater. Her vision blurred for a moment. The pale light and shadow blended. There was nothing on the stair . . . Then, in an instant, her sight cleared and she realized that she was staring at Linda's crumpled body.

The house's stillness touched her again, pulsating in long breathing waves. Unknowable currents. Secrets. Fears. Anguish.

What these walls knew . . . what these walls

had seen . . . And now . . . Linda . . .

The purse dropped from Claire's nerveless fingers.

Dora said, "What's the matter? Claire!" And then, stumbling at the foot of the stairs, she screamed, "It's Linda!"

Claire said dryly, "Go into the living room, Mom. Please. Sit down there."

Rea came close, pressed her shoulder to Claire's. "Is she dead?"

"I don't know . . . I think . . ." Claire stopped herself. She could feel Rea's shivering. She mustn't go to pieces now. She had too much to do. She pushed Rea towards the living room. "Stay with Mama, Rea."

When the girl left her, Claire moved slowly closer to the stairs. She forced herself to climb them. One, two, three . . . Midway up, she leaned down to Linda, touched trembling fingers to the girl's throat. Cold flesh. Still, unmoving. There was no pulse.

Only then did Claire allow herself a direct look at Linda's face. Seeing it, she felt a shudder in her heart. Linda's blonde hair, usually so smooth and pale, was in wild disarray, and matted with dark stains. Her small mouth was agape. Her eyes were open to slits showing dully in mounds of torn flesh. Her cheeks were bruised. Black thumb prints encircled her neck.

"Oh, Linda," Claire whispered. "I'm so sorry." And even as she spoke, Claire thought of Margo. Margo's poor broken face, torn flesh. What connection had there been between Margo and Linda? What had begun with Margo's death that had ended with Linda's murder? And had it ended?

From the doorway, Rea said, "Claire! Linda was supposed to go home. Why didn't she?"

"I don't know." Claire came down the steps. "I'm going to call for help."

Even as she spoke to the police station, she asked herself, when will it be over? How will it end? Why is this happening to us?

And then, within only moments it seemed, she heard the now too familiar sound of a siren wailing in the distance.

By the time seven days had passed the first high peak of fear had muted. Claire and Dora could read the newspapers, and listen to the radio. Carrie had gone back to her typing in the evening, and Rea immersed herself in *Gone with the Wind* one more time.

But no one forgot the night that Linda was found dead on the stairs. The memory of her death lingered on, drifting like a shadow through everyone's mind.

The first police who had responded to Claire's frantic call had been to Hannah's Gate

188

before. They remembered that there had been a burglar in the house. They remembered too that Margo Desales, once a resident there, had been murdered. They were immediately in touch with Detective William Eagan, and he, along with other men in the Homicide Squad, arrived soon after.

They spent hours at Hannah's Gate, questioning Dora and Rea and Claire. When Carrie came home, they went over the same ground with her.

By then, Linda's body had been examined, photographed, and taken to the morgue for an autopsy. They searched Linda's room, and when Claire led them to it, Detective Eagan's eyes flicked sideways at her, and he said, "So Linda took this room?"

Claire remembered the day when Linda had asked if she could have the big back room, remembered helping to move her things.

"It didn't bother her?" the detective asked.

Claire shook her head.

"I guess there's no reason it should have."

Yet now, thinking of it, Claire was uneasy. She knew Linda hadn't liked Margo, but still . . . wasn't it unfeeling to move into Margo's room without any second thoughts?

Late the next day Detective Eagan telephoned Claire. The results of the autopsy had come through. Linda had died of severe head injuries, had been savagely beaten about the face, and had been choked. She hadn't been pregnant, had no signs of being raped, and was, in fact, a virgin.

Claire asked if the detective had any leads.

He said there were none. When she insisted that the murder must be related to the killing of Margo, he said, "I agree that there's too much of a coincidence here, but I don't have anything to go on yet."

"And so . . . ?"

"You've had a burglar before. It looks as if that's what happened this time too. Only Linda was home."

He would say nothing more.

Brett was there when the call come. He had driven to the house as soon as he heard the news, and had returned every day since for a brief visit.

Now, when Claire put down the phone, he asked, "Anything new?"

"Nothing. He's back to the burglar again." She sighed. "He agreed it's too much of a coincidence, but said there's no evidence to support any other theory."

Brett looked worried, his dark brows drawn. "There's got to be a connection."

"I agree. But I don't know what it is, or where to look for it."

Soon after that, Linda's parents came to

190

claim Linda's body, to take her home for burial. They were stunned, saddened, bewildered. Linda's father said, "I was against her coming here, but she wanted to be part of the war effort and everyone said it would be all right. But she wasn't used to big cities, nor to big cities' ways. I was afraid something bad would happen to her." Linda's mother wept into an embroidered handkerchief.

Claire had another meeting with Detective Eagan. He seemed even more tired than usual. They once again went through the 'Is anything missing?' and the 'Why was she here if she was supposed to be going out of town?' As well as the 'Who knew she was going to be away? And who knew she wasn't? And who were her friends? Who did she see most?'

In the end, it was the same as before, when Margo died. All questions. No answers.

Brett had his own interview with the detective. The results were the same. The detective agreed that on the surface it could appear that there must be some tie between Margo's death and Linda's. But he could see none. Until he had reason, by which he meant facts, to change his mind, he would have to consider Linda's death an accident that had occurred when a possible robber realized she was in the house. Not that, he added hastily, Linda's death would be forgotten. He would, of course, continue studying the case, re-checking, questioning the neighbours and Linda's employers, to see what he could learn.

Brett had to act as if he were satisfied with that, although he feared that Linda's case would slowly be moved from the front of the desk to the back, soon to be quietly forgotten.

He didn't mention his qualms to Claire. There seemed no point to it. At the same time, he grew more and more fearful for her. Too much had gone on at Hannah's Gate for him to suppose that anyone there was beyond danger. He couldn't bear to think that some evil fate might await her in the future.

Once again it was as if nothing had happened. At least, that's what everyone pretended. Claire went along with that. It was the only way.

Both lodgers' rooms remained empty. Dora spoke of renting them; she needed the money. But a lethargy had descended on her. She couldn't bring herself to get the rooms ready again. She couldn't get herself to advertise them either. It would mean meeting people, establishing new bonds, new routines. She couldn't deal with it. She didn't want to.

Claire understood and didn't try to push her mother. In time Dora would be ready to handle things. Meanwhile it was just as well she didn't.

Suddenly it was December 7th again, but of 1943 this time. Two years had passed since the Japanese attack on Pearl Harbor.

Claire was at work when she noted the date. Her hands dropped away from her typewriter for a moment. She thought back to that Sunday afternoon when she'd first heard the news: Casey listening to the radio, Rea at his feet, she in a chair nearby, Ian and Leigh upstairs, Dora in the kitchen. Claire remembered wondering what was going to happen to all of them, knowing they'd never be the same again. It was true, and the end was still nowhere in sight.

A week before Christmas Casey returned home to Hannah's Gate. He looked well, younger than ever. He said nothing of his still secret determination to leave Dora for good.

For a day or two Dora brightened. She brushed her hair, made up her face. She wore her black dress with the big white lace collar. She told him about her several visits to Anna Taylor, and about how she planned to rent out again the two rooms now available, also about how much Carrie Day knew about Big Jack. She confided her fears that Claire would end up an old maid. "There's this Brett Devlin," she said. "You'll meet him, I'm sure.

He's crazy about Claire. But she doesn't bother with him. She writes to Leigh almost every day. And what if he never comes back? Then where'll she be?"

Casey said, "It's her life. You can't live it for her."

"But if she doesn't marry soon . . ."

"Leave it alone," Casey said, yawning.

"You don't care if she's an old maid."

"There are worse fates. She could be married to a man she hates."

Dora pretended she hadn't heard him, and went on to speak of other matters. The house, the yard . . .

That was the night he told her he was leaving the next morning, and Claire heard the angry whispers again.

He missed Ian's arrival by a few hours.

Dora, red-eyed and tense, wandered through the house, murmuring. "We could be murdered in our beds, and he wouldn't care!" That had been her main argument to Casey. She needed him. Rea and Claire needed him. Something terrible was happening at Hannah's Gate, and he was leaving them alone. Casey answered, with terrifying dispassion, "Don't you realize there's a war on?"

Ian listened to what his mother told him, but said very little. Until he came home, what he had heard of Margo's death, and Linda's, had seemed unreal to him. But now, even though he was aware of the news in a different way, he couldn't dwell on it. His mind remained far away. So much had happened to him in the past few months that he felt like a stranger at Hannah's Gate. Only two things concerned him now. The first was his work. The second was Luz Delgado. And, in natural order, it was the first that had led to the second.

One morning at Oak Ridge he'd been told that the transfer he had requested was granted. He was now assigned to the U.S. Engineers Office in Sante Fe, New Mexico. He knew immediately that his actual destination was Los Alamos.

With stunning swiftness, he stepped off a train at a tiny town called Lamy. There he saw a railroad station, a diner, a few rundown adobe houses, and the burnt out remains of a Harvey House. A herd of goats grazed in the red fields nearby. An Army truck picked him up and drove him to Santa Fe. After he'd presented his papers, he received a pass, and then another government truck took him north to a town called Pojaque, where they turned left on to a narrow dirt road. At a place called Otowi, they crossed an old bridge. Half an hour later they stopped at the first of several guard houses. It was manned by military police wearing battle helmets and carrying guns. On both sides of the guard house, stretching as far as he could see, there was a seven-foot chain linked fence topped with three strands of barbed wire. At regular intervals, there were signs saying U.S. Gov. Property, Danger — *Peligro* — Keep Out.

They drove through pine and juniper, crossing choppy hills, dry ravines, and blood-red *mesas*, always climbing. Soon they reached the Pajarito Plateau from which they could see Frijoles Canyon and the Puyé Cliffs, and in the distance, to the east, the Sangre de Cristo Mountains.

Los Alamos had once been a private school. There were a few buildings left from that time. The new ones were of clapboard and frame, clustered around Ashley Pond, and spreading out from there. He was soon settled in one of the green barracks-like structures. He had a room to himself, for which he was grateful. It held minimal furniture: a bed, a table, two chairs. It had a wood stove, a tiny bathroom with a shower. It seemed luxurious because he'd expected far less.

He immediately plunged into work, quickly infected with the anxiety of those around him. The project had to be completed as soon as humanly possible. American lives depended on it. There were constant meetings, in the early mornings, late at night. Without pause experiments, calculations, and measurements continued.

Still, he had an occasional day off, sometimes even two, for visits to Santa Fe. On one of those trips he met Luz Delgado.

She was riding the G.I. bus that left the Hill, as Los Alamos was called, early on a Saturday morning. He sat behind her, and noticed the shape of her head beneath its crown of thick dark braids. When she turned, he caught a glimpse of a high cheekbone, a long straight nose. Her skin was olive, but with a faint undertone of pink.

He was attracted to her on sight, and determined to know her. Unlike Leigh, who had always been easy with girls, Ian had been shy. Now, though, he felt different. He made sure that he left the bus before her when it stopped at the La Fonda Hotel in Sante Fe. He was waiting for her when she got off. It was easy to engage her in conversation after asking her for directions to a good place for lunch. So that, for him, was the beginning of their affair . . .

Now, at home in Hannah's Gate, he learned that he had just missed seeing his father. He had dropped a note to Casey when he arrived in New Mexico, thinking that they'd be able to get together. He'd had no answer, and supposed that Casey was away on a field trip. He decided he would try to contact Casey again when he returned to the Hill.

Meanwhile there was little he could say. When Claire asked him about his work, he told her he wasn't at liberty to discuss it.

She nodded, remembering that a neighbour had told her about an F.B.I. agent who had asked about Ian.

After a day or two, he became restless. So, even though he had several days left of his leave, he decided to return to Santa Fe. He gave Claire a new address — Box 1663, Santa Fe, New Mexico — told her to be careful, kissed Dora and Rea goodbye, and was soon gone.

Two days later he sat in the lobby of the La Fonda Hotel, waiting for Luz, who had promised to be there when he arrived. She turned up after an hour, but when he saw her hurrying past the potted palms, slender, her long legs flashing beneath her full skirt, he forgot his anger.

"I told them I was sick," she said, her slanted green eyes sparkling. "Very sick," she added. "So we shall have two days." She slid her hand under his arm. "Come on. I missed you."

As they went to the tiny house off Garcia Street that she borrowed from her cousin for their meetings, she told him how much she had missed him, told him how she planned to prove it to him. She spoke in words that he'd never heard a woman use before. Had it been anyone else, he'd have been disgusted. But in her mouth those same words were exciting.

She banged twice on the door, then unlocked it. Inside, she called, "Fred? Fred, it's me. It's Luz," and then turned to Ian, "It's okay. He remembered. He won't bother us." She was referring to her cousin. "Hurry, Ian. Hurry, hurry," she commanded, and meanwhile, with the door closed and locked, she began to undress him, her fingers warm where they touched his flesh, her cheeks burning hot when she buried her face in his throat. "Ian, hurry! I want you!"

Days later, when Ian had returned to work on the Hill, she was in the small house off Garcia Street again. That time she was there with Fred Delgado. He was a heavy-set man a few years older than Ian. He had a dark beard and thick curly dark hair. His face was full, the cheeks ruddy. He said, "What did you get?"

"Thirty dollars," she told Fred. "But there'll be more later."

"Okay," he growled. "Just remember who you belong to."

Her green eyes were unreadable. "He's a very nice boy, Fred. But this is business. So you behave yourself."

"Sure," he answered. "I'll behave myself so long as you don't forget you're my wife. And I'm not letting you go."

With Casey and then Ian gone, Hannah's Gate seemed even more quiet than usual. There was a sense of expectation, of incompletion.

When the telephone rang, Claire leaped to answer it, always hoping that Detective Eagan would call with information. But the calls were from Anna Taylor, from Brett, occasionally from Jeremiah Merrill.

It was the same with the mail. Every evening Claire leafed through the few letters. Then, though, she wasn't looking for word from the detective. She hoped for a note from Leigh. Evening after evening she fought her disappointment. Soon, she told herself, she would hear from him. She would know how he was, and where. And soon the war would end. Leigh would come home again.

At New Year's Dora made her usual supper of black-eyed peas with ham hocks, and told the usual stories of her youth, while Carrie listened avidly, and contributed stories of her own.

Brett was there that night, and lifted a glass of wine in a toast. "To 1944. May it end in peace."

"For all of us," Dora added. When she emptied her glass, she went on, "Thank you for bringing the wine, Brett. It was kind of you."

Winter dragged into spring. Lines grew longer in the grocery stores; tempers grew shorter.

Claire's working hours were increased. She didn't mind. The busier she was the less time she had to think.

Rea suddenly became clothes and make-up conscious. She borrowed sweaters from Claire, experimented with a new hair style. Dora, who had complained before that the girl was too slovenly, now complained that she was too vain.

In March Claire once again dug up her garden to prepare to plant vegetables.

Logan came out to talk to her and Rea.

He had been watching, waiting. Nothing had happened. He was still uneasy. Very soon, he expected to receive his orders. When it was time, he had to be free to do what he was supposed to do. Everything depended on it. Yet he wasn't easy in his mind. There were loose ends, or possible loose ends. He wasn't sure. He found himself thinking of Margo, of

Linda, of the diary that might or might not exist. He was attracted to Claire and somehow repelled by her at the same time.

She, unaware of his thoughts, answered his comments briefly. She was planning a letter to Leigh. She always thought ahead about what she would write. She'd tell him about Ian's visit, give him the new address. She'd mention her father too. She could describe the new Rea. She would speak of her job, maybe tell him about seeing 'Going My Way' with Bing Crosby. And of course she'd describe the victory garden she was working on now. She wouldn't mention Margo, and she'd say nothing about Linda. She wanted her letters to be cheerful. No matter how she was feeling, she was determined to sound fine for him.

When Logan excused himself and left her, she hardly noticed. She finished the day's work and went inside. Having washed her hands at the kitchen sink, she went into the study. From upstairs, she heard Carrie typing. Carrie, Claire thought, was serious about her writing. Hardly a day went by that Carrie didn't work on one of her short stories.

But then Claire forgot about Carrie. As she stepped into the study she saw that the portrait of Big Jack Gowan had been moved. It hung crooked on its hook, and along its right side there showed a broad strip of clean and unfaded wallpaper.

She stared at it, plunged in sudden chill. She remembered finding her grandfather's books out of order, as if someone had searched through them. She thought of the broken lock on the door of the storage shed. She could hear again Linda accusing Margo of looking in her drawers, and Margo saying Linda had been in *her* room. Both girls were gone, but something was still happening.

She became aware that the sounds of Carrie's typing had stopped.

In the sudden silence, the rattle of March wind at the window seemed thunderously loud.

Claire tried to shift the portrait. It was heavy, hard to handle. There were kinks in its wire. It couldn't have slipped sideways by itself. Someone had had to struggle with it to move it aside.

When she finally had the portrait straight, she stepped back to look into Big Jack Gowan's eyes. If only he could talk . . . if only he could tell her . . .

With a sigh, she turned away.

Chapter 12

The date was June 6th, 1944.

Leigh squinted at his wristwatch. It was one o'clock in the morning. He yawned. He'd have liked to stretch his legs, but he could barely move. He was hemmed in by men, who like himself had been crouched in readiness in these tight quarters for hours.

Would this be it? No one knew. But all were expectant, prepared. They had exchanged addresses, paid debts, prayed, and slept, the night before. They'd even had a special meal of steak and eggs. Now they waited.

The sky was a grey canopy overhead. A cold drizzle fell steadily. The seas were rough, occasional waves spilling over the gunwhales. Some men were seasick, vomiting into paper bags. Others groaned behind clenched teeth.

Leigh hunched forward, holding steady against the constant rocking. Shoulders pressed against his.

A small picture grew in his mind. A woman's face. It was narrow at the chin, lips faintly smiling. Jeri. He quickly erased it, made his mind empty. He had become very good at that in the past months.

He hadn't been back to London since he'd fled from the bombed out house. He'd been found by a military policeman staggering along Oxford Street that same night, unable to speak or to identify himself. He was hospitalized for several weeks. As the days passed, he slowly recovered. His memory came back, but he learned to erase those thoughts with which he couldn't deal. He was allowed a few more weeks of recuperation and was then sent to a base near Rye.

By then the south of England was a huge arsenal. Hidden in the forests were stacks of ammunition. There were ambulances, armoured cars and trucks, camouflaged to be unseen from the skies, lined up bumper to bumper on the moors. The valley floors were covered with railway stock, locomotives, tankers, and freight cars.

Through the month of May men gathered at loading points near Newhaven, Brixham, Plymouth and Portsmouth. Finally, under a grey night sky, they set out on transports across the channel to a rendezvous called Picadilly Circus south of the Isle of Wight. There they re-grouped and headed for Normandy in five lane convoys. Later these convoys split into ten lanes, two for each beach, Omaha and

Utah, for the Americans, the others for the British.

The armada was made up of 5000 ships. There were fast new attack transports, slow freighters, small ocean-going liners, channel steamers, hospital ships, weathered tankers, swarms of tugs, shallow draft landing ships carrying fast landing craft for beach assault, mine sweepers, coast guard cutters, buoy-layers, motor launches. Seven hundred and two warships escorted the convoy, which included two floating harbours called mulberries, which were to assure delivery of men and supplies until a port was taken.

Twelve miles off the coast, they anchored, waiting again. The tide had to be low enough to expose German beach obstacles. The wind had to be right. The sky had to be cloudy.

Earlier, low-flying planes heading for France had flown over. They carried pathfinders paratroopers with blackened faces, sent to mark the drop zones for later jumpers.

At 1:15 A.M. a full scale air assault was launched by American planes.

At 5:30 A.M. warships fired at German coastal targets. Great pillars of black smoke rose in the air. The sky glimmered with flashes of light and leaps of flame as pillboxes, bunkers and redoubts were hit.

Then, from the command ship, two messages came. "Away all boats . . ." was the first. After a moment's pause came the second, "Our Father, which art in Heaven, hallowed be Thy name . . ." It was 6:30 A.M.

The transports moved closer. Men poised over the scramble nets. When the order came, they raced down them and into the landing ships. The landing ships sped towards shore. At the same time a huge fleet of Spitfires, Thunderbolts and Mustangs swooped in to strafe beaches and headlands, creating air cover for the infantry.

The L.S.T.s bumped ground. Leigh, with the others, hit the choppy water, holding his carbine high. The weight of his pack, canteen and extra ammunition almost dragged him under. The stench of oil smoke scorched his throat. The noise was deafening. The boom of the warships' guns, the high whine of the planes, the crash of waves, shouts of anger or anguish, were brain-dazing blows. He managed to struggle against the choppy seas to his feet. Behind him, the dark water parted in long white wakes, and the L.S.T.s moved off.

He reached shore, part of a quick-moving mass. Before him the beach erupted in a sheet of fire. From the skies came a rain of dirt. He kept going, barely conscious of the men falling around him, of the bodies that lay in the surf, the floating helmets, packs, spilled rations. He was barely conscious of the agonized screams, dismembered flesh and blood. But he was absorbing it, and later, far away, he would remember.

He fired his carbine, racing on, zig-zagging towards the protection of trees that loomed ghost-like in the gray mists. Then the brain-numbing noise seemed to fade. Pale dawn edged the forest. He plunged into it, heaving a great breath of relief. In that same instant, he sensed danger and swung to face it. He was too late. The dark bush to his right exploded into staccato flashes. Heat seared him. The grey dawn burst into inky blackness.

It was 3:30 A.M. June 6th, when word of D-Day reached Washington. Lights suddenly flashed on over the city. The telephone lines were busy. Radios were tuned in.

Several hours later Claire was dressing when Rea pounded at her door, shouting, "They've done it, Claire! The invasion's begun!"

She hurried downstairs, following Rea. Together with Carrie and Dora, they bent over the radio as the news came in.

Six weeks later, just after Franklin D. Roosevelt had been nominated for an unprecedented fourth term as president, and had named Harry S. Truman to be his vice-presidential running mate, Jeremiah Merrill came to see Claire.

It was a late July twilight. The air was a hot and humid blanket, faintly lemon-scented by the last of the blossoms on the two old magnolias that stood next to the house.

As Claire opened the door at his knock, her hands went cold.

He was grey-faced, his pale eyes red-rimmed. His shoulders, usually squared, were bowed.

She had spoken to him on the phone several times, but she hadn't seen him since just after Letty Merrill died.

"Mr Merrill," she said in a dry whisper. Her heart had climbed into her throat as soon as she recognized him. "Come in." She led him into the living room.

He sat down, put his hat aside, and looked at her without speaking. He wasn't a large man, but now he looked smaller than ever. He had a well-shaven face, light eyes, and a ruff of thin hair ordinarily combed carefully across his pink scalp. Now his hair looked as if he had forgotten to brush it. His cheeks were flushed, but his lips, tightly compressed, seemed very pale. He was carefully turned out, his seersucker suit fresh, his shirt white and unwrinkled. But his blue tie hung crooked under his collar, as if he'd repeatedly pulled at it.

At last she asked hoarsely, "Is it Leigh, Mr Merrill?"

He said, "Yes. It's Leigh. He's been listed as missing in action."

She sank into the sofa, her knees suddenly melting under her. "Leigh? Missing?" She had never allowed herself to think of the possibility of this moment. Yet it had been in her mind all the while, she realized now. It was familiar. She felt that she had heard those words before. Still, the scene was unreal. She didn't believe it. That's why she felt this way. She didn't believe it.

Jeremiah went on, "We don't know anything. But when his group re-formed as planned, he didn't respond. Nothing . . . that is, nothing of his was found." Jeremiah's tired voice faltered. "The invasion . . . that's when, perhaps, with the attendant confusion . . . It's impossible to be certain of anything at this point. Perhaps, later . . ."

"Missing . . . that's what you said," she whispered. "He could be a prisoner." She drew a deep breath. The sense of unreality was receding. The air was lightening. "That's it, Mr Merrill. He's been captured."

"It's possible." But Jeremiah didn't seem to believe it.

She heard the doubt in his voice. "It has to be that," she insisted. "If he was dead, killed . . . then I'd know. I'd feel it. I'm sure he's okay." Even as she said the words, hesitantly, thinking aloud, the certainty grew in her. Leigh couldn't be dead. She would feel it. If he were gone from her life, a part of her would be gone too. She would know. "I'd feel it," she repeated aloud. "I'm sure he's okay. One of these days, soon, the Red Cross will be in touch with you. Or Leigh himself will get word out. We'll hear from him."

Jeremiah smiled faintly. "You may be right, Claire. I pray so. He's all I have. All that's left of my family. Just Leigh."

She pressed her trembling hands together. She thought, Leigh's all I have too. He's all I want. Nothing bad can happen to him. He can't be dead.

Later, when Jeremiah had gone, she took Leigh's picture from her dresser. She held it tightly. You've got to be all right, she whispered to his smiling face. You've got to be. I love you.

From the beaches in Normandy, American and British forces pressed on to fight in the cobblestoned roads and stone houses of Vierville, Colleville, La Madeleine and Ste Marie-Église.

211

On August 15th another force of Americans landed in southern France between Toulon and Cannes. The liberation of Paris was accomplished on August 25th.

Brussels and Antwerp were freed on September 4th, and on that day Leigh half-crouched against a wooden shed, his head and face wrapped in dirty bandages. His face burned, his body ached. It had been weeks since his wounds were perfunctorily treated, weeks too since he'd heard any news. But there was a restlessness in the prison camp now. The guards were nervous, occasionally pausing in their rounds to whisper quickly to each other.

The roar of planes swooping low filled his ears. He squinted up at them, faintly smiling. American fighters. Give them hell, he thought.

By mid-September there had still been no word about Leigh.

Claire calculated it to be three months and one week since he had been listed as missing in action during the invasion of Normandy. But she didn't think of him as missing. She called it being held prisoner of war. No matter that France, and now Belgium, had been overrun by American and British forces, and at least three camps had been taken, their inmates freed. No matter that Leigh hadn't been among them, and that no one from his unit knew what had happened to him, Claire remained certain that he was alive, that he would soon return to her.

She spoke often to Jeremiah Merrill, hoping for news of Leigh from him, but also buoying his sagging spirits.

One day he took her to the Cosmos Club on LaFayette Square across Pennsylvania Avenue from the White House. They were served lunch in a quiet dining room.

He fiddled with his cutlery, pudgy hands shaking slightly. "I've been trying to find out about Leigh.

"Considering how the fighting is going now, I expected it to be easier than it has been. But there are still pockets of resistance. And it's very difficult to get through. I guess the strings I've pulled haven't been the right ones. And somehow I haven't wanted to push too hard. There are so many of us in the same boat."

"Maybe soon . . ."

"You still have hope, don't you? You still believe he'll come back."

She said fervently, "I . . . I have to. I can't give up."

"But what if . . . have you thought . . ."

"No," she interrupted. "No. Please. We mustn't talk as if . . ." It was the big unmentionable. She wouldn't think it, say it. No. Leigh *had* to be all right. Soon, oh, God, please make it soon, the war would end. Then Leigh would come home. It was what she clung to.

Jeremiah said gently, "If you ever need me, remember that I'll help however I can."

They went on to speak of other things. He talked of the coming election. He believed Franklin Roosevelt would win. He hoped so. But he greatly feared the president wasn't well. When Jeremiah had seen him last, he had the feeling that something had gone out of the man. Hopkins, none of the others, mentioned it. But Jeremiah was uneasy. Even so, he didn't think Thomas Dewey was the right man for the White House, the man to deal with the world as it would be when the war was finally over.

After that Sunday, Claire saw Jeremiah occasionally. They had lunch together. She invited him to dinner several times. Soon she became aware that there was a warmth between them. In spite of the big difference in their ages, they were friends. And he was important to her because of Leigh. He was a link to Leigh. She supposed it was the same for Jeremiah. For him, she was a link to his nephew. Their times together were satisfying, and brought some cheer into the drabness of her life.

It had been over a year since Margo's death, somewhat less since Linda's. Claire no longer heard from Detective Eagan, and had, long before, stopped calling him. Only Brett's casual visits were left to remind her of what had happened.

Then, one night when Claire was looking for something to read in her grandfather's study, she realized that once again his books had been disarranged. Plutarch was at the front of a shelf instead of at the back. Plato was in with Longfellow. She took down both volumes and examined them, slowly turning page after page. Unable to find anything, she returned them to where they belonged. It was just as it had been before. The slight changes that proved to her that someone had been looking for something. And, as before, she thought immediately of Margo's diary. Her blood began to throb in her pulses. She had thought those terrible days behind her, gone into the past, but now they had come back.

She found Rea in the kitchen and asked, "Have you been looking at Grandpa Jack's books?"

"Who? Me?" Rea was startled. "What would I want with those old things?"

"Somebody moved them around."

"Then ask Carrie," Rea said. "She's always

got her nose in some book or other, hasn't she?"

When Claire mentioned Big Jack's library to Carrie, the woman's eyes widened. "Of course I've seen your grandfather's collection of books. And I don't mind telling you, I wish they belonged to me. But I'm a guest in your house. I'd ask first if I was to borrow any of them. It wouldn't be right otherwise." Her soft slurred words were earnest, innocent.

Claire said hastily, "Oh, I know you'd ask, Carrie. I was just wondering. But if at any time you want to read his books, you're welcome to them. You know that."

"Thank you," Carrie said. Then: "He's such an interesting man, Big Jack Gowan. I always admired him so. Everybody I knew did."

"Did you ever meet him?" Claire asked.

"Oh, no!" Carrie sounded shocked. "How could I? I was just a child, and never in Washington then, before he died." She went on, "But you do remember him, don't you, Claire?"

"Just as an old man. Not at all the way my mother describes him."

"He was very important. He must have had loads of friends."

"I suppose so." Claire wasn't interested in talking about Big Jack. He had nothing to do with what was going on now at Hannah's Gate, she was sure. "My mother would know."

"Yes," Carrie sighed. "She would, wouldn't she?"

Claire was struck by a false note in Carrie's response. Dora had spoken about Big Jack dozens of times to Carrie. Claire had heard some of those conversations. She was sure there had been many others. She asked herself why Carrie was not pretending that those conversations had never occurred. It didn't make sense. But it was one more thing for Claire to think about.

The following weekend, very early on Sunday morning, Claire heard the sound of Carrie's walk on the stairs. It was a solid, heavy tread, not to be mistaken for Rea's dancing step, or Dora's slow, cautious one.

Claire looked out to see Carrie duck around the car, then stop at the storage shed at the end of the driveway. The broken lock had never been repaired, Claire knew. Now Carrie hurried into the shed. It was full of boxes and trunks. Some dated back to the time of Dora's marriage to Casey. Some were even older, having once belonged to Big Jack. There was nothing of value among those mouldering cancelled bank checks, water and gas bill receipts, old newspaper clippings, stacks of *Saturday Evening Post* Magazines, and piles of *Liberty*. Then what was Carrie looking for?

Claire went downstairs. From outside the shed, she heard the sounds of Carrie's movements. The shifting of a box. The ripping of paper. All accompanied by soft murmurings as Carrie spoke to herself. A whispered, "No . . . no. It can't be. But somewhere . . . for sure . . . oh, no . . . so many . . ."

Claire pushed the door open. A tide of stale air swirled around her face. The place was full of shadows. A curtain of grey motes hung over stacked crates. Carrie turned, eyes wide. She stammered, "I was . . . I was looking for a hammer. I want to hang a picture in my room."

"You were looking for Margo's diary," Claire burst out. "Why don't you tell me the truth?"

"Margo's diary!" Carrie's eyes filled with honest amazement. "What are you talking about? Why would I care about her diary?"

"That's what I'm asking you," Claire retorted. But now she was sorry she'd allowed herself to accuse Carrie. Plainly the woman was astonished by what Claire had said.

Carrie said, "Besides, after all this time, the diary would have been found, wouldn't it? If there ever *was* a diary." She couldn't stop talking about it. She was so relieved that Claire thought that was what she had been looking for that she had to keep repeating it. "Margo's diary! Honestly, Claire . . ."

"If you want a hammer, you're in the wrong place. Come on."

She led Carrie out of the shed, pulled the door shut. She'd buy a new lock, just to keep people out, she decided. She said nothing about that, however, but took Carrie inside to the basement tool room. "There, up on that wall, is where we keep the hammer. And whatever else you'd need to hang a picture with."

"Oh, thank you," Carrie said sweetly, ignoring Claire's tart tone. "I'm sorry I bothered you."

She took the hammer, and went upstairs to her room. She had already had a framed picture ready. Just in case. The just in case had happened. She tapped a nail into place, hung the picture on the wall. Also just in case Claire decided to check up on her.

Then she sank on to the edge of her bed, breathing hard. She'd been frightened at first. Not sure of what Claire would do, what she would think. But the minute Claire mentioned Margo's diary, Carrie had stopped being afraid. *That* had nothing whatever to do with Carrie. Besides, that was finished, ended, done. Why was Claire still wondering about it? There couldn't be any reason to. But, either way, it had nothing to do with her, with Carrie.

Still, Claire's suspicions *did* trouble Carrie. She wondered if she ought to give up her search. Perhaps it had all been nothing more than her mother's imaginings. But she was doing no harm. And it was comfortable at Hannah's Gate. She had a room to herself, her typewriter, her privacy when she wanted it. She hated to leave without knowing one way or another. She'd had questions all her life. Now, finally, she was in the one place where the answers lay, if indeed there were answers. And there had to be. She was somehow sure of it. Her mother couldn't have been so far wrong. Carrie sighed. She could try to be more careful, but she couldn't give up now.

The following Sunday Brett came by to see how things were. He had stayed away for a few weeks, telling himself that he must be careful not to wear out his welcome. But finally he'd given in to himself. He wanted so desperately to see Claire. Just to see her. Be with her.

Rea wandered in while they were talking. She wore a blue angora sweater and saddle shoes with matching blue angora socks. Her dark hair was caught back in a pony tail.

"Hi, Brett," she said brightly.

He greeted her, then went on speaking to Claire.

220

Rea listened for a while, then said. "The war is the only thing you two ever talk about."

Neither of them answered her.

She smoothed her hair. She crossed and re-crossed her legs, fidgeting as if bored.

Brett noticed, and wished that she would stop being so much the younger sister, and just disappear.

Claire noticed and realized that Rea had a crush on Brett, and was trying to get his attention.

But both Brett and Claire were astonished when Rea suddenly burst out, "What's the matter with you? Why don't you talk to me too? Can't you see I have opinions and feelings? Why don't you act as if I do? Why can't you listen to what I have to say. At least Logan does. He pays attention!"

Claire said quietly, "I'm sorry, Rea." She didn't explain that while she talked about the war with Brett, she was thinking of Leigh. Only half of her was here. The other half was far away. She couldn't say those things with Brett sitting there, so she said no more.

Brett too apologized. Then he went on with the conversation, this time making sure that he included Rea in what he was saying to Claire.

But Claire no longer listened. She had realized that in spite of Dora's admonitions about

Logan, Rea and he did seem to spend a surprising amount of time together. Now she began to wonder about that, particularly about the 'why' of it. What she didn't know was that Logan spent that time with Rea adroitly pumping the girl for information about Hannah's Gate, and Claire.

It was the same evening. Claire had a guest, one of her co-workers in the Department of Engineers mail room. The girl was a classifier, and had worked at the desk next to Margo's.

Logan arrived home in his car, and called in at Hannah's Gate, hoping Claire was alone.

Rea let him in, chatted with him before leading him into the study. As soon as he realized that Claire had company, he said he'd only stopped by for a minute, and soon departed.

After he had left, the girl said, "You know, Claire, I've seen him before. It was with Margo. But a funny thing happened. Afterwards, when I told her about seeing her and some man at the Domino Bar, she said she'd never been there. She was really insistent. I couldn't understand it. I was certain it was her. And now that I've seen Logan Jessup, I know he's the man she was with."

Claire agreed that it had been odd for Margo to deny having been to the Domino. In fact, Claire knew for sure that she had been there.

She'd told Claire about it herself. And there'd been Domino Bar matches in her purse. And Claire knew too that Margo had dated Logan a few times. Why should she pretend she hadn't? Claire wondered if the pretence could possibly have been a ruse to throw anyone interested off. Perhaps Margo and Logan had had an affair. She had been pregnant when she was killed . . .

Later, as she was preparing for bed, Claire heard the wistaria scrape against the wall. The wistaria . . . Rea had said she saw Margo climb down it. That's where she herself had got the idea.

Margo and Logan, pretending to have broken off while they had an affair . . .

Margo and Logan . . . the diary . . .

Claire tiptoed down the hall to Rea's room. She knocked softly, bracing herself for the argument she knew must come. At Rea's call, she went in.

Chapter 13

Logan was in his back yard when Rea returned from school that day.

For a while, she watched him from the window. She liked to look at him when he wasn't aware of her presence. It gave her a chance to see what he looked like when he was alone. It gave her a glimpse of another Logan. One that had a deep impenetrable expression. Mysterious. A man no one really knew. To know *that* Logan made her feel strong. It gave her some of his power. The Logan everyone else knew was open, friendly, always smiling. She found it interesting that the 'alone' face was so hard, while the 'public' face was just the opposite. She would have thought it would have been the other way around. Why hide when you were by yourself? That was what she felt about his 'alone' face. That he was concealing his real self. She watched for a little longer. Then, having refreshed her make-up and combed her hair, she went outside.

She had been nursing her anger at Claire ever since the night before, stoking it with memories of other slights. She was fed up with being treated like a child. She wasn't a baby any more, but that's how Claire, and everyone else too, insisted on treating her.

She could have told them plenty if they'd asked her. But no, they pretended to think she was deaf and dumb and blind. Claire knew she wasn't stupid. Why did she hide things from Rea? Well, she would show her, and all of them. She didn't know how, but she would.

Claire had said, "Rea, when did you see Margo climb out of the window?"

Rea had been cautious, wondering what Claire was driving at. "I'm not sure."

"Did you see where she went?"

Rea had shaken her head.

Claire stared into her eyes. "Tell me the truth. Did you follow her?"

"I certainly did not," Rea had retorted, feeling virtuous. That was true. She hadn't followed Margo. She hadn't needed to.

"And you didn't see where she went?"

"How could I? It was always dark."

"Did she climb out often?"

"I don't know." Rea had paused, waited. When Claire was silent, she asked, "Why? How come it matters now?"

"I don't know," Claire had said. She seemed to gather herself. "Listen, Rea, I want you to be careful about Logan Jessup."

"Careful? Why?" Now Rea had begun to

understand. It had to do with Logan. Margo and Logan. She had had to fight back a laugh. If they'd paid attention to her, they'd have known about that a long time ago. And she supposed she ought to have told. But they'd made her so mad, treating her like a stupid child. Now it was too late. If she said anything now . . .

Claire had said, "We don't know anything about Logan. Where he's from. Who he works for. I don't want you to spend so much time with him."

"Why not?" Rea demanded.

"I've just told you."

"I don't see what you're driving at," Rea said, although she saw that Claire was worried, maybe even scared. Claire thought Logan might be dangerous, so she was trying to protect Rea.

"There's something about Logan I don't like," Claire had said.

"If you don't tell me why, then I don't see why I should listen to you," Rea answered, thinking she was very reasonable. She didn't need protection. She could take care of herself. And all she wanted was to know what was going on. So she added, "Has it to do with Margo?"

Claire averted her gaze. "I'm beginning to think it does."

If she'd gone on, explained, Rea would have told Claire that Margo had gone to Logan's house. Not once, but many times. And that was after she'd said with bored indifference, "Oh, Logan, he's too dull. I don't want to waste my time on him."

But Claire didn't explain. She had said, "Never mind about Margo. Stay away from Logan from now on."

Rea hadn't answered aloud. But inside she seethed. There it was again. Talking down to her. Treating her as if she didn't count. Claire did it all the time now. And Brett Devlin did it too.

Logan Jessup was the only one who paid any attention to her.

That was very nice, and she enjoyed it. But just the same, she knew what she was going to do. It was like a big puzzle. If you couldn't get all the pieces to fit, you could work on it forever and still not get anywhere. When that happened there was only one thing you could do. You could shake the pieces hard, again and again. Then, with everything disarranged, you had to start from scratch. Usually, that time, everything would fall into place.

Everything would fall into place, she was thinking, as she walked toward Logan, smiling.

He turned, and his 'alone' face fell away. He smiled at her. His blue eyes were bright, almost the same colour as the heavy sweater he wore. She wondered if he could possibly be what Claire seemed to think he was: a dangerous man, a murderer. Briefly, her resolve weakened. She reminded herself that she was going to show them all. And nothing would stop her.

When he had greeted her, he asked how she was.

She said, "I'm so mad I could spit."

"How come?" He asked seriously.

She looked away from him. She wished she could blush. That would have been useful now. But since she couldn't, she made the best of it by looking embarrassed. "My family. My mother. Claire. They're always on my back."

"That's how families are," he said philosophically. And added, "It's because they love you."

She burst out, "They just don't understand how I feel about you!"

"About me? What have I got to do with it?" His voice was very deep. His eyes were puzzled.

"Oh," she cried, putting her hand over her mouth. "Oh! I didn't mean to say that. I didn't want to tell you."

"Tell me what?" he asked softly.

"They don't want me to . . . well, you know . . . to be so friendly with you."

Logan was immediately alert. This could be important. He had to find out. But he didn't want to be obvious about it. Still, there was a way to ask. He made his face bewildered. He made himself somehow boyish. "Me? Not be friendly with me? I don't understand, Rea." When she shook her head sadly, he went on, "What have I done? Why do they feel that way?"

"Claire's got the idea . . . oh, it's so silly, Logan. And maybe that's just an excuse. Maybe she's just jealous."

Logan wished Rea had finished saying what she had been going to say instead of switching off to the jealously thing. Claire wasn't jealous of Rea, he was sure of that. He wondered, for a moment, if even Rea believed that. It seemed unlikely. But it wouldn't do to challenge her now. Not when he had to find out why Claire had taken to warning Rea against him. It meant she was suspicious of him. But why now? What had happened?

He remembered when Rea had told him that Brett said Margo had kept a diary all her life. So Claire had known about that for a long while. But did her suspicions mean that something had changed? Had she found the diary, for instance? He didn't want to ask. He didn't want to bring that up directly.

So he allowed himself a warm smile. Okay, he could go along with this and see where it led him. "Jealous? Claire?" he said. "Maybe. But you know, Rea, I think you probably misunderstood. It wasn't me she was talking about. It could have been anybody. I'll bet she was just using me as an example. She was trying to teach you the caution that any young, beautiful girl should have."

Rea threw back her head, laughing. "Beautiful!" she crowed.

Still, he wondered what was going on. He asked himself why, suddenly, would Claire have begun to suspect him? What could she know?

It was too bad he hadn't been able to wrap it up long ago. But he'd had his duties to perform. They came first. They continued to come first. Even now, with the war going badly for the Führer at the moment, Logan had to continue. When the time came, and with it his orders, he had to be ready. Even if these so temporary losses in Europe were to increase, his mission would be necessary. Perhaps it would be even more important than ever.

He saw the White House in flames, its portico and roof blown away. Thick black smoke poured from its shattered windows. Roosevelt would be dead, of course. The mission would be accomplished.

A squirrel chattered along the fence. He smiled at it, reached into his pocket for peanuts, and said to Rea, "Yes, that's it. Claire wants you to be careful about any man. And she's absolutely right."

At the same time, he was considering various contingency plans he had worked out many months before.

Just after election day, Logan appeared at Hannah's Gate. His blond hair was carefully combed. He was carefully dressed in a dark blue suit. His tie was maroon, his shirt white. He had decided against telephoning first. A 'no' was harder to say face to face than across impersonal wire.

But Claire had no difficulty in saying that she was unable to go to the movies with him. She was polite, but firm. She was, she told him, expecting a guest. She didn't suggest he try another time.

He soon left, realizing that he would have to change course. He didn't know what she knew, but he was certain she would never let Rea or herself be alone with him. That being the case, he would no longer afford to wait.

Rea had lingered about when he was there. He was pleasant to her, but distant. Fuming, she watched him leave. What was he up to? Why had he asked Claire to go out with him? Was it because she, Rea, had re-arranged the pieces of the puzzle? She was suddenly a little frightened. Maybe it hadn't been such a good idea.

Then Brett Devlin arrived. Rea remained obstinately in the room, dropping small remarks, trying to capture Brett's attention. Like Logan, he was polite. But he wanted to talk to Claire alone. Finally he asked her to go for a walk with him. She agreed, and they set out.

It was a brisk evening, starless, with only the pale lamp lights rippling along the deserted road through the leafless trees.

Claire told Brett about Logan's visit and invitation, and her refusal.

"I'm glad you didn't accept. I don't trust him."

"Neither do I. I've been trying to get Rea to stay away from him. But she thinks he's wonderful." Claire paused. Then: "I admit he *is* nice to her."

"I don't trust that either."

"If only we could find out more about him . . ."

"I should have. A long time ago. I didn't because I concentrated on Margo's diary." He was silent for a moment. "I told you about

232

Angelo Niro, remember?" At Claire's nod, he went on. "His wife, Rose, has never forgotten what happened. She's alone still, bitterly unhappy. Even her memories of Angelo are tainted. I want her to think of him with love, and in peace, so she can go on with her life. I thought Margo's diary could help her. But it looks as if I'd better forget that now. I'll see what I can learn about Logan instead." Brett slid a hand under her arm, drawing her close. "There's another thing I ought to have spoken of a long time ago." He looked into her face. "I should have said . . . said how I feel about you. That I'm . . . I'm in love with you. I have been since I first saw you. Surely, by now, you've guessed?"

"Oh, Brett," she whispered. "I'm so sorry." She looked pained, frightened. She attempted a smile, but her face felt frozen. "I *did* try to let you know that . . . I . . ."

"You're interested in someone else?"

"Yes," she said. "Leigh Merrill. You've heard us speak of him."

"Of course. And I understand your feelings. But I had to tell you how I feel about you anyway."

"There's always been Leigh," she said gently. "As far back as I can remember."

"So there's no chance for me." He gave her a sudden wink. "Okay. That's behind us now.

We go on as before. I want us to be friends. I mean it, Claire. I'd rather we were in love and going to be married. But, if not, then so be it."

She said, "Oh, thank you, Brett. I do need my friends."

He smiled at her, and they went on walking, arm in arm.

Claire remembered when she had suspected that he himself was somehow involved in Margo's death. He'd said he was related to her, but that had only been an excuse to explain his interest in her, her diary. Now she understood. He was a man of deep and lasting loyalties. He'd believed in Angelo Niro, and wanted to clear his name. He pitied Rose Niro, and wanted to help her.

Brett said suddenly, "I wonder just how much of a check the Homicide Squad did on Logan."

The street was dark, empty. The windows of the few houses on Honey Locust Lane were still unlit. Claire pulled her coat more tightly around her. She had worked later than usual that evening. She was tired and cold after the long wait for the over-crowded bus.

The trees cast deep, swift-moving shadows. It was so quiet that she could hear the hum of traffic on Connecticut Avenue although it was several blocks behind her now.

She had her head down against the wind, her eyes fixed on the broken pavement. There was a faint hiss suddenly, only a whisper of sound. Startled, she stumbled. A black cat shot across her path, brilliant green eyes flicking upward in a venomous glance as it dashed away.

She had begun to laugh, recovering herself, when there was another whisper of sound. The steady wind suddenly shifted, coming from her right. A dark shadow, big and bulky, raced towards her from the mouth of the alley. She flung herself away as it sped past, lightless, enshrouded in blackness, so that she couldn't see the driver.

It disappeared into the night. She clung to a tree, breathless, shivering. It had been so close. She had felt her coat sucked toward the car. She had felt the pull on her legs. She had almost felt herself falling beneath those fast turning wheels.

Finally, she went on. Her knee joints seemed made of jelly. She looked from one side of the road to the other. She studied the parked cars. Nothing. No one.

Earlier there would have been men in uniform coming home, and groups of girls returning from work. But now, no one stirred.

Had there been a reason for that car to come

235

out of the alley just as she passed. Had someone tried deliberately to attack her? Had someone sat there, in the dark, waiting for her appearance? Or had it been an accident? An absent-minded driver, forgetting to put on headlights, in a hurry, rushing through the alley in the dark, not even realizing, perhaps, how close he had come to her.

She wanted to believe it had been a near-miss accident that could have happened to anyone. But she wasn't sure. Maybe it had to do with Margo, with Linda . . .

She told no one at home what had happened. As the week passed, she tried to forget about that night, forget the sudden drowning fear she had felt.

Brett called to tell her that he had started the ball rolling on questions about Logan. It would take a while, even with his connections in Capitol Hill, he was sure they would eventually get the information they sought.

Then, on a Saturday morning, Claire set out for the grocery store with Dora's shopping list. She was driving down the hill on Honey Locust Lane towards the avenue.

Stewing beef, she was thinking. Nineteen cents a pound. Potatoes. Five cents a pound. She would get three pounds. A big sack of dried lima beans. She had a ten dollar bill in her purse, and hoped it was enough.

As the car picked up speed, she pressed down on the brake. The car didn't slow. She pressed even harder. Nothing. She jammed her foot down with all her strength. The pedal was at the floor, but the car's momentum increased.

She had only an instant in which to decide. She tightened her fingers around the steering wheel. At the first opening in the line of closely parked cars, she headed towards the curb, hoping to bump it, to stop herself. The car hit, jumped the curb, and slammed into a tree with a mind-numbing crash.

She sat at the wheel, stunned, bruised. What had happened? Why hadn't the car stopped? What made the brakes fail?

Several people came running, excitedly shouting questions, offering help. She climbed out. The car's front end was damaged. One headlight smashed, the bumper dangling.

But she was unhurt, except for a steering wheel bruise on her chest, long red marks on both her knees.

Someone called the AAA for her. A truck came and towed the car to a garage.

Poor Ian, she thought. He loved that old Chevy. She'd have it fixed no matter what it cost.

Later, when the mechanic told her how much the repairs would be, she asked, "Can you tell why I couldn't get the brakes to work?"

He said, "They're both damaged. It could have happened when you hit the tree, I guess. Or maybe before. But don't worry. The insurance will cover that too."

She thanked him, arranged to pick up the car at the end of the following week, and went home.

This time she mentioned that she'd had a small accident, and the car was in the garage. She said nothing more. But she was sure that the brakes hadn't failed by accident. And that her near miss the week before hadn't been an accident either. Someone was trying to kill her. Someone connected to the murder of Margo and Linda.

But who could it be? Could Carrie be the one? No. Claire couldn't convince herself that she had anything to fear from Carrie. The woman didn't have the strength to have killed Margo and Linda. She didn't drive, knew nothing about cars. Briefly, unwillingly, Claire considered Brett. No again. Her intuition refused the thought. But how did she know? Perhaps his declaration of love for her had only been a cover. Maybe he had other reasons for returning again and again to Hannah's gate. But she couldn't make herself seriously suspect Brett. What he had told her about Angelo, about Rose Niro, rang true. No one could have made it up. She kept coming back to Logan. Logan, who lived in the house behind Hannah's Gate. Logan, who'd gone out with Margo at least once . . .

Now, early in December, Claire stood at the window of Margo's old room. She looked down into the yard, looked at the old Merrill house that Logan now occupied.

Only the night before Brett had told her that if Logan ever lived in Chicago, it was strange he'd left no trace of himself behind. His birth had not been registered there. He had not attended public schools there. He'd never had a driver's licence there, or registered a car. That was all that Brett had learned thus far. It wasn't much, he said. But it was a beginning.

Logan hadn't lived in Chicago. He'd lied about that. Claire wondered what else he'd lied about.

She imagined Margo climbing down the wistaria, going to meet someone in the shadows of the yard. Slowly, within the frame of Claire's imagination, that someone became Logan. But why should they hide their affair? Why would Margo have to sneak out at night? Why had she denied ever being in the Domino Bar, being there with a man who was undoubtedly Logan?

On impulse, Claire threw the window open. She climbed up on the broad sill. The wistaria was December bare now, its leaves and blossoms gone. She stepped on to the thick notch formed beneath the window by old gnarled limbs. The vine whispered, groaned, scratched against the house. Sounds she had heard for most of her life. Sounds that suddenly developed a sinister significance. She had heard them often when Margo was alive. But she had heard them since then too. Rea, having seen Margo leave that way, had done the same. Perhaps, in spite of her promise to Claire, she still climbed out through the wistaria.

After Margo's death, Linda had stayed in this room, looked from this window, past the vine, and down the long slope. Thinking back now, it seemed to Claire that Linda had somehow changed once she moved in here. What had happened? What had she seen? Standing on the notch, fingers tightening around a limb to steady herself, Claire pretended she was Linda. As always, her eyes went to the Merrill house.

Then, for no reason that she ever knew, she raised her head and looked up, and saw, beyond arm's reach, a large squirrel's nest. She had never realized there was a nest in the wistaria, although she had known that

240

there must be one somewhere at Hannah's Gate. Now she could picture Logan tossing squirrels peanuts. See them dashing along the fence. Remember tiny tracks in the grass after a snow fall.

So here, high above the window, in the wistaria, was where the animals lived.

Claire stood in the tree for a moment longer, looking at the house where Leigh used to be.

A wave of longing swept her. If only he were home. If only she knew where he was, how he was.

She stepped back into the house and wandered restlessly from room to room. How long would the war go on? How long before she saw him once more?

Dora was knitting again with the blue wool that was to provide sweaters for the Free French Army. Carrie must be working on a new story because there was the tap tap of her typewriter coming from her room. Rea was finally doing her laundry.

Claire made herself a cup of tea, drank it slowly, and then resumed her uneasy wandering through the house.

At last she returned to the room that had been Margo's. Again she paced the floor idly, opened the closet, closed it, turned away. Finally she threw open the window once more, and stepped on to the gnarled notch of the wistaria. Carefully, holding her breath with each step, she climbed up slowly from limb to limb. The vine gave with her weight, swaying beneath her, sighing and scratching and whispering against the house.

After what seemed a long time, she was within reach of the squirrels' nest. She tried to see into it, but couldn't. She coughed aloud. Spoke a few words. There was no response. No chattering. No agitated rustling. She assumed the nest was empty now. Finally, she gingerly slipped her hand into it, hoping that she was right, that the squirrels were out foraging or had abandoned it. She was ready to pull back at the slightest sound or movement. But there was nothing. At last her burrowing fingers touched something rough, gritty. They closed around a package, drew it out.

It was about eight by ten inches in size, very thick, and wrapped in a waterproof canvas tied with a red ribbon. The ribbon's dye had run when soaked with rain, and the canvas wrapping was stained as red as blood. Margo's blood or Linda's, Claire thought grimly.

She climbed down, stepped inside, and closed the window behind her. Quickly she untied the ribbon, unwrapped the stained canvas. A wave of dizziness swept her when she saw that she held in her hands the diary that Margo Desales had written.

Unbelievably, by purest chance, she had found, after all this time, the diary that might provide the answer to Margo's murder.

Claire went to her own room, locked the door behind her, and sat down to read Margo's words.

The packet was so thick and heavy because it went back years and years. Claire flipped forward quickly. Washington, 1942 . . . Some of it Claire already knew. Some she had guessed. But as for the rest . . .

Her eyes widened. She bit her lip. Poor Margo. Why had she become obsessed with Logan Jessup? With this terrible and dangerous man? Hadn't she realized she was playing with fire?

Margo wrote about the first time she talked with Logan in the garden, about her first date with him, and how their affair had started. She wrote about going to the Domino with him, and how he had insisted that she pretend to have dropped him because he didn't want anyone to know about their relationship. She wrote about her feelings for him, in bed and out of bed. She said she had for him the same wild crazy hunger that she'd had for Angelo Niro. Angelo hadn't wanted her, so she had paid him back and ruined him. She'd do the same to Logan, if she had to. Further on, she told the diary that she thought she was pregnant, expressed her relief when she discovered that she wasn't. She put down the date on which she again suspected she was pregnant. This time she said she was glad. It gave her a hold on Logan. She described a night when she was determined to see him, and had ended up eavesdropping on him, hearing him and another man talk. And then, as Claire's skin crawled, she read what Margo had said about Logan being a member of an underground German group, a spy for Hitler, and finally about her certainty that he would marry her to keep his secret safe. But she didn't intend to tell him what she knew, she wrote, at least not yet. There were other entries. Several about Carrie. She was peculiar, Margo wrote. And so was Linda. Why was she always sneaking around? Then there was more about Margo's feelings for Logan. The diary ended at that point.

Claire closed it with trembling fingers. She tried not to think of it. But a picture crept into her mind: Margo, flinching away from Logan's big fists, falling, her face bruised, bleeding . . . Linda's mouth stretched wide to scream, to fight for breath . . .

Logan. So he must have killed Margo when she threatened to expose him if he didn't marry her. Then he must have been the person who had been searching for the diary all along. He must have been discovered by Linda on one of his forays, so he had killed her too.

But how would he have known about the diary? Claire wasn't sure. Margo might have told him herself. When she was younger, according to Brett, she had told some of her friends about it. That's how Brett had known she kept one. But there was Rea too. Rea could have told Logan, not realizing that it would matter to him. Perhaps not even realizing that she had said it. Maybe Logan was so nice to Rea because she was a source of information for him. Rea knew about the diary, Claire knew, because she herself had told the girl that Brett had asked about it.

Why had Logan become suspicious of her? Why did he feel she was a threat to him? He must think that. Else why would he have tried to run her down? Why tamper with the brakes on the car?

Or was she allowing her imagination too free a rein? The diary proved none of her speculations. It only gave Logan a motive for killing Margo. No more than that. Yet it seemed to Claire that one step led to another. From Margo's death to the black car rushing out of the alley, to the runaway ride down Honey Locust Lane.

Holding the diary tightly, Claire went

downstairs to call Detective Eagan. He wasn't in, so she left her name and telephone number. She stayed up late, waiting. When, by midnight, she had heard nothing, she called again. He still wasn't there. She thought of speaking to someone else, but decided it would be too complicated to try to explain. So, before going to bed, she made her plans.

In the morning, having slept little, she hid the diary in her biggest handbag. She would stop first at the office to explain that she must have a few hours off. Then she would call Brett, tell him what she had found, ask if he could meet her at police headquarters, so he could describe himself his efforts to get information about Logan, when she turned the diary over to Detective Eagan. The detective, she was sure, would know how to proceed. If he wasn't in, then she and Brett would have to speak to someone else.

She dressed in warm clothes — a black skirt and a pale green sweater with a dark green scarf. She buttoned her heavy coat to the throat, and stuffed knitted gloves in her pocket. Dora stopped her when she was leaving the house.

"Claire, come and see this," she said worriedly.

"I'm in a hurry, Mama," Claire said. Her bag seemed to burn beneath her arm.

"Oh, please, you've got to look. It's the craziest thing!"

That made Claire give in. She allowed her mother to lead her into the backyard, to the gate between the Lovings' property and the house on Afton Place. There were two good-sized holes near the gate, one on either side of it next to the posts.

"What does it mean?" Dora demanded. "Who's digging in the yard?"

"I don't know," Claire said. "We'll find out about it later. There's something I must do now."

But, as she turned away, she sent a quick glance at Logan's windows. Was he now looking for the diary by digging in the yard? It was improbable. But, perhaps . . . Meanwhile, she had to go.

Carrie was looking down from the window. It was her own fault, she thought. She oughtn't to have been so impatient. If she'd waited, she'd have had time to refill those damnable holes. Then nobody would have known about them.

She squeezed the thin scrap of paper in her fist. She'd found it in the lining of the old Bible in Big Jack's study. She was sure that the fading spidery handwriting was his. 'Be sure to remember. Hannah's gate.' Hannah's gate. At first, she hadn't caught on. Hannah's Gate, she'd thought. God, why couldn't he have been more specific? Because she was certain the note referred to what she was looking for. But suddenly it struck her. He didn't mean the house. He meant the gate. Small g. The gate. It hadn't been near the posts. But she was still sure it was there. As soon as she could, she'd get the shovel out and try again.

When Claire reached the office, she was told that there'd been a phone call for her. A man. He'd left no name, but said he would call back. Brett? Could it have been him? Why hadn't he said where she could phone him? She went to tell her supervisor that she had to be away for a few hours. A family emergency. When she returned to her desk, the call for her came through. The instant she heard it, she recognized Logan's voice.

He had considered it from every angle, and had decided he could wait no longer. Perhaps he had already waited too long. It didn't seem likely because nothing had actually happened yet. No one was following him, no tap on his phone. He was certain of that much because he had checked. But now there was no time left. Claire Loving had to have guessed. Under his careful questioning, Rea had explained to him how suspicious Claire was. Too bad he'd been unsuccessful when he'd tried to run her down, or when he damaged the car brakes. A fatal accident, and it would have been over. As it was, he had to act. He might soon have to go on another trip. His orders could come through any day. He expected a German counter attack. That would change everything.

He made his preparations during the night. Then he returned to the house.

He was ready and watching the next morning when Rea left for school only a few minutes after Claire had started downtown. He got into his car and caught up with Rea, smiling at the sight of her tall slim figure. Her hair sparkled like black coal in the sunlight. She was alone. He pulled up alongside her. "Rea! I'll give you a lift."

She hesitated for the slightest moment. Maybe she should listen to Claire. Maybe Rea had tossed the pieces of the puzzle around enough for something new to develop. Then she grinned happily, climbed into the car. "Oh, Logan. Thanks." It was broad daylight. Logan couldn't hurt her on Connecticut Avenue. And besides, why should he? She wasn't involved. None of this mess had anything to do with her.

"Has Claire gone to the office?" he asked.

"She left just before I did."

"Good. I need to talk to her. Will you give her a call for me?"

A soundless alarm went off in Rea's head. Call Claire? What did Logan have to speak to her about so urgently that he couldn't wait until evening? Rea said, "She doesn't take personal calls at the office. She's not allowed to."

"She will, if it's from you."

Rea shook her head. "I'd better not. And we have to get going. I don't want to be late for school."

His deep voice was regretful. "You mean you won't do a friend a favour, Rea?"

"What's it about, Logan? You can talk to Claire tonight."

She sounded very adult suddenly. He realized that he'd never thought of her as grown up. Now he saw that she was. She wore make up, a young woman's clothes. She wasn't the child he'd always thought of. Suddenly he imagined her with her dark hair hanging long and loose . . . imagined her as Esta had been, tempting him, but always beyond reach. Shaking that memory away, he stared at Rea. It was too bad she was so grown up. It made her more dangerous to him. Although he was sure she knew nothing. Not yet anyway.

He said, "I must talk to Claire. Please . . . don't argue. I'll find a phone, and . . ."

"But I won't call her." He recognized the mulish tone in her voice. He'd heard it before. "Unless," she added, "you tell me what this is about."

She didn't intend to call Claire, no matter what he told her. She realized now that her meddling might have been a mistake. She'd thought she'd be the one to bring the truth to light. She'd be the heroine, and everyone would admire her. But now it seemed that she'd only placed Claire, and herself too, in a bad spot. Because Logan was no longer the man she had known for the past couple of years. He was a stranger, icy, determined, scary.

He glanced quickly up and down the street. Then he seized her by the shoulders. "Listen to me! We're going to call Claire. Now."

Rea's eyes widened. Her mouth trembled. She said, "Logan, why?"

His fingers tightened.

He pulled her close to him, so that he could drive with one arm around her, holding her tightly against his hip.

"I'm going to find a public phone. You'll get out of the car with me, and we'll make the call. Do you understand?"

"Yes." She was too frightened now to continue her protest. "Yes. I understand."

Chapter 14

Claire wasn't there the first time he called. He glanced at his watch. He would try again in ten minutes.

He took Rea by the hand, his fingers crushing hers. "We'll go up and down the block. You'd better keep your mouth shut."

They walked for five minutes south, the wind stinging their eyes. Then they turned, walked five minutes north, the wind thrusting them on. He pulled her with him into the phone booth, leaving the door half open. He held her within the circle of his arm. She hated being that close to him, although once she had thought she would like it. When he got through to the switchboard, he asked for Claire, said it was a family emergency.

In moments he said, "I must talk to you, Claire. Meet me at the corner of Virginia Avenue at 21st Street. The northwest corner, in front of the small grocery store. Be there in three-quarters of an hour."

"I can't get away that quickly," she protested. "I'll need permission to leave." She needed time to reach Detective Eagan. By afternoon, by evening . . .

But he was saying, "You must meet me now."

"What's the matter? Why can't it wait until tonight?"

"Okay," Logan said. "You decide."

Claire wondered if he knew she had found the diary. Could he have seen her climb into the wistaria? Could he have watched as she searched the nest above her window? Or did this have to do with the holes her mother had showed her near the fence posts?

Logan, meanwhile, put his hand on the back of Rea's neck. His fingers dug in.

She tried not to gasp. She folded her lips tightly, closing her eyes although they leaked tears down her cheeks. But, after a few seconds, she cried out.

"Rea!" Claire's heart gave a great leap in her chest. The room was warm, but she was suddenly caught in currents of icy air.

"You'd better come . . ." Rea said. "Logan's gone crazy. And I'm so scared."

Logan asked, "Shall we continue the argument?"

Claire said shakily, "All right, Logan. I'll meet you. But I'll need an hour, no matter what you say."

He purred, "It's nine now. At ten o'clock, come to the northwest corner of Virginia Avenue and 21st Street. And be sure to be alone."

"I'll be there. And I'll be alone," Claire said. "Just don't hurt Rea. Don't frighten her any more. She can't help you. But I can. And I will. So wait for me."

"Oh, yes," he said.

The phone went dead. Her connection to Logan, through him to Rea, was gone.

For an instant she was still, gathering herself. Then she took up the phone again. Her first call was to the Homicide Bureau. When she asked for Detective Eagan she was told that he had been shot the night before, was in the hospital now, and couldn't be disturbed for any reason.

The speaker asked what she wanted, offered his help with whatever her problem was. But when she told him her name and address, he sighed. Oh, yeah, he remembered. The Desales case. The Grant case. And there'd been another girl too. All on file now, no leads, nothing.

She glanced at her watch. It felt as if an hour had already passed, but she still had fifty-five minutes. She mustn't waste any more time. What should she do? Once she had met Logan, what would happen? What did he want? How could she defend Rea, defend herself?

There was only one other person to whom

254

she could turn for help. She dialled Brett, hoping he was in his Capitol Hill office, hoping that if he weren't, he'd left word about where he could be reached.

Now she heard his voice. "Brett Devlin."

"It's Claire," she gasped. "Logan has Rea." She went on, quickly describing to him the call she'd had, what Logan had said to her, how Rea had sounded.

When he spoke of the police, she told him about her call to the Homicide Bureau, that Detective Eagan was injured and in the hospital.

He was silent for a moment, then said, "This is going to be dangerous. You'll have to be as careful as you can." He went on to tell her that she was to meet Logan as arranged. But she was to wait until the very last possible moment. The very last. Brett would leave the office now. He would call her on this telephone as soon as he was in position to watch her meet Logan when she got to him. After Claire had talked to Brett then, she was to start out. But not before. Even if she were to be a few moments late.

"Do you understand?" he asked.

"Yes. I'll wait here until after I talk to you again."

It was then 9:25. She still had thirty-five minutes left. While she waited to hear from

Brett, Claire looked at the diary again. She turned the pages slowly. Carrie's name suddenly seemed to leap out at her. Carrie Day. Margo began by describing Carrie's move into Hannah's Gate. What she looked like. Fat, hopeless, sort of dumb. She said she was a writer. What a laugh, Margo commented. What did she know to write about, poor Carrie? Then, quite suddenly, the tone of the entries changed. Margo became suspicious. Why was Carrie always turning up in funny places in the house? Was she following Margo, spying on her?

Claire remembered that Rea had said you never knew when Carrie would be ducking into the study, and remembered too the morning when Carrie had searched the shed, ostensibly looking for tools with which to hang a picture. Carrie . . . what could she have to do with Logan? They were a very unlikely pair. But Carrie could have been Logan's eyes at Hannah's Gate. Claire dismissed the notion. Logan didn't need Carrie. He had had Rea to act as his eyes. That's why he was using her as bait right now.

Claire turned the diary page, but there was, suddenly, no time to read any more.

Brett called to say he was in the grocery store at the corner of Virginia Avenue. He had seen Logan drive past the place twice, slowing down, but not stopping. He hadn't been able to see Rea in the car with him. Brett said he would stay where he was, watching for Claire. By the time she met Logan, Brett would be ready to follow, if that was necessary.

"Stall as much as you can. Talk to him. Ask questions. But be careful, Claire."

She put the diary into her desk drawer. On top of it, she placed the short note she had written earlier. It directed whoever found the diary to give it to the police. She glanced at her watch. She had five more minutes.

She put on her coat, pulled on her gloves, and set out, walking slowly.

When she reached the corner where she was to meet Logan, it was exactly ten o'clock. As she looked around, she saw his car drift slowly down 21st Street, pause at the light, then make a right turn into Virginia Avenue. She stepped forward, waved. He pulled into the curb.

She saw no sign of Rea. She went around the car to the driver's side, leaned at the open window. "Logan, where's my sister?" Her heart was beating quickly. Her coat collar was damp with perspiration. Passing cars trailed clouds of bitter fumes. She hoped Brett was in one of them, but didn't dare look lest she arouse Logan's suspicions.

"Don't worry about Rea," Logan said to her, smiling. "Just get in."

"What have you done with Rea?"

"She's safe in the boot. Mad as hell, but okay."

Claire hoped he was telling the truth. But she wasn't sure. She was afraid to believe anything he said. As she passed the boot, going around to the passenger's side of the car, she gave it a quick light tap. There was an instant answering thud from inside. Rea had heard, had answered. At least now Claire knew where she was, knew that she was all right.

In the car, Claire said, "Okay, Logan, tell me what you want. Why did I have to leave work to see you? What's so important that you scared Rea half way to death to get her to make me come out to talk to you?"

He drew her closer to him. She shuddered at his touch, but said nothing. Margo's written words whispered through her mind.

She kept herself from looking back, from seeking the reassurance of a glimpse of Brett. She knew he was somewhere about. He had said he would be, would be in a position to follow, if necessary. She knew she could rely on him. The one thing she mustn't do now was lose her nerve. She had to keep Logan believing that she had been frightened into coming alone, as he'd ordered. That he had nothing to fear from her, or from anyone else.

He drove out of Virginia Avenue, then along Canal Road. As they passed Fletcher's Landing, she thought of the girl who had been found there murdered. Did her death have anything to do with Margo's? Was Logan remembering her now? Claire sneaked a look at his face. It was expressionless. She couldn't read anything there.

She didn't know where he was going. Some place out of town. But which direction? West? North? A car passed, then a small truck. She still didn't allow herself to look back.

Soon they were on MacArthur Boulevard. She caught a glimpse of the canal through the bare trees.

After a long silence, he said softly, "If only your kid sister weren't so smart . . . Then we wouldn't be here. Now. Together. And neither would she."

"What's Rea got to do with this? She's only a child." Claire felt a tiny glimmer of amusement even then. Rea would resent that terribly. But if Claire could only persuade Logan . . .

He laughed. "She hasn't been a child for some time. But she's not as clever as she thinks she is. She, with her small hints . . . a bit here, a bit there . . . teasing me. Logan Jessup saw through her very quickly."

"Teasing you about what?"

"I knew about the diary all along, Claire."
His voice was low, reasonable. "How could
you suppose otherwise?"

"You're not making sense, Logan. What
diary?"

He slid a hard blue gaze at her. "Don't deny
it. I know you know. I told you, I've known
all along. It was Margo." His voice became
hard, to match his hard blue gaze. "It's ridic-
ulous for you to lie to me, Claire. Margo herself
told me about the diary. And she told me that
you knew about it. That you, Claire Loving,
even suggested where she should hide it for
safety."

It was a lie, of course. Margo had only said
she'd written the diary. Nothing about Claire.
But if he could make Claire believe that he
knew, then he could get her to give it to him.
Then, when he had it . . .

Claire gasped. "Oh, no! It's not true. You're
lying. I know nothing about Margo's diary.
If there ever was one." She thought quickly,
then said persuasively. "Logan, have you considered how frightened Margo must have
been? She just wanted you to think . . ."

"It doesn't matter," he said. "You,
Rea . . ."

"But why?" Claire cried. "What happened?

260

She loved you, didn't she?"

"Love," he sneered.

He allowed himself the brief luxury of imagining ahead. Claire, bound, her auburn hair tousled around her face. Her silken smooth body . . . But no, not now. He wouldn't spend thought on that now. It was for later, when he was through. Or nearly through.

He swung the car into a dirt road. They had long since left the city and small country towns behind. Now wide empty gray fields spread out to the horizon from a stand of tall trees that learned over a narrow creek.

"Where are we?" she asked.

"You can see for yourself."

She almost recognized the place when he stopped before what appeared to be an abandoned stone house. Almost, but not quite. Some time, long before, she'd been there, she thought.

And then, as he opened the car door and stepped out, she remembered. It had been when she was very young. Rea was still an infant. The family had picnicked close by. Ian had fished in the canal. It was probably the last maintained lock. Swain's lock. Beyond it, there would be the Potomac River. Although she couldn't see it from where she stood, she heard the sound of it now.

When they'd come here, some of these cottages had still been occupied. There'd been boats tied to tiny landings along the creek. Seneca Creek.

Now she wondered if Brett had seen Logan turn in. If he'd been able to follow. She hadn't dared look back even once. Logan might have noticed. She knew only that Brett couldn't have stayed too close to them. He would have been easily noticeable on a road with so few cars.

"Get out," Logan told her.

He opened the boot, and pulled Rea out. "We're going inside," he told both girls. And, with a hand curled around the back of Rea's neck, "If you try anything, either of you . . ." He gave Rea a hard shake.

He pushed her ahead of him, paused to turn a key in a shiny new lock. He didn't touch Claire, knowing he didn't have to. She would follow wherever he went, as long as he had Rea with him.

Inside it was dim, musty. There was a table, a couple of broken chairs. He shoved Rea into one, jerked his head at the other. For a moment, it was very quiet. He sat down, stared at the two of them, his hands folded in front of him on the table.

Then he said softly, "I'm at the end of my patience. So tell me where the diary is. That way you will make it easy for yourself."

Claire had to stall for time, to give Brett a chance to catch up. She had to assume that he was nearby, would soon be able to do something. But what to say? How to deflect Logan's attention?

He said, "Rea will suffer for your silence, Claire."

"She doesn't know anything," Claire cried.

"But you do. And she knows more than she should." He dropped his voice. "Don't you understand? Now it isn't only the diary. It's you. And Rea herself."

Claire looked carefully around the room. The window was small, webbed with grey at its corners. As she watched, she saw a single white flake of snow drift by. The hearth on the wall behind Logan was littered with rusty cans. A poker leaned against it. A big metal bedspring leaned against the wall behind Rea. A splintered broom lay in a far corner.

She faced Logan. "You don't have to be afraid of us. I promise you that neither Rea nor I will ever speak of you."

"You surprise me. I didn't think you were stupid. How could I trust you?"

"Why not? I've told you. We're not involved, Logan."

"When you're both dead, having suffered a very sad accident, then I'll be able to trust you. Until then, I think not." He took the gag from Rea's mouth. "Perhaps you'll be more sensible, Rea."

She flashed him a black look of fury, wet her lips. She didn't look at Claire. But Logan did.

He watched Claire as he held Rea's arm and began, very slowly, to twist it.

"Stop," Claire cried.

"You're not important," he said. "Rea isn't important. Only my mission matters. Nothing will stop me."

As Claire leaned forward, Rea screamed, "No, no, don't tell him. He'll kill us when he doesn't need us!"

But there was no longer any reason to pretend ignorance. There was only a need to play for time. Claire asked Logan, "But why did you have to kill Margo? Surely there was another way."

"She threatened me," he answered. He too felt no need for lies now. Claire would die. Rea would die. There would be no witnesses left. He would be ready when his orders came.

"Threatened you?"

He shrugged, didn't answer.

"And Linda?"

"Oh, that was a pity! She was crazy, that one. But there was nothing I could do. She was supposed to have gone away, like the rest of you, for the weekend. But she was there when I went to look for the diary." He looked into Claire's eyes. "I didn't believe in the diary. Not for a long time. But then Rea said that Brett knew about it. He'd heard about it long ago. So I had to believe." He shrugged. "After that, what could I do?"

"But what made you think I knew about it?" Claire asked.

He smiled. "Rea told me. Although she didn't realize that she was telling me, I think. I told you — a little here, a little there. I saw you were suspicious, so I knew you must have the diary." He rose. "And now, tell me where it is. We'll get it together."

Claire didn't hesitate. She saw what was in Logan's eyes. She gave the room a single swift glance again. Snow was falling more heavily at the window. The poker lay on the hearth. The rusted metal spring leaned against the wall behind Rea. She said tonelessly, "I found the diary last night. I took it to work this morning. It's in my desk."

There was a brief silence. Then he said, "It's lucky I was unsuccessful when I tried twice before to kill you. If I had, I'd never have found the diary, would I?"

"You don't have it yet," Rea snapped, and kicked back her chair.

The instant Rea moved Claire grabbed the table, thrust it up and over, at Logan. Rea meanwhile was on her feet, reaching behind her. She pulled at the rusted bedspring. It tilted forward slowly.

At the same time Claire seized the poker. She swung it at Logan just as the bedspring fell on him.

He went down. In the same instant, the wooden door splintered and burst open. There was a swirl of snow flakes, a cold wind. Brett seemed to dive into the room.

He threw himself on Logan, who had managed to extricate himself from the springs. The two men crashed to the floor, rolling and pummelling at each other. Then Logan broke free and was up, racing from the stone house towards his car. Brett went after him, angling across his path to head him off. Logan changed direction, disappeared into the brush. When Brett next saw him, he was at the lock. He jumped down to the tow path, dropping out of sight.

But soon Brett saw him again, and knew that he was gaining. He would be able to bring Logan down in a moment.

Logan knew it too. He left the path. There were sounds of him breaking through the brush, crackling in the leaves, the tumbling of stones.

Then, quite suddenly, there was a snapping sound, and a deep boom. Immediately there came the heavy thud of falling earth. The long echoes faded slowly. At last there was only the soft whisper of the snow.

Brett, following the trail Logan had left behind in his headlong flight, suddenly found himself teetering on the edge of a high crumbling bank. A single glance below made clear to him what had happened.

Logan had come this far. He hadn't realized that the earth dropped at this point. When he got too close, the bank fell away. Logan had fallen with it.

Now he lay near the edge of the river. His legs were twisted at an odd angle. He was completely still, except for one hand that floated on the small ripples reflecting the disturbance of the cave-in.

Claire and Rea caught up with Brett.

"We'll need help," Claire said.

"It's on the way by now," Brett told her. "I wasn't the only one following. I got a friend of mine to come along too. An off-duty Capitol policeman in a truck. He'll have radioed in by now."

The two girls followed Brett when he slowly climbed down the bank. His bad leg was hurting now. He had to take his time. But finally he knelt beside Logan, touched him, searched for a pulse in his throat, his wrist. There was nothing. Logan was dead.

The falling snow thickened, soft and white and silent.

In the distance there were sirens.

Rea pressed close to Claire, and burst into tears when Claire took her into her arms.

Chapter 15

The snow was still falling in the early afternoon when Claire, flanked by two F.B.I. agents, retrieved the diary from her desk. Her hands shook as she tore up the note she had left with it. She remembered how frightened she had been, hearing Rea's anguished cry over the telephone. Now, weak with relief, she could only marvel at the miracle of their escape.

By then, the house on Afton Place had been searched from basement to attic. Even the two potted plants on its front porch had been examined.

Claire and Rea had spoken only a few words to the Maryland State Police before they were told the F.B.I. had to be notified. Very soon after, a team of four agents arrived at Swain's Lock. They studied Logan's body, photographed it, and it was taken away.

As they were driven back to the city, Rea and Claire and Brett were questioned closely. The stop for the diary took only moments. From there, they went on to the Justice Department to make additional statements.

A few hours later, when the snow had stopped, and a blue twilight had descended on Hannah's Gate, Claire and Rea stood at the back window, with Brett, and watched while tall silent men moved quickly, carrying box after box from the house Logan had lived in.

The agents had said little. But, plainly, from what Claire had told them, from the diary, and from the cache of arms and explosives found in the attic, they had learned enough to satisfy them that Logan Jessup had been at the centre of a sabotage operation that had not yet been carried out. When they were finished, they closed up the house.

Soon perhaps, Claire thought, when he had permission to do so, Jeremiah Merrill would either rent it again, or sell it, as Leigh had suggested.

The unmarked cars pulled away. Afton Place was dark and still.

Rea turned to Brett, her eyes shining with tears. "Oh, Brett, how can I thank you? You saved my life! You saved Claire!" She threw her arms around him, her face warm and silky at his throat.

He looked at Claire. He had begun to love her the first time he saw her, when he came to Hannah's Gate to ask about Margo. He still loved Claire. But he knew there was no chance for him. Her thoughts, loyalties, and hopes were fastened on Leigh Merrill.

Brett patted Rea's cheek in a brotherly gesture. "It's over," he said. Now he thought about Rose Niro, beginning to plan the letter he would write to her, the letter he hoped would free her from the past and allow her to be happy again. Angelo had been innocent. Margo had lied. Her diary proved it. Brett saw the words as he planned them. He would end, 'Rose, forget it. It's done.'

Claire too was thinking. It's done. Yet she felt a strange uneasiness underlying her relief.

Over the next few weeks, her uneasiness grew stronger. Although she tried to avoid thinking about them, there were still many unanswered questions.

She remembered how the books in Big Jack's study had been disarranged. Not once, but several times. Could Logan have done that? She remembered the holes in the earth near the gate posts. She thought about her feeling that the china had been moved around in the tallboy. Maybe Logan had been searching for the diary in all those places? But it seemed somehow unlikely. It even seemed to her that sometimes things had happened when she knew that Logan was away on one of his short trips. If he hadn't been around, he

271

couldn't have crept into Hannah's Gate, could he?

It was time to forget Margo, Linda, and most of all, Logan. They were gone forever out of her life, gone from Hannah's Gate. Yet she continued to wonder. Were they truly gone? Was it over? The dark tides in the house seemed as strong as ever to her.

Still, as the Allied armies crossed the Rhine, and she followed the war news, anxiously studying her maps of Europe, her life seemed to return to near normal. She went to the office each day, waited for news of Leigh, spoke to Jeremiah often and saw him occasionally.

Carrie continued to work nightly at her typewriter after coming home from the Library of Congress.

Rea daydreamed constantly about Brett over her homework.

Dora spoke bitterly of Casey, until finally she had a letter from him, saying he would be home for a few days as soon as he could arrange it.

But months passed. Christmas, and then New Year's Eve, came and went.

In late January Claire left her office at five o'clock as usual. She raised her face to the icy wind. The sky above was black. The slender young trees at the curb glistened with frozen sleet. Her heart seemed to skid down to her toes. When would this black winter end? When would the war end? Would spring ever come?

It seemed to her on that January evening that the drab cold would last forever. But weeks passed. The days grew longer. Forsythia began to flower on the lawns, and cherry blossoms showed pink petals at the Tidal Basin.

Finally, early in April of 1945, Casey wrote to Dora to say that he would be arriving at the end of the week.

In a flurry of excitement, she cleaned the house, prepared his favourite foods and spent long hours telling Carrie about her meeting with him, and how they'd fallen in love, and married, and how, once he was home, everything would be all right again.

But Casey never did come home. On a warm April day, he kissed Maria in New Mexico and hugged Carlos before leaving for Lamy to board the train. At Chicago he had to make the usual change. He took a cab to the B & O station, and settled down in its waiting room to spend the two hours until his train was to depart for Washington.

He was glad to sit down. He'd been feeling tired. He began to think maybe he should forget Washington and return to Hobbs. He didn't feel up to dealing with Dora, to explaining to the girls. But he knew it would be better to get it over with. He was going to tell Dora he wanted a divorce. If she wouldn't release him, then he would desert her, for good.

He wanted to be free to be with Maria and Carlos. One way or another, he intended to be.

He was thinking of that when he felt an aching numbness in his hand. It spread swiftly up his left arm. Then, suddenly, an enormous hot pain exploded in his chest. The sounds of the station faded away. The lights dimmed slowly. He whispered, "Maria . . . Carlos . . ." and fell sideways, sliding from his seat to the floor.

"He's gone," Dora said, weeping hysterically. "Gone forever." She was remembering Casey as he'd been when her father first brought him home. "He'll never come back now."

The home office of Geostat phoned only hours after Casey died. Maria, in the small New Mexican town, heard nothing until several days later when a lawyer called her from Albuquerque. She too wept when she heard the news. She too remembered Casey as she had first seen him. Tall, slim, his face weathered by time and sun, his dark eyes agleam with admiration, and later warm with love.

But Dora knew nothing of any loss but her own. She was inconsolable.

Ian came home for two days. It was a sad and painful time for the whole family. Rea and Claire did the best they could, but their words didn't help, except that in concentrating on Dora, they found momentary respite from their own grief.

Even weeks after the funeral Dora paced the house, crying and murmuring to herself. She hardly seemed aware of what had happened, when, on April 12th, news was announced of President Roosevelt's death in Warm Springs, Georgia. She listened blankly, then turned away from the radio.

To Claire it seemed that the whole city came to a momentary, heart-stopping pause. She herself felt the same awful emptiness she had felt when she learned of her father's death. What would happen, to her, to everyone else now? She had no memories of any other president. She couldn't imagine what the White House would be like without Franklin Roosevelt. American and Allied troops were surging eastward across Europe. Would Harry Truman, taking the presidential oath that day, be able to lead them to victory? Would the war end soon? When would Leigh come home?

On April 29th, the Dachau concentration camp was liberated. Soon photographs of stacked bodies, bodies the Germans hadn't had time to dispose of, flashed around the world.

Gypsies, Jews, Catholics, all types of political opponents of Hitler, had been murdered in the millions. Millions more had been worked to death, starved, tortured, gassed, burned in ovens. Everything and more than had been rumoured for years was now proven true.

Dora seemed incapable of taking in or understanding that horrible news. As Casey's small estate was settled, she became more distraught. She couldn't understand why he had left so little money. There'd been only a few hundred dollars in their joint bank account. He had cashed in his life insurance policy, she learned, and had then taken out a new one, but for half the original value. She received a cheque for ten thousand dollars, having expected close to twenty thousand.

"But there must have been more," she insisted. "I don't understand."

Claire didn't understand either. But she, and Jeremiah too, after she consulted him, agreed that if Casey had other assets, he had hidden them well.

With Jeremiah's help Claire had been able

to trace the last withdrawal from the joint bank account Casey had with Dora. There'd been a cashier's cheque written on it for five thousand dollars. That cheque had been made out to Casey, and he had cashed it in an Albuquerque bank. There was no record of what had happened to that money, and no way to find it.

Hannah's Gate had been left directly to Dora by her parents, and had remained in her own name, so the family had that. They had little else.

Dora's agitation continued. One night Claire found her walking in the yard, wringing her hands and weeping. Claire led her inside, tried to reassure her. But nothing helped.

Dora no longer noticed that Rea came and went as she pleased. She barely responded when Claire spoke of Leigh, of the war, even when Carrie talked of long ago days in Mississippi.

Claire began to dread returning from the office, fearing for Dora and her safety. Too often, she found Dora pacing the rooms in the house, peering into cupboards and chests, always searching for the money she thought must be there, since it seemed to be nowhere else.

Soon Claire wondered if Dora, all along, had been doing this. Searching. Examining. Had

Dora disarranged the books in Big Jack's study? Had she moved the china in the tallboy? But why would she have done that before Casey died? Then, one evening, she heard sounds of digging in the yard. She raced outside.

Dora, panting, sweating, shivering, stood over a hole several feet deep near the gate in the fence.

"It's got to be somewhere," she said.

Close to tears, Claire tried to persuade her mother to go inside. But Dora was adamant.

"The money's got to be somewhere," she repeated. "Where's a better place for Casey to hide it than right here?"

Claire said quietly, "Mama, listen. You know it's impossible. Dad wasn't here at Hannah's Gate."

"When he visited . . ."

"I don't think so," Claire said.

"I don't care," Dora cried. "I know something's wrong. We never had much, but we had more than he left us. There's got to be an explanation."

Claire saw that the only way to convince Dora was to prove her wrong. She took the shovel. "Okay. If you think it'll be worth it, then we'll look. And when we don't find anything, we'll forget it."

Dora said nothing. She stood there expectantly, fingers braided tightly.

Claire dug until the hole Dora had made was a trench several feet deep. It took her a long while. But just as her strength and patience were nearly gone, she heard the clang of metal.

"You see!" Dora cried.

Now Claire too felt rising excitement. What if her mother had been right? What if her father had hidden the case away in the ground, and told no one? Then doubt swept her. How was it possible? It had been years since this area of the yard had been disturbed. The grass was thick and strong.

Still, judging by the sound of it, something was there. She dug on, more quickly now. Soon she went down on her knees, Dora beside her, both of them scooping dirt away from a long metal box.

When, finally, they pulled it from the earth, they saw that it was old and rusted. It had been there too long for Casey to have buried it. Claire was certain now that it could never have belonged to her father.

But Dora twittered excitedly as they took the box into the house and set it on the kitchen table. "I knew it. Now you'll see . . ."

The lock was stuck. Claire forced it open with a knife. The hinges squealed as she pried at the lid. Finally, she managed to force it up.

Inside there were faded photographs, mouldy letters tied in a faded and rotten green string. An odour of decay arose from the scraps and shreds. It was as if she had opened an old grave, Claire thought.

Unbelievingly, Dora sifted quickly through the damp contents. Her mouth shook. The colour slowly drained from her face. There was no money. Nothing of Casey's was here. When, at last, she was sure, and forced to believe it, she collapsed, sobbing, into a chair.

It was then that Carrie appeared in the kitchen doorway. Her sandy hair was dishevelled, her blue eyes wild. She'd watched from her attic window as Claire dug the narrow metal box from the place near Hannah's gate, just where Big Jack's note to himself had said it would be. She'd watched in rage and horror. The box was hers. She deserved it. How dared Dora and Claire try to take it away from her!

Now she screamed it aloud. "That's mine, and so is everything in it." She made a grab for the box, but Dora was up, on her feet, her face scarlet. She seized the box.

There was a momentary struggle. The box slid from both their hands, fell from the table, and spewed its contents on the floor.

Carrie swooped down. She grabbed the faded photograph. "You see! It's my mother!"

Dora looked, and shrank back. A familiar face . . . once loved, then hated. "It's Fergie," she whispered, horror in her voice. "Fergie! And you're her daughter!"

So the box had been Big Jack's, not Casey's. And neither of the men, not father nor husband, had left anything but memories. Some good, some bad. And here was Fergie, back in Hannah's Gate one more time. Dora repeated, "You're her daughter, aren't you?"

Carrie didn't answer. She knelt, touching the piles of letters, the pictures. She looked through them, letters from her mother to Big Jack Gowan. Letters he'd saved. Photographs taken many years before. She stroked them all. Letters, photographs, scraps of rotting paper, shreds of ribbons, even the flakes of a dried maple leaf. At last, she said wonderingly, "And there's no money! Mama always said Big Jack had lots of money for us, but he was never able to get it to us. She said some day we'd find it. And we'd be rich, and live in a house bigger than Hannah's Gate." Tears flowed from her eyes, silvered her round cheeks. "He loved us. She always told me that. And he wanted to take care of us. But we never saw a cent of the money he had saved for us. And now I know why. Because it never existed. It was a dream Mama had. Just a dream."

"Money," Dora said bitterly. "They'd said he'd taken bribes. They destroyed him. But there were no bribes. And no money either." But she was thinking of Casey now, asking herself how it had come about that there'd been so little left for her.

Claire asked, "Carrie . . . what happened? Why did you come here? Why did you pretend to be someone else?"

"I always wanted to believe Mama's dream, and so I did. When I came to Washington to work, I was determined to get that money for myself, if I could find it. I heard that you all were renting out rooms. I came to stay, knowing I'd find it much easier if I lived in the house. But I couldn't find it. I looked everywhere I could think of. Everywhere. Even in Margo's room. In Linda's." Her voice broke. "Finally I found a note your grandfather left. 'Hannah's gate.' Small g, it said. And I realized it meant near the gate. So I understood. But I still couldn't find it. And now, now I see it was all for nothing." Carrie raised her head and looked at Dora.

The two woman exchanged a long silent stare. Until this moment they had been friends. There had been a special warmth between them, the bonds of a shared past. Now there was nothing. Dora knew that the woman she had considered her friend was actually her half sister. The secret, unacknowledge daughter of Dora's father, Big Jack Gowan. And all those years after Fergie had left Washington, he had heard from her, had letters, pictures. He kept them, buried them for safety. He had loved Fergie . . .

Now Dora said coldly, "You're nothing to me, Carrie Day. Nothing. And you never will be. So get out of my house."

"Yes," Carrie agreed. "That's right. We're nothing to each other." It didn't matter that they'd had the same father, Dora a child of his youth, Carrie a child of his mature years. It didn't matter that the same blood ran in their veins.

That night Carrie packed. The next morning she moved out.

Dora said in a relieved voice, "We'll never see her again, thank God."

But Claire wondered if Big Jack's legacy could be so easily disposed of.

Chapter 16

At news of Hitler's suicide and Germany's surrender six days later, crowds gathered in Washington to sing and dance and kiss under waving flags, celebrating the coming of peace to England and the European continent. But there was a bittersweet edge to the joy. The war was not yet over. Fierce fighting continued in the Pacific theatre.

Through the days that followed, Claire waited breathlessly for word of Leigh.

But a month passed. Then, as she left work one evening, she found Jeremiah Merrill awaiting her. She was immediately frightened. Was something wrong? Had he heard about Leigh?

Then he smiled. "Good news. I've heard from the Red Cross. Leigh's in a prisoner of war camp. He was injured, but he had treatment. He's all right, Claire!"

She closed her eyes tightly against a sudden rush of tears. Oh, thank you, God, she thought.

Jeremiah said, "You never gave up."

She shook her head.

"I'm afraid I almost did."

"When will he be home?" she asked, fearful to voice the question but unable to stop herself.

"Maybe a month or two. There are so many to bring back."

"Oh, Jeremiah, thank you for this." She felt as if she were coming awake after a long nightmare. Leigh was safe. He'd soon be coming home.

Jeremiah held her hands tightly. "Thank you for caring about Leigh. And for your faith that he'd return. I know it helped."

He drove her home, and that night she wrote a long letter to Leigh, using his old A.P.O. number. She walked down to Connecticut Avenue to mail it. She watched it slide down the chute. Now she had to wait again.

Ian opened his eyes when Luz touched his cheek.

"You sleeping?" she demanded.

"Sorry." He smiled at her. "I was more tired than I realized."

Her long dark hair fell like veils framing her face. Her green eyes glowed at him. "Oh, poor baby," she crooned. "You work so hard."

Beyond the dusky curve of her bare shoulder, he saw the thin blue curtain billow at the window. "I've got to get back to the Hill."

"Oh, no," she pouted. "Not yet. Not so soon."

"I'm sorry, Luz."

"Why? The work goes on and on. What differences does it make? One little hour, maybe two."

She didn't understand, and there was no way he could explain. The one hour, the two, might matter more than anyone knew. With the fighting in Europe ended, it was even more important to get ready.

"But Thursday then, Ian?"

"I'll be working," he said.

Disappointment clouded her eyes. She flounced away. "Oh, that's not nice. You promised me."

"I can't help it. It'll probably be a week before I can get away." He couldn't tell her where he'd be, what he'd be doing. He didn't even allow himself to think too long on it. He opened his arms to her. "Come back, Luz."

She exaggerated her pout, but crept close to him, tangling her legs in his, wrapping her arms around him, so that he felt every curve of her lithe body against his. "You're bad," she murmured against his mouth. "Oh, my, you are bad. But I love you. I really do love you so much, my sweet bad Ian." The soft words were crooned into his car, her breath warm and sweet. He turned, holding her more closely, and said, "We'll get married as soon as we can, Luz."

"Yes," she breathed.

"I'm going to make you happy."

"Oh, yes," she said, and laughing, "I'm going to make you happy too."

Later, dressing quickly, he told himself that he should let Claire and the family know what he was planning. He'd already known when he'd returned from his father's funeral. But that hadn't been the time to talk about Luz, about his decision to marry her. His mother had been too upset, frightened. Claire and Rea had been preoccupied with trying to help her. He could have stayed longer, but he'd been impatient to get back to Luz. He'd wanted to hold her in his arms, press her legs apart and bury himself between them. He'd left a day earlier than he'd had to so that he'd have extra time with her. Time in the small house off Garcia Street.

They'd had a wonderful half day together. She'd been excited by the necklace he'd brought for her under the portale at the Governor's Palace on the plaza in Santa Fe. She'd been grateful for the hundred dollars he pressed on her to help with her sister's doctor's bills. The money he earned didn't matter to him. All he cared about was Luz. Even his father's death seemed unreal. He wished he'd made a greater effort to contact Casey when Casey was in southern New Mexico. He knew that if he'd really tried he could have located his father. But he hadn't, and now it was too late. He told himself not to think about that. He had Luz, didn't he?

He kissed her goodbye, and hurried to La Fonda Hotel to pick up a bus for Los Alamos. It would be days now before he got back to Santa Fe.

Luz was dressed. She wore a black satin blouse, long full sleeves draped around her slender arms, the deep decolletage exposing the curved tops of her breasts. Her skirt was white, full, belted with a woven red sash. She leaned close to the mirror to paint mascara on her long eye lashes. When she heard the door open, she turned, smiling.

Fred Delgado said, "Well?"

"He's still talking of marrying me."

Fred grunted. "What did he give you?"

"Nothing," she said. She threw a shawl around her shoulders. "Ready?"

"Hey, wait a minute," he said. "What do you mean 'nothing'."

"I didn't ask him."

"You crazy? What's this all about if you

don't get anything from him?"

"I don't want him to feel like I'm digging him for money, Fred. That will spoil it. He'll get mad."

"I'm going to get mad if you don't have anything to show me pretty soon."

"I will," she said airily. "Just leave Ian Loving to me." In a day or two, if she had to, she'd give him half the hundred dollars Ian had given her. But only half of it. And she wasn't going to tell Fred about the necklace. That was hers. But she knew she'd better not be too greedy. Next time she saw Ian, and got something from him, she'd turn it all over to Fred. That would shut him up for a while longer.

Fred caught the two ends of her shawl, pulled her close to him. "Listen, you better not get any cute ideas. This is business, remember?"

She giggled, "Come on, sweet man. Let's go buy us some drinks."

Trinity was the code name chosen for the site. It was in the New Mexican desert in an area called the Jornada del Muerto by early Spanish settlers. Only a few low shrubs and an occasional spiky cactus grew there. The sun was hot and brilliant.

Ten miles from its base camp, at what was

spoken of as Ground Zero, resting in a special cradle, and protected by three wooden and one canvas wall, was the atomic bomb known as Fat Man.

For this moment there had been months of preparation. During the night before, there had been thunder growling over the Oscura Mountains to the east, and lightning had zigzagged across the sky. But it was quiet now at 5 A.M.

Ian, with a group of men at base camp, stared at the tower in the distance. Even with the heavy welder's glasses he wore he squinted in the glare of searchlights focussed on the tower's top.

It was still cold. Most of the men wore sweaters or coats. Their subdued uneasiness of the night had been replaced by rising tension.

With the others, Ian settled in a shallow protective depression.

A calm voice began the countdown. Ian held his breath, but his own lips moved, counting too. And soon: "Five twenty-nine fifty-seven. Five twenty-nine fifty-eight. Five twenty-nine fifty-nine. Now!"

Eyes closed momentarily, Ian felt an explosion of light, the heat of it on his body. When he looked, a huge greenish sun was flashing upward. It rose to eight thousand feet and spread, touching the clouds. A dazzling glow poured over earth and sky. The ball of fire climbed higher, changed from deep purple to orange. A giant mushroom cloud formed and expanded to another one above it. High still another grew, until, finally, it disappeared into the sky.

Meanwhile a hurricane wind swept the desert, and a deafening roar rolled across the distances. The greenish light faded. Dawn came as the mushroom cloud dissolved. The loud roar diminished to faraway murmurings in the mountains.

At Ground Zero the desert had become a white-hot saucer hundreds of yards in size. The sand was a new substance, green and unbreakable.

Ian was dazed, awed. The test had been successful. Around him, the others began to smile. There was scattered applause. Men jubilantly hugged each other. They had done it! The bomb worked.

But Ian, turning away, was suddenly frightened. This was no ordinary bomb. War-making had moved on to a new, more dangerous level. An entirely different world was about to be born.

He was to remember that thought on August 6th, when President Truman announced, "Sixteen hours ago, an American airplane dropped one bomb on Hiroshima . . ."

That day, hearing of the devastation, Ian felt tears sting his eyes. He studied his hands. Had they participated in that work? Had his mind, anxious to save lives, shared in that destruction?

Later he learned that 60,175 people were dead and missing. Four square miles of the busy city had been completely vaporized.

Within a few days Russia declared war on Japan, and soon after American forces dropped an atomic bomb at Nagasaki.

On August 14th the president announced the surrender of Japan.

A gigantic celebration swept Washington. Horns blew, crowds gathered, shouting and laughing. The bars and restaurants, banks and shops, spilled joyful customers into the streets. Bands played beneath waving flags. Cars filled the roadways and finally came to a standstill. Streetcar bells and exploding fireworks added to the din of shrieking celebrants. Torn phone books and newspapers drifted like confetti on the air.

The chaos spread across the country. Everywhere there was joyful laughter, dancing, music.

It was the same in Los Alamos, but beneath the relief and gaiety, there was a sombre quality. The Hill's mission had been accomplished, but what now?

Ian told himself that it had been a trade-off. Thousands of American soldiers' lives had been saved by the two bombs.

Later the same day, he set out for Santa Fe to see Luz.

It was a Saturday morning in September. Golden leaves drifted along Honey Locust Lane. The two magnolias next to Hannah's Gate were studded with glistening red seed combs. The wistaria vine hung limp at the window.

Claire sat in the study, reading the newspaper. Suddenly she raised her head. The house was so still. It was as if the whole world had died. She had a quick vision of a rising mushroom cloud; black, terrible to look at.

She jumped when the telephone rang.

Jeremiah said, "Leigh's here, Claire. He's safe, and fairly well. But he'll need a little time. I know you'll hear from him soon."

Joy closed her throat so that she could only whisper her thanks. It was only later that she asked herself why Leigh hadn't called himself, why he hadn't come to see her the moment he arrived.

When Jeremiah put down the phone, he sighed. Poor Claire. Jeremiah didn't know what had happened, what was to come. Leigh was changed. Whether that change was permanent, Jeremiah didn't know.

He had come to the apartment five days before. Very thin, his hazel eyes burning and bloodshot. An ugly scar, jagged as a shaft of lightning, marred his jaw.

Jeremiah welcomed him joyfully, then said, "I know you want to call Claire. Go ahead while I see to your room."

"Claire . . . yes . . ." Leigh answered.

Bewildered, Jeremiah waited. He remembered when he returned home from the First World War. He'd been afire with eagerness to see his family, friends, the girl he'd left behind. Never mind that she'd married someone else while he was in France. That first day he hadn't known about it.

But Leigh didn't call Claire that night, nor the next.

More and more Jeremiah saw how different he had become. He was drinking hard, smoking feverishly. He did nothing but pace the apartment. Something was wrong. Jeremiah didn't know what it was.

When, finally, he spoke about Leigh coming back to the office, Leigh buried his face in his hands. "Jesus Christ! Give me time," he groaned. "I don't know what I'm going to do."

"I didn't mean right away," Jeremiah said

hastily. "I just want you to know your desk is ready whenever you're ready to take it over."

At the end of five days, Jeremiah knew he must call Claire himself. It wasn't fair to her not to tell her that Leigh was safely back. So he spoke to her, heard joy in her voice, and hoped that Leigh would go to see her soon.

Leigh was thinking about it, gathering his courage by having shots of whiskey every now and again. He was continually just a little drunk. Not staggering, falling down, shouting drunk, but glittery-eyed, tense and touchy drunk.

He had to see Claire, he told himself. She was waiting for him. He had to face her.

Jeri was gone. The child they had made between them was gone. So he had to deal with Claire. He didn't know if he wanted her or not. How could he know? There'd been Jeri, hadn't there? Or maybe he'd dreamed that. It almost felt as if he had. England was far away now, another world. It had been years since he'd seen Claire. He'd been a different man then. She'd been a different woman. How could he know how he felt?

So finally, at the end of the month, he brushed his hair, and went to Hannah's Gate.

As he climbed the steps to the porch, the

place seemed smaller, shabbier too. The sign leaned at a tilt, and needed polishing. The white woodwork at the windows was stained and grey. He rubbed the scar on his jaw thoughtfully. What did that mean? What had happened? Or was the change only in him? Did he imagine that Hannah's Gate had withered with age? Or had it actually happened? And what about Claire? Had she changed too? His uncle had given him all the details of Margo's death, and Linda's, and Logan Jessup's involvement. He'd told him too about Claire and Rea's narrow escape. The whole Loving family had been through a lot while Leigh was away, Jeremiah had said. Leigh supposed that their experiences had marked them, just as he had been marked by his. But how did they show it? What would Claire be like now?

Then, bracing himself, Leigh knocked at the door. He held his breath until it opened. A tall beautiful young woman stood there. A young woman. He realized she was Rea. She wore a short orange wool skirt, a white blouse with an orange scarf looped under her collar. Her lipstick was orange too. She screamed, "Oh, my God, it's Leigh! Claire! Leigh's here. Mama, come on!" Still calling the others, she threw herself into his arms.

He staggered, hugging her awkwardly.

She'd been a child when he left. Now she was grown up.

Then Claire was there, smiling tremulously and holding out her arms. Claire. Her auburn hair was as soft and silky as he'd remembered, smoothed back from her forehead and falling to below her ears, still curled under in the pageboy she'd worn when he went away. Her brown eyes were warm, glistening.

Everything about her seemed the same. Still, he knew he must be wrong. She had to be different. Things had happened. *He* was different, wasn't he? But he went into her arms, and bent his head to kiss her, feeling her lips tremble under his.

She led him into the study. "Sit down, Leigh."

She had seen how bloodshot his eyes were, how his hands shook. It shocked her. He'd never been a hard-drinking man before. But she reminded herself that he was only recently out of a prisoner of war camp. He'd had a difficult time. He must be reacting to it. She asked him how he was, about his wounds.

He touched the scar on his jaw. It was still red, but no longer tender. He remembered, suddenly, the smell of burning, bodies adrift in the surf, and then the sharp explosion that had brought him down.

"It wasn't much," he said aloud. "I'm okay now."

But there was a dullness in his hazel eyes, and an intense restlessness inhabited his body. He was always moving, his fingers tugging his hair, smoothing his jaw, feet shuffling.

Over the next few weeks, Claire realized that the jaw wound he'd had was indeed nothing. He had other wounds, wounds that left scars that didn't show, but they were in him, in his flesh and in his mind.

He was like a stranger, so changed that it was as if the years of their growing up together had been wiped away.

She tried to catch him up with what had happened. She spoke of Margo, Linda, Logan Jessup. He turned away, saying that his uncle had already told him. He jammed his hands in his pockets, and stood at the window, looking down the slope at his old home.

It was vacant again now, although it had been briefly rented for a year or so after Logan's death.

Claire asked when he would move in.

"I'll stay with Jeremiah for a while," he said.

"And the house?"

He shrugged. "I don't know."

Already she realized that she felt differently about him. How could she not? When she hardly seemed to know him.

Yet, remembering their closeness before he went away, the feel of his body against hers, she tried to ignore her unease. He was the only man with whom she had made love, to whom she had given her body and soul. And he needed her. She was convinced that he needed her now as never before.

Chapter 17

They were sitting close together in a booth at the Roma. A candle flickered on the table. The straw-covered Chianti bottle was nearly empty.

Leigh's eyes reflected the light. He'd had several drinks before dinner, most of the wine, and now he had a Scotch before him.

He was thinking about Jeri. She was gone. He had to forget her. He needed and wanted someone. He looked into Claire's heart-shaped face. She had waited for him. He'd told her not to. He'd warned her that he mightn't be the same man when he returned home. But she'd waited anyway. She'd waited for *him*. At least he thought she had. It was hard to be sure. How did he know what she'd done while he was gone? What about Brett Devlin? He acted like a family friend, at home and comfortable with Rea and Dora Loving. But Leigh had observed how he looked at Claire. Let the damned draft dodger look, Leigh thought. A lot of good it would do him.

Claire was asking, "Do you remember the last time we came here?"

He didn't, but he took her hand.

"I remember everything," he said softly. His eyes were on her breasts.

A blush rose on her face. She had been remembering too. Not their last visit to the Roma, but their two bodies together, her cheek pressed into his shoulder, his hands stroking her . . .

"I want you so," he went on. "I can't wait any more. I don't want to."

She was unable to speak. She wanted him too. But something within her, a faint intuition, warned her. Perhaps this wasn't the time. Perhaps they should wait a little longer. He hadn't yet spoken of marriage, or of making plans.

"We can go some place, Claire. The two of us."

She realized that he wasn't speaking of marriage now either. Hurt flowered in her. Wasn't he as anxious as she was to have their love known and recognized? What should she do? What should she say?

He saw her hesitation. He whispered urgently, "Don't refuse me, Claire. I need you as I've never needed anyone in my life." He'd thought the memory of Jeri was dead. But it was with him still. He had to be cleansed of it. He had to save himself by forgetting. He needed Claire.

It was because she saw that need that she allowed him to take her to a hotel. She had thought that by now they'd have made plans for their future together. She'd supposed they would have told her mother, Jeremiah, everyone, when they would be married.

Now, instead, she told herself, never mind. It isn't time yet. We'll make our plans soon. And she said softly, "Yes, Leigh. Whatever you want to do."

They left the restaurant, and after stopping first at a nearby liquor store, drove to a downtown hotel.

As she followed him into the carpeted room, she thought of the motel they'd gone to before he went away. Grimy and cold, the unshaded bulb hanging from the cobwebbed ceiling. This room was clean, the big bed covered with its blue satin, the windows hung with matching drapes. The surroundings made no difference. She was with Leigh again.

He poured drinks for both of them. She still had the taste of wine in her mouth. She accepted the glass he gave her, took a single sip and set it aside. He drank his, refilled it, and emptied it within moments. With another drink in his hand, he sank on to the edge of the bed, looking with burning eyes, at her and through her at the same time.

In his mind, he saw Jeri's small shoe. The

gorge rose in his throat. But he kept silent. His thoughts whirled on. That July, that August, that September. The light snow falling . . . the mud . . . the long weary miles . . . flameouts and burn outs, explosive embers leaping for the sky . . . the squeals and shrieks and thundering . . . and the sudden deadly stillness . . . the barn where he'd been able to hide for a little while, and being taken prisoner . . . the memory of Jeri and what she'd done. He couldn't talk about her. He couldn't talk about the war. Not to Claire. She'd never understand. He didn't even want her to.

So he sat in silence, slowly emptying the bottle, while she watched him in growing bewilderment. Finally she said, "Leigh, what's wrong? Tell me."

He shook his head. "Nothing, Claire. Nothing."

But he continued to stare at her. He didn't speak. He didn't reach for her. She had dreamed for so long of making love with him again. Of feeling his body against hers, his mouth devouring hers. She had wanted him with her whole heart. Now, though, he seemed a stranger. A grim unsmiling stranger.

She said unsteadily, "Leigh, I think we should go." He was a stranger, and hurt in his soul, with scars from wounds she couldn't see. She needed time to understand.

303

He said, slurring the words in his drunkeness, "Don't leave me. I love you." It was clear to him now. He had to have Claire. Only she could free him from the memory of Jeri. He had to have her. He drew her to him, pulling her down on the bed. He said thickly, "I'm not going to let you go. I can't."

"All right," she said softly. "I'm here. I won't go." She drew his head down to her shoulder, holding him gently, feeling his heart pound against hers.

Within moments he fell away into a deep snoring sleep, leaving her more alone than she'd ever been in her life.

When she was sure he wouldn't hear her, she rose and combed her hair and powdered her face. It was just as she was letting herself out of the room that she heard him say, "Jeri . . . Jeri . . ."

She understood the name to be Jerry. Jerry who? Was he a friend? Had they been together, buddies in the war? Did Jerry too have unseen scars that still marked him? Had he too come home a stranger to those who loved him?

On the street, Claire hailed a cab and had herself driven home.

Chapter 18

When Leigh awakened late the next day, his head ached and his hands shook. Waves of nausea rose in his throat. Why had he let himself get so drunk? It was past noon before he had shaved and dressed and reached Jeremiah's apartment.

He listened at the door before entering. He didn't want to run into Jeremiah. His uncle would want to know when Leigh was planning to go to work. It was easier to avoid Jeremiah than to keep saying he needed more time.

When he was sure Jeremiah had gone to the office, Leigh went inside. He waved away the housekeeper's offer of breakfast, or lunch, or whatever he wanted.

He had to see Claire. To apologize for being such a fool. For getting so drunk and going to sleep. He supposed she'd be at work. But when he called to get her office number, Dora told him that Claire was at home. She hadn't felt well that morning. Leigh thanked her and put down the phone.

He had to talk to her.

As he drove up to the house, he saw Brett

Devlin and Rea on the front steps. She had her hand on Brett's arm, and was looking earnestly into his face.

Anger stung Leigh. What the hell was Brett doing here? Why was he hanging around? Okay, he'd helped Claire when she needed it. But that was over now. He'd done his good deed. Why didn't he ride silently away into the sunset? Leigh jerked his head in silent greeting at Rea and Brett, and ran up the steps.

When Dora opened the door at his knock, he muttered an apology and made for the stairs. He knew Claire's room. He headed for it, knocked and threw the door open.

Claire turned from the window. Her hair was tousled, her face not made up. She wore a pink robe, and pink slippers on her feet. Brown eyes wide, she watched as he crossed the room to her.

"What can I say?" he asked, close but not touching her.

Silent moments passed. At last she said, "We don't need to talk about it."

He put a hand lightly on her shoulder, making a physical bridge between them. From downstairs, he heard the murmur of voices.

Damn Brett Devlin, Leigh thought. If he comes up here now, he told himself, I'll pitch him down the steps. Limp and all. He'd had enough of draft dodger Brett and his polio.

The unconscious jealousy of before became conscious now. Damn Brett! Claire was his. He took a deep breath. "I'm sorry I got so drunk. I'm sorry I passed out like that. It just hit me."

She looked towards the window at the fading October light streaming through the nearly bare wistaria vine. She whispered, "I thought . . . I thought it was maybe because . . . because you didn't want me."

"Claire! Jesus! How could you think that? I just got so drunk. The wine . . . the whiskey . . . I didn't know what I was doing. And it'll never happen again. I swear to you, I'll never have another drink again. I love you. I need you."

She looked at him for a long still moment. He loved her, he said. He needed her. That was what she wanted to hear. She pressed both her hands to his cheeks, her fingers soft as petals against his skin. She held him, and looked into his eyes. "Can you stop drinking, Leigh?"

"Of course," he said fervently.

"And you promise?"

"I'm finished for good with liquor," he said.

But was it just the drinking? Or was there more? Who was Jerry? Why did Leigh dream, whispering Jerry's name? Still, having heard the silent voice that asked those questions in

307

her mind, she said, smiling, "All right, Leigh. Let's forget last night."

A grin flashed across his mouth. His eyes grew bright, a shining hazel flecked with gold. He said quickly, "Now I'll ask you what I've been thinking about all the time I was away. I'll ask you to marry me, Claire." He hugged her, pressed her close, swung her around the room in a crazy dance, laughing.

She laughed with him. His mood was so contagious, his hope impossible to ignore. And yet . . .

He understood her hesitation, and was determined to overcome it. Nothing was going to get between them. He said softly, "You begged me to marry you. I ought to have done it then. I'm asking you, begging you, now — what's changed?"

She didn't answer, but he knew what was in her mind. He seemed different to her. He'd been drunk and had gone to sleep when he should have been making love to her.

"It was the liquor," he said. "And I've promised. I won't touch a drop of whiskey again."

Later she would remember that promise, remember the whole conversation, and she would think incredulously, and I believed him! My God, I actually believed him!

But now, as he swung her in a wild dance

around the room, she only knew that she had always loved him. He was the only man to whom she had given herself, so that, in a way, they were already married. What had happened the night before didn't matter. She knew only that he needed her. She said, "Yes, Leigh. Of course I'll marry you."

With the decision made, Claire's apprehensions became joy. But, to her surprise, neither Dora nor Rea were as enthusiastic as she had thought they would be. True, neither of them expressed their reservations aloud. Yet she had the feeling that they wanted to. And when she told Brett, he sighed, "I always knew there wasn't any chance for me. I wish you every happiness, Claire. And if you ever need me . . ."

She remembered the terrible moment when she had thought that she and Rea would die at Logan's hands, and how Brett had catapulted through the splintered door to save them.

"I'll never forget what you did," she said.

Later, she discussed her plans with Dora. She and Leigh wanted a small wedding. Just the family, at home, in Hannah's Gate. And, she went on, Leigh wanted to sell the Afton Place house and use the money to help him get started, since he didn't want to return to work for his uncle. So, she told Dora with a question in her voice, she and Leigh wondered if they could stay here, with her, at least until Leigh was settled in the small new law office he was thinking about.

Dora was relieved. Money was short. With Leigh and Claire contributing to the household expenses they would be able to manage well enough.

They picked a date at the end of November, and later that same evening, Claire sat down to write to Ian. He was Leigh's best friend. She wanted him to come home, to be with them to celebrate their marriage with them.

But Ian never received the letter. The same night that Claire had written to him, he had left Luz, promising they'd get together at the weekend, saying, "We'll make our plans then. Okay?" And she had answered, "Oh, yes, Ian. However you want it, whatever you want." And she'd laughed. "Imagine it! You and me. Mr and Mrs Ian Loving!" And later she had told her husband, "I'm going to get a divorce and marry Ian. And you can't stop me!"

"Wait until he hears about the divorce," Fred sneered.

"He has heard. What does he care? You and me, we've been separated for a long time. It's nothing to him."

Fred growled, "You said it was for the money, Luz."

"I've changed my mind. Why should I stay married to a nothing like you when I can be married to a somebody like him?"

At ten o'clock that night Ian looked up at the star-filled sky. A meteor left a long slanting trail against the dark. An icy wind swooped down off the Sangre de Cristo mountains. He tightened his coat at the neck, and started across San Francisco Street, heading for the La Fonda Hotel, where he could catch a shuttle for Los Alamos.

A car whipped around a corner, accelerating wildly. It struck him a direct and solid blow, flung him back across the sidewalk and through the plate glass window of a drug store. Before passersby could read the mud-smeared numbers on its licence plates, or recognize the rage-twisted face of the man at the wheel, it was gone.

Ian died on the way to St Vincent's Hospital, never knowing that Fred Delgado had run him down.

It was almost impossible for those at Hannah's Gate to accept Ian's death, to believe he was truly gone. He hadn't been overseas during the war. He hadn't been exposed to enemy fire. He had been in New Mexico, working at the job that the Army had ordered him to. Neither his mother nor his sisters had ever imagined him to be in danger. But he was dead. There was no way to bring him back.

After a delay of seven weeks, Leigh was able to persuade Claire into going ahead with the wedding. Thus, on January 1st, 1946 at six o'clock in the evening, Claire and Leigh were married in Big Jack Gowan's study at Hannah's gate.

At the stroke of midnight a new year had been ushered in, and with it a new world. For Claire a new life was about to begin.

She looked beautiful. Her auburn hair glowed. Her eyes were brilliant with happiness. She wore a pale two-piece dress of teal-coloured silk, the jacket short and snug at her breasts, with a narrow ruffled edge at her tiny waist. Her fine legs were shown off by the short straight skirt.

She and Leigh exchanged their vows, then kissed.

Then Jeremiah, who had been best man in Ian's place, put an arm around Claire's shoulders. "I wish you every happiness. I'm joyful to have you as my niece as well as my friend." He shook hands with Leigh, congratulated him, and then added seriously, "My boy, I'm sorry you won't rejoin my office. But if you decide you want to in the future, your desk will be waiting for you."

"Thanks, Uncle Jeremiah." Leigh was amiable but cool. He'd already made his feelings clear. He wanted to be on his own. Jeremiah ought to accept that decision and stop trying to have his own way.

Jeremiah had provided champagne and a small supper. It was served by a cousin of his housekeeper.

When Claire saw the tall black woman fill the champagne glasses, she glanced quickly at Leigh, a tremor of unease quivering through her.

He accepted the glass, saw her looking at him, and smiled. "Our wedding toast," he told her.

But when the toasts had been made, he had another glass. And later, on the train to New York for their two-day honeymoon, he insisted on going into the club car and having still more to drink, insisting that he had to toast his bride again, while she, growing more concerned, turned a glass of ginger ale in her cold hands and wondered what was going to happen.

By the time they reached the hotel where they were to spend the first night of their marriage, his eyes were glittering and his voice had roughened.

While she unpacked he ordered a bottle of whiskey from room service. It was brought too soon for Claire. But he was anxious. He opened it immediately, and poured two drinks. She hadn't even sipped hers when she saw that he had finished his. "Leigh, you promised."

"My wedding night! Jesus! What do you want of me?" Then he grinned. "It's okay. I'm fine."

He took her into his arms, held her tightly. She told herself that it wasn't his fault that the war had changed him, that his memories made him drink. With time, he would become again the man he had been before. It was easy to believe that as he pressed his mouth to hers, and became once more her tender passionate lover.

Leigh moved in. He was sober and considerate. He decided that Dora needed help with the house, and arranged for Irene Beston, the young girl who had served the wedding supper, to come in once a week. He did chores around Hannah's Gate that had been left undone for years. He teased Rea, and courted Claire.

A week after he put the house on Afton Place up for sale, it was sold. But on closing day, he backed out. "I can't do it," he told

Claire. "We'll manage some other way." So the house stood vacant, while he and Claire stayed on at Hannah's Gate.

He rented a small office. Claire made curtains for the single window, painted bookcases for his law books. Then the staff of the Office of Engineers was cut. Claire was laid off.

The same thing was happening all over Washington. There was a shrinking back from wartime expansion. Less traffic in the streets. Fewer people in the restaurants. The supper clubs, once standing room only, were nearly empty.

Claire wanted to apply for a teaching job. But Leigh didn't want her to work. He needed her at home. He could support her, he swore. But it soon became evident that his law practice would scarcely support him, much less take care of her, and help her mother and sister, and maintain Hannah's Gate.

He spent virtually no time in his office. When Claire reproached him, saying, "You must be there in case there are calls. Your uncle will surely refer . . ." Leigh would glare at her and yell, "I don't want my uncle's help, damn it!" Or say sarcastically, "What do you know about practising law? When did you get your degree?"

She wouldn't answer, and soon he would say sheepishly, "I'm sorry, Claire. I didn't

315

mean it. I try not to lose my temper, but with so much on my mind . . ."

The apologies came more and more frequently. Claire began to hate them, knowing them to be empty words.

Near the end of their first year together, he began drinking seriously again. She didn't know it that Friday afternoon when she was supposed to meet him at Garfinckle's to pick out a birthday present for Rea. He didn't show up. Claire waited nearly two hours before she went home.

Leigh wasn't there, and he didn't come home that night, nor the next.

Claire, frightened, paced the floor and peered from the windows. She couldn't imagine what had happened. She didn't want to call the police. She had had to do that too often in those awful months after Margo and Linda were murdered.

When, very late Sunday night, Leigh came staggering in, she was glad that she had trusted to her instincts and done nothing but wait for him. He was still a little drunk. His eyes were bloodshot, his hair dishevelled. His unshaven face was grey. "I was delayed," he said.

"I was frightened for you."

"I'm home now," he told her.

Rea, listening from the upper hall, came halfway down the stairs.

"But where were you?" Claire asked. "What happened?"

"Nothing happened. And where I was is none of your damn business."

Face flaming, Rea exploded, "Don't talk to my sister that way! Who do you think you are!"

"And it's none of your damn business either," Leigh yelled. He pushed past Claire, past Rea, and stamped up the steps. In a moment there came the crash of the bedroom door slamming shut behind him.

Rea said into the silence that followed, "He's crazy."

Claire didn't answer her.

"Throw him out," Rea said. "You don't need him."

"But *he* needs *me*."

Rea made a contemptuous sound. "You're as crazy as he is."

The next morning, when Rea was getting ready to leave for her new job, Leigh came down. He was shaven now, his hair brushed. He smiled at her as if nothing had happened. "Tell you what, Rea, if you say you're sorry, then I will too."

"I don't have anything to be sorry for," she retorted.

"You've got a big mouth for a little girl," Leigh said sharply.

"I'm not a little girl any more," she told him. And then: "And your mouth is worse than mine."

"If you don't like it, you can get out," Leigh told her. "I live here now."

"I'm going to get out as fast as I can," she said sweetly.

She meant it. She had already decided. She didn't know how she would do it, or where she would go, but she was determined that she wasn't going to live in Hannah's Gate, not as long as Leigh Merrill was there.

Soon after, Brett stopped by. He mentioned that he was planning to move to Boston in six months to become a partner in a public relations firm, where his Washington contacts and connections with Congress would stand him in good stead.

"You're going away?" Rea said incredulously. "You mean you're really leaving?"

He smiled at her. "It's not the end of the earth, Rea. I'll be back."

"You won't," she said, and following him out to his car when he left, said, "I can't believe you'd do this to me."

"Rea, stop it." He smiled at her. "Enough of your tricks."

She smiled too. "It's not one of my tricks, as you call them. I mean something specific. I always thought you'd teach me to drive, and now you won't."

"Leigh will."

Rea gave a mock shiver. "Oh, no! I wouldn't want him to. He'd yell, and we'd fight even more than we already do."

Leigh's unsteady temper was no secret. The whole family knew of it. So naturally Brett did too.

Claire was too proud to admit how hard Leigh was to live with. But Rea cared nothing for Claire's pride. She had her own plans. She'd loved Brett, wanted him, ever since he'd saved her and Claire from Logan. And even stronger than love or wanting was her determination to escape Hannah's Gate. Brett was a way out. So she set herself to win him.

He taught her to drive, using his car. They spent a lot of time together. Hours when they had both finished work. Saturdays. Sundays. The day she passed her driver's test and got her licence, she threw her arms around him, her long black hair spilling over his shoulder. She cried, "Oh, Brett, thank you, thank you." And: "Oh, I love you so."

He felt her young eager body against his, and looked into her laughing eyes. She was so young, just eighteen now to his thirty-five. He had always thought of her as Claire's kid sister. But he saw that she was grown. A warm, lovely woman. He had loved Claire a long time, and kept his need submerged, his hunger concealed. Now that he had given up hope for good, here was Rea, her love a blessing. It was natural to turn to her.

He said nothing then. But several weeks later, just two weeks before he was to leave for Boston, he asked Rea to marry him, and she replied instantly that she would, that she'd been afraid he'd leave without having asked her, and she would have to chase him to Massachusetts to propose to him.

She shrugged away Dora's protest that Brett was too old for her.

Claire asked Brett if he was sure he was doing the right thing for him, and asked Rea if she loved Brett. He said he was doing what he had to do. He wanted to marry Rea. He hoped Claire didn't object. Rea laughed at Claire's question, saying, "Oh, poo! Love! What are you talking about?" And then, smiling sweetly, "But don't worry. I'll be a good wife to your Brett."

So about eighteen months after Claire married Leigh, Rea, like her sister, took her vows in Big Jack's study, with only the family present, and then she and Brett left for Boston.

It was three years before she came home again, and by then things were very different at Hannah's Gate.

Chapter 19

In the year and a half that Leigh and Claire had been married they had seen Jeremiah Merrill regularly. He was determined to help Leigh establish himself, whether Leigh wanted his help or not. He went about his goal with careful tact, involving the younger couple in his social life, gradually introducing them to his close friends, and then, more slowly, to his business associates.

He made sure that they felt at home and welcome in his two-storey apartment on Connecticut Avenue, where Leigh had lived briefly at the end of the war. It was there that they several times met President Truman, and his wife, and their daughter Margaret, and several members of the president's kitchen cabinet.

At first Claire wasn't comfortable in that company, but soon she found that they were people much like herself, who spoke of the news of the day, of Washington, of the homes they had left behind. And she could always make small talk with Margaret, who was a history major at the George Washington University.

321

It seemed more difficult for Leigh. He was forever restless, the first to suggest that it was time to leave, having been the last to arrive. He made no effort to be friendly, even fended off the overtures made to him.

But Jeremiah never became discouraged. He was fond of Claire. Leigh was his only nephew. He wanted the best for them, and was determined they should have it. So he regularly included them in his entertainments.

Claire, wanting to reciprocate, hoping to draw Leigh closer to Jeremiah, often asked the older man to Hannah's Gate for family dinners.

A month after Rea and Brett were married, on a hot night in late June, Claire and her mother sat with Jeremiah in Big Jack's study. The air was close, filled with the lemony scent of the magnolia blossoms on the trees close by the house.

Claire looked at her watch for the third time in five minutes. She was uneasy. Leigh was late.

Jeremiah saw the glance, and smiled at her. "Now, don't fret, Claire. I have all evening."

"I suppose a client's holding him up," she said. But she wondered. He had so few clients. There was little to keep him in the office. Still, he hadn't had a drink in over a month. Maybe her fear was unjustified. She'd begun to feel the worst was over. He was becoming himself again. Yet she had been disappointed so many times in the last year and a half. So her ears strained for the sound of the car in the driveway, and she silently prayed that he hadn't forgotten that his uncle was to be there that night, that he hadn't stopped for a single drink that had become two, three, four.

As soon as Leigh walked into the house, she knew that her hopes had been in vain. She heard the clatter of his footsteps on the oak floor. The defiant stride and sudden hitch, which meant he had paused to steady himself by touching the wall. Once in the room, he looked at Jeremiah. "How are you tonight, Uncle?"

"Good evening, Leigh." There were sudden deep grooves in the older man's well-shaven face. His pale glance touched Leigh, while his manicured nails beat a light tattoo on the arm of his chair.

Leigh sat in the place that had been Big Jack Gowan's first, and then Casey Loving's. He stretched out his long legs. "I'm sorry I'm late. Something came up."

"Of course," Jeremiah said.

Dora said she would see about getting dinner on the table, but Leigh said sharply, "No, not yet. We should have a drink first, as civilized people do." He turned to Claire. "Will you?"

She hesitated, knowing that Leigh had had as much as he should have, and perhaps even more.

Jeremiah said, "I'll join you this evening, Leigh."

She went to the sideboard, brought back a tray with a decanter of water, a bottle of Scotch. Dora hurried out for ice, then retreated to the kitchen again.

Leigh poured himself a strong Scotch with a single cube and proceeded to empty the glass.

Claire saw that he had forgotten to serve Jeremiah. She hurried to remedy the oversight. Leigh didn't even notice that. He seemed nearly asleep until Jeremiah said, "To your very good health. Both of you."

Then Leigh refilled his glass. He laughed. "Oh, yes. To both of us!"

When Dora called that dinner was ready, he protested. His uncle had said they were going to be civilized that night, hadn't he? He glared at Claire. "Please explain to your mother what that means."

"Never mind," Claire said gently.

Jeremiah made a coughing sound. His eyes moved from Claire's face to Leigh's. It wasn't the first time he'd noticed that something was wrong. Nor the first time that he'd heard that ugly note in Leigh's voice either. He'd thought, more recently, that the boy was settling down. But now . . . He let the thought trail away. At the first opportunity, he would talk to Leigh. Perhaps the boy didn't realize how much his drinking affected him.

When Claire didn't go to speak to her mother, Leigh yelled, "Damn you! I mean it! Tell her to hold dinner until I'm ready."

It was no use trying to placate him. If she did as he ordered, he would find some other excuse for making a scene. She had seen the pattern too many times to mistake it.

She said apologetically to Jeremiah, "Shall we go in?"

The two of them went to the dining room, leaving Leigh behind.

He continued to drink, while the others had their meal, making small talk, speculating about who President Truman would choose to run for vice president on his ticket the following year. But Dora, passing the bread tray, ignored the conversation and kept looking anxiously at the door.

When they had finished dessert and coffee, Jeremiah got to his feet. "Ladies, thank you. I'm sorry this evening wasn't what you'd planned." Before leaving he stopped to speak to Leigh. "I think we should get together, my boy. Say one night over the weekend?"

"If you like," Leigh said.

"Yes. Please. Shall we say eight o'clock. My apartment, on Sunday?"

"Okay," Leigh said truculently. "Eight o'clock. Your apartment. Sunday."

In the days that followed Leigh brooded about the coming appointment. What did his uncle want? What would he say to Leigh? What would Leigh say to him? Had Claire complained? But what could she have to complain about? So he drank. So what? Plenty of men drank more. Jeremiah was old. What did he know?

By Sunday, Leigh had worked himself into a rage. He had several drinks before going to Jeremiah's. As he rang the bell, he considered telling Jeremiah that he wouldn't stay. He'd come only to say his uncle should mind his own business. Then, Leigh thought, he'd walk away.

But when Jeremiah opened the door, Leigh decided he might as well remain. He'd keep his temper through the lecture that was to come. After all, Jeremiah had always been good to him, and he was Jeremiah's only relative. Leigh owed him the chance to lecture. He'd give the old man his due.

"It's just us," Jeremiah was saying. "It's the housekeeper's night off."

Leigh followed him up the narrow staircase to the second floor of the apartment, and into Jeremiah's office. Leigh had been there many times, but now he was struck by the luxuriousness of the room. The carpet was a thick Oriental, the sofa and chairs soft and deep. A vase of pink roses scented the air. How different it was from Hannah's Gate, where the furniture was old, the carpet threadbare.

"I do a lot in here these days," Jeremiah said, noting Leigh's look around. "The boys handle the office for me." He smiled slightly. "I'm beginning to feel the need to slow down." Still smiling, the older man went on, "Wish you'd decided to come in with us. I'd like to see another Merrill on our sign."

Leigh said nothing.

"And, I hope you know," Jeremiah added, "the door is always open to you. Any time you change your mind . . ."

"No. But thanks." Leigh wanted a drink to keep him going. But he didn't want to ask for it.

Jeremiah sat in the corner of the sofa, waved Leigh to a chair close by. He tented his plump fingers, and said gently, "I'm worried about you, my boy." Even though there was no accusation in the words, heat immediately burned through Leigh. Jeremiah went on, "I know you had a difficult time overseas. The

327

fighting. The prison camp. They're bound to leave marks on a man. But, Leigh, you must work through it. Your wife . . . Claire . . . she isn't to blame. She's not your enemy. She loves you deeply."

"You don't have to tell me that," Leigh said. He touched the scar on his face. Memories rose in his mind. Red mist . . . burning fires . . . He said thickly, "But you weren't there. You can't understand."

"But I was . . . in the first war . . . Flanders . . . " Jeremiah took a deep breath. "I understand better than you imagine. Still, you must put the past aside. Allow the memories to fade, Leigh."

"What do you want from me?" he demanded.

"It's not what I want. It's what you must do to save yourself." When Leigh didn't respond, the older man said, "My boy, this attempt to drown your pain in alcohol will destroy you."

"Has Claire complained to you?" Leigh asked coldly.

Jeremiah looked surprised. "Of course not. Do you believe I can't evaluate the evidence of my own eyes?"

"I know you mean well," Leigh said. "But I'll live my life as I wish. Not as you think I should."

"You'll throw away your life if you continue as you are," Jeremiah said. "You don't realize what you're doing."

"It's none of your business," Leigh told him heatedly. He rose. "You've done me a lot of favours. I'm grateful. But that doesn't give you ownership over me. Nor allow you to tell me what to do."

Leigh strode from the room. He wasn't going to listen any more. Even his uncle couldn't talk to him like that. Nobody could. Just as nobody understood. It had been a mistake to come, to be reasonable and polite. It had been a mistake to listen to Jeremiah even for an instant.

Jeremiah hurried after him. "My boy, please . . ." He caught Leigh by the arm as he started down the stairs.

Leigh thrust him away. "I don't want to hear any more," he yelled. "I've had it with you, with everybody. Leave me alone."

At his angry push, Jeremiah staggered and tripped. He stumbled over the edge of the top step, and went rolling and crashing down the stairs to land at the bottom. There was blood on his mouth when he raised his head. His face was grey, his pale eyes staring. He croaked, "Help me, Leigh!"

Leigh walked slowly down the stairs. He stepped over the older man's fallen body without a glance, went to the door and left.

At midnight, when the telephone rang at Hannah's Gate, Leigh was in a drunken stupor and didn't hear it.

Claire did. She ran down the steps, fright quickening her breathing. What had happened? Who was calling so late? With sinking heart, she grabbed the phone.

Jeremiah's housekeeper told her that he had apparently fallen down the stairs, and had had a stroke. The emergency squad had just pronounced him dead.

"We'll be there as quickly as we can," Claire said. Poor Jeremiah. How sad that he should die. He'd seemed so vigorous. She would miss him. He'd been a good friend to her.

She went up to Leigh, tried to waken him. It was no use. He only mumbled, and thrust her away. At last she gave up. She'd go alone.

He heard her voice from a long way off. He understood her words. But he didn't want to know. He didn't want to believe it. He felt her tears fall on his cheeks, and thought they were the red drizzle of blood, burning his flesh again.

Three weeks later, Leigh said wonderingly, "I'm a very rich man, Claire. Jeremiah left everything he owned to me. The apartment building where he lived. The stocks. The bonds. The bank accounts. His share of the firm even. We're on easy street now, Claire."

He didn't permit himself to remember that last time he had seen Jeremiah alive, the last words Jeremiah had spoken to him. He would never, as long as he lived, allow himself to remember that he had stepped over Jeremiah's fallen body and left him to die alone. But he never forgot it either. That knowledge was sealed deep into his soul.

"He loved you," Claire said.

"Yes," Leigh agreed tonelessly. "Yes. He did."

So, from what had been near poverty, the family was suddenly wealthy.

Leigh stopped even the pretence of practising law. He gave up his small office, sold his share of Jeremiah's firm to the other partners, and began to develop plans for expanding Hannah's Gate. Soon he was busy putting those plans into effect.

Since the house was actually Dora's he made a great show of consulting her at every step. Always, she would agree, but doubtfully, plucking her chin with thin fingers, saying, "If you think it's all right, Leigh . . ."

By the time Rea returned home after three years in Boston with Brett, the Merrill house on Afton Place had been torn down, and in its stead, a large swimming pool had been installed. A small three-bedroom house, used as a cabana, had been built next to it. An eight-foot brick wall enclosed the property at the back and front. Temporary fencing lined both sides of the house. For Leigh was bargaining with the neighbours to right and left. He wanted their land. He wanted a full block, square and deep, to be the final setting of the jewel that he envisioned Hannah's Gate would be.

That summer he put everything on hold, thinking he might be called back to serve in Korea, when North Korea sent an army across the 38th parallel, and President Truman supplemented a United Nations force with American ground troops. But Leigh heard nothing, and he soon put out of his mind the possibility that he might have to serve again.

In November of 1950, two Puerto Rican nationalists tried to assassinate the president at Blair House. He was unhurt, but one of the men was killed, the other captured.

Washington was still buzzing with that event when Rea arrived. She didn't explain, at first, that she had left Brett and was home for good. She introduced her six-month-old son, Keith, and settled in. Keith was a square, happy child, with a big head covered with a fine light fuzz, and Brett's dark smiling eyes.

When Claire spoke of the resemblance, Rea frowned. "I think he looks just like me."

Later Claire realized that she should have known from those few words what Rea planned. But she didn't think of it then. Her mind and heart were focused largely on Leigh.

They had many good days together. There were weeks, months even, when they were as close as man and wife could be. But she never knew when he would suddenly begin to drink. Then, he would once again become the stranger who had returned to her from the war.

It was after Rea returned with Keith that Claire saw how obsessed he was with the idea of having a family.

He realized that he had always needed a replacement for the child Jeri had aborted. Now, without mentioning the lost child, he told Claire, "I want children. I need them."

"It will happen when it's supposed to," she said.

"How do you know? Maybe there's something wrong with you. We've been married four years and nothing's happened."

There had to be something wrong with her. It couldn't be him, he knew. He'd fathered a child before. And besides, although he wouldn't admit it to himself, Claire was too perfect. Too kind, too loving, too pretty. She had to be flawed. And that must be the flaw, she couldn't have children.

Aloud he said, "Rea didn't have trouble getting pregnant."

"Don't worry about it," Claire said. "We have time."

"But I *do* worry," Leigh answered, frowning. "How long do you think I want to wait?"

It was a conversation they had often. He continually made it clear that he blamed Claire for their childlessness. But she suspected it might be that he was so often drunk when he made love to her, and she was so frequently concerned about that, that it became impossible for her body to conceive. She kept her suspicions to herself, however.

Rea had been home for two months when Brett came to visit, to see Keith, and to ask her to return with him to Boston.

She refused. She had tried to be a good wife to him, but it was no use. She didn't want to be married to him anymore. Saddened, but accepting, and blaming himself, Brett left for home alone.

Afterwards Claire told Rea, "I'm afraid you're making a mistake. Brett's a good man."

"Yes, he's a good man," Rea retorted. "But I don't like being second best. And that's what I always was to him. Second best. Because he really wanted you."

"Rea! That was a long time ago. He married you. He loves you."

"I know what I'm talking about," Rea answered. And then: "But that doesn't matter. I'm going to get a divorce. And, by the way, Claire, you should do the same. We've both made mistakes, but I'm the only one doing anything about it. Your Leigh Merrill is crazy. The best thing you can do is admit it, and bail out."

"Don't say that, Rea. I couldn't leave Leigh. I wouldn't even want to."

Rea gave her a long level look. "If you had any sense you would."

She picked up Keith, and retreated to her upstairs bedroom. She didn't want to talk about it any more. Not about Claire. Not about herself. The truth was, Brett bored her. He was a good man, a good husband. He was loving to her and the baby, and gave them everything. But the years between them were a barrier she couldn't breach.

She had had to escape Hannah's Gate, to get away from Leigh. He was too bossy for her taste. Let Claire put up with him. Rea wouldn't. So she married Brett. But three years with him had been all she could bear.

He'd bought a neat saltbox in the Boston suburb called Newton. She'd learned to clean and cook. When Keith came, she learned about formulas and diapers. And now, at twenty-one, she couldn't stand that life any more. No matter what happened, she wasn't going back to Newton, and Brett.

Soon she began to explore Washington. She became a familiar figure in the cafes and bars and bookstores around lower Connecticut Avenue. Wherever she went people stared at her. She was striking, tall and slim. with a long tangled mass of black curls. She wore a small peaked cap pulled low over her right eye, and narrow black jeans with a body-hugging black knit shirt. Dora was a willing baby-sitter, so she was free to do as she pleased.

The following spring she saw a man named Vance Ward at a poetry reading, and the same evening, saw him again in a Connecticut Avenue bar. She sat alone in a dim corner, sipping a beer. The place was empty except for Vance and two other men, who sat not far from her. They were all in their twenties, dressed in boots and open-necked shirts. Vance was the oldest of them. He had a thick black moustache, heavy dark brows. His face was weathered, with a small white scar etched into one eyebrow. What she heard of the men's conversation was loud, punctuated by obscenities.

Rea listened openly. She smiled when Vance turned to stare at her. After a while he came to sit in the empty chair at her table, asking,

"Expecting somebody?"

She shook her head.

"You like poetry."

"Yes. I guess you do too."

"I was thinking that you're good to look at," he said. "I thought it at the reading, and here too. So I decided to take a chance. Is it okay if I stay?"

"Why not?"

He grinned. "Listen, I can tell you why not. If you want me to. There are plenty of reasons. But instead of telling you, I'm going to let you find out for yourself. How's that?"

"That sounds good," she said.

They saw a lot of each other for the next six months. Vance drank large quantities of beer, but he only smiled more, laughed more, talked more, he worked only when he was out of money. He wrote long, unrhymed, not quite coherent poetry. When he couldn't pay for his beers or food, Rea did. She borrowed cash from Claire to keep going. She spent nothing on clothes, either for Keith or for herself. As long as she had enough to pay for Vance's beer, an occasional book, rent, and sometimes petrol for his old motorcycle, she was content. That's all she needed. It didn't amount to very much.

Leigh questioned her about Vance, not liking his thick moustache, not liking his different clothes, boots and motorcycle. Rea answered Leigh's questions flippantly, ignored his opinions, and stayed away from him as much as she could.

One night, when she came home very late, Leigh was waiting. He caught her by the hand. "Hey, Rea, just wait a minute."

"What do you want?"

"What're you up to? I've got a right to know. You're living in my house."

Ordinarily she wouldn't have argued with him. But that got to her *My* house, he'd said. *My* house. It wasn't his. He had no right to say that. She exploded, "*Your* house! Are you crazy? It's my mother's house. My *family* house. And always has been."

"But I pay the bills," Leigh said silkily. "That gives me some say." He slid his arm around her waist and leaned close.

She could smell the whiskey on his breath.

"Let go of me," she said loudly.

"You used to like me well enough," Leigh whispered. "So don't act as if I'm poison now."

"You *are* poison now," Rea cried. She pushed past him, and fled up the stairs.

Within a few days, she was gone. Vance told her that he was pushing on. He'd been in Washington long enough. He'd heard that his old buddies, Bill Burroughs and Al Gins-

338

berg, were in Mexico. He was heading that way too. He laughed when she told him she was going with him.

Soon after, having tied a few changes of clothing in a bundle, she kissed Keith good-bye, climbed on to the pillion seat of Vance's motorcycle, and clinging to his waist, rode away from Hannah's Gate with him.

Chapter 20

In the first three months after she left, the family had two postcards from Rea. One was from El Paso; another had been mailed in Tijuana. Neither of them spoke of when she would return. Neither asked about Keith, nor mentioned Brett.

Brett had come to Washington as soon as Claire realized that Rea had gone away for more than a few days. He intended to take Keith home to Boston with him.

The boy was then nine months old, Dora doted on him. Claire cherished him. But for Leigh, Keith was the son he didn't yet have.

The three of them persuaded Brett to leave Keith in their care temporarily. They reminded him that Rea would surely return soon. They pointed out all they could do for the child. He finally agreed, but stressed that it was only for the time being. Meanwhile, he said, he would visit Keith once a month.

Time passed. Rea didn't come back. Leigh began to resent Brett's visits. What if he insisted on taking Keith away? Leigh worried aloud to Claire, who said, "Remember that

Keith is Brett's son."

For a long while, Brett said nothing. Plainly he loved the boy. Claire enjoyed seeing them together. Brett's eyes shone as he watched Keith toddle around the room. Yet he never indulged Keith as Leigh did. If the boy wanted to play with the picture of Leigh in its silver frame, Leigh allowed it. When Brett was there, the picture was taken away, and building bricks offered instead.

In those brief visits to see Keith, Brett saw more than his son. He saw Leigh Merrill too. Having never known him before the war, he knew only the Leigh of the present. A changeable, bad-tempered man who drank too much on occasion, and when he did, became ugly and abusive. To strangers. To Dora. Even to Claire.

At first Brett had hoped Rea would soon return. That he and she would live together again with Keith. He was so much older than she. He ought to have known that would be a problem. He must allow her time to mature, since it was he who had taken her young adulthood away.

He permitted Keith to remain at Hannah's Gate because he knew that was best for the boy. So, although he missed being with his son, he contented himself with his visits. Gradually, though, he gave up hope. There had been no word since the two cards from Mexico.

Now, two days after Dwight Eisenhower's inauguration as president, and three days after Brett had departed for Boston, Claire let herself into Hannah's Gate.

She heard the sound of voices from the new television set that was in the study. It was a large mahogany box with a good-sized screen that showed black and white images. Dora was fascinated by it, and watched it for hours each day. Keith enjoyed it too.

Claire looked in at the two of them.

"We've been having a grand day," Dora said, smiling. "And you?"

"Fine. I managed all my errands." That was what she had said she was going to do when she went out. But it had been more than that. She repressed the urge to shout out her news.

Keith pointed at the image on the screen. "Man," he said clearly, indicating a trouser-wearing woman.

When Claire left them, Dora was trying to explain why the girl wearing trousers was a girl, and not a man.

Claire hurried upstairs. She would tell Leigh first. She was so happy. She knew he would be too. She'd suspected for six weeks that she might be pregnant. Now she was certain. She had just come from the doctor's office. She'd said nothing beforehand to Leigh. She didn't want to disappoint him lest she be mistaken. She had never given up hope during the seven years of their marriage. Now that hope was justified.

Leigh wasn't in their room. She looked out and saw him on the terrace below, frowning at a sketch pad. He was planning some new improvement, she supposed. He had been able to buy the house to the east, so soon he would extent the wall along the property line. One day he'd be able to buy the house to the west, and Hannah's Gate would finally have expanded to fill the block.

The area had changed since he and Claire had grown up here. The houses had become too expensive for young couples starting out. Nowadays they moved to development houses and garden apartments in Silver Spring and Arlington, the close in suburbs.

Yet Cleveland Park looked the same as always. The trees were rich with blossoms in the spring, and lilacs and daffodils glowed on the lawns.

Baby Merrill wouldn't remember Hannah's Gate when it had needed new window trim and layers of paint. It would never know of the war, nor the depression before it. It would never hear of Margo Desales nor Linda Grant nor Logan Jessup.

Claire shuddered. That was in the past. It was the future she should think about. She went to the mirror. Even though she was in her early thirties, she had the fresh glow of a girl. She put on fresh make-up, ran a comb through her hair. Now she was ready to tell Leigh. Her heart beat quickly as she went downstairs.

"We could have a greenhouse there," Leigh said, by way of greeting. He pointed to the still-raw earth where the next door house had been. "What do you think?"

"That would be nice." She smiled at him. His hazel eyes were bright. He had that intense expression he often had when he spoke of his plans for Hannah's Gate. It was a good day, she knew. She hoped that was an omen of things to come.

She had meant to lead him inside, to sit him down and prepare him by saying she'd been feeling funny for a little while. That she hadn't said anything because she hadn't understood what it meant. But now she blurted, "I'm pregnant, Leigh!"

"You're . . . you're . . ." He looked stunned. As if he couldn't take in her meaning. His face paled, then flushed. "You're pregnant!" he said, and seized her, swung her into his arms. He danced around, hugging her to him.

"You're pregnant, Claire! Finally! You're going to give me my son. Oh, yes! I can feel it. I know. I'm going to have my son!"

"I don't know what we'll have," she said, laughing. "Except that it will be a baby. And whatever its sex is, we'll love it."

"He's going to be a boy," Leigh said adamantly. "How can the Merrill name be carried on, unless it's a boy? And the name will be carried on! We're the Merrills of Hannah's Gate. There'll always be Merrills here."

Gowans, Claire thought. First Gowans. Then Lovings. And now Merrills. Hannah's Gate belonged to all of them. But she said nothing. She was struggling with a sudden fear, burying it as it rose in her. Leigh was happy. That was the important thing. The baby's sex wouldn't matter. He'd love the child once he'd held it in his arms. He'd be good with it, to it, as he was with Keith, no matter what.

Leigh immediately began to speak of his plans for his son. In the days that followed he expanded on them. He brought home infant toys and clothing, always in blue. He worked on a nursery, sketching austere furniture, plain curtains, a freize of soldiers in modern dress and knights-at-arms, to be painted above the moulding on the walls.

He stopped drinking to excess, and became

totally concentrated on looking forward to August, when Claire expected the baby. A pleasant sense of contentment cocooned all of them that summer.

Then, at the end of July, just after the armistice ending the Korean War was signed, when Claire, heavy and ungainly, had begun to count the days to the end of her confinement, she received a phone call from Tasco in Mexico. A distant voice, speaking heavily accented English, informed her that Rea was dead.

The conversation remained forever a blur in Claire's mind. She knew that she had been told that Rea was staying at a tiny inn with a man named Vance Ward, and several others. She had fallen ill. The others had departed. A few days later, the owner of the inn had found her dead in her room.

Claire knew that she spoke of arrangements, the return of Rea's ashes, and that she thanked the man for letting the family know what had happened. She knew that she called Brett immediately, and broke the news to him as gently as she could. But mostly she remembered the pain of loss. Of Rea's being abandoned to die alone.

She often wondered about Vance Ward, and what had happened to him. She never learned that from Mexico he went to San Francisco.

In 1959, flying high on LSD, he stepped off a fifth-floor balcony, and was dead when passersby reached him. By the time that had happened, he had only the faintest memory of Rea, the girl with long black hair whom he'd called his old lady and said he loved.

There was one thing, though, that Claire always remembered: Leigh saying with no sympathy, no regret, "She should have stayed where she belonged."

In due course, the urn containing Rea's ashes arrived. Brett came the following day.

They held a small private funeral service, and Brett and Claire took the ashes to Chain Bridge and let them float on the wind until they disappeared into the Potomac River.

Afterwards, driving back, Brett told Claire that he wanted to take Keith home with him, and the next day, blowing kisses and laughing, the child went away.

The house seemed empty without him. Claire and Dora keenly felt his absence. Leigh seemed to have dismissed him from his mind and heart. He spoke only of the baby to come.

In mid-August, Claire felt the first of her labour pains. Leigh wasn't at home, so she called the doctor, told him, and then had a taxi drive her to Columbia Hospital. It was a short and swift ride downtown. Her labour was short too. Within three hours, the nurse was smiling at her. "You have a beautiful little daughter, Mrs Merrill."

A few hours later, as Claire held the baby girl in her arms, Leigh came into the room. He was red-faced and grim. He said coldly, "I wanted a son." With those curt words he turned and left.

He walked down to Pennsylvania Avenue to a bar, and stayed there, drinking until they closed the place. Then, barely able to stand upright, he went back to Hannah's Gate.

He ignored the little girl when Claire brought her home. Claire named her Elianne. She had a small amount of pink fuzz on her head. Her eyes were large, and scaldingly blue. Soon they changed to a deep soft brown. She was a good baby. She slept a lot, rarely cried, ate what she was given, and thrived.

But Leigh wasn't impressed. He didn't care. Elianne, his firstborn child, should have been a boy. He never allowed Claire to forget that she had disappointed him, denied him what he most wanted.

Even later, when, in 1956, she had Gordon, the son he hungered for, he said, with rancour instead of gratitude, "Finally you've given me what I want."

It was the same in 1958, when she had their youngest child, David.

But, if he had nothing but anger for her

most of the time, he doted on Gordon and David.

From their first hours they could do no wrong, and as they grew older it was the same. He didn't see that Gordon was headstrong, blind to all but his own whims, nor that by the age of three, David was subject to uncontrollable tantrums. They were his sons, extensions of himself. And he remembered the child that Jeri could have had for him, but didn't.

On rare occasions Brett brought Keith to visit. Claire came to dread those times because, after Keith and Brett had gone, Leigh would speak of Rea. She'd been a tramp, he'd say. Else why had she run away? Why had she abandoned her husband and son?

"There's bad blood in your family," he'd tell Claire. "Look at your grandfather, Big Jack, and his Fergie. Getting himself an illegitimate child. And her coming here, Carrie Day, to Hannah's Gate, to get what she could." Leigh's sneering laughter would ring out. "And there's you too. You slept with me before we were married."

"Leigh," she protested, "I loved you."

"Whatever the reason, you did it." His eyes would narrow. "Not much different from Rea, are you?" And later, when Elianne was older, he would say to Claire, "She's got Rea's temperament. She even looks like her." And then, overriding Claire's protests, would go on, "You'd better keep a firm hand on her."

Now, once again, long past her growing up years, Claire sensed dark currents spreading through Hannah's Gate, and heard angry whispers in the night. This time though they were her whispers, hers and Leigh's.

Claire slowly turned the pages of the magazine. From beyond the window, she heard the voices of three-year-old David, and Gordon, now five. Soon Elianne would come home from Eaton School, where Claire herself had attended the lower grades. For an eight year old, Elianne was very self-sufficient. Claire felt she was too solemn, and tried too hard to please.

Claire brought her attention back to the magazine. Suddenly a familiar name leaped out at her from the mass of print. Carrie Day! The byline above a short story. It had been so long since Claire had thought of her. Where did she live now? Was she still in Washington? It was hard to imagine what she looked like now. Sixteen years had passed. Carrie would be fifty-one.

Claire read the story. It was labelled fiction, but within the first two paragraphs, Claire saw familiar facts. The house described was

Hannah's Gate, although it was called by another name. The girls were Margo, Linda, and Claire, although they too had different names. There was a murder, but this time there was no Logan Jessup. The character representing Linda was the killer. It was a strange twisted story of jealousy and hatred.

Chilled, Claire finished reading it. Then she took the magazine into the kitchen. It was Irene Beston's day for doing the heavy cleaning. Claire murmured an excuse, and buried the magazine in a waste bin. She didn't want Dora to see it. Any mention to Carrie Day upset her mother.

Dora pretended that there had been no Carrie Day, no half-sister, and no Fergie. Claire agreed that it was better to let the past die. If only Leigh could do that, how much better off he would be. But she knew that he couldn't. Even after all these years, though he never spoke of it, she knew he was plagued by memories of the war.

Now the front door slammed and Elianne raced in. She was tall for her age, very slender. Her eyes were still too large for her face, deep brown and shining. Her hair had darkened to the same shade of auburn as Claire's, and covered her head in thick curls and waves. "Mama," she cried, "I've decided! I'm going to be an astronaut when I grow up!"

351

★ ★ ★

It was mid-October a year later.

Leigh said heavily, "We'll have to build a bomb shelter."

Dora paled. "A bomb shelter? Here? At Hannah's Gate?"

"You can't imagine what it's going to be like," he said.

Claire said softly, "Leigh . . . the children . . ."

"They might as well know." He looked at Gordon, then David. His eyes passed over Elianne as if she were invisible, although she sat at the table just opposite him. "You boys are going to have to help me. It's so we'll be safe from those Cuban missiles President Kennedy is talking about."

"But where . . . how?" Dora asked tremulously. "I don't understand."

"Of course you don't," Leigh told her. His eyes narrowed with memory. "But I do."

A few days before, President John Kennedy had announced that reconnaissance photographs showed sites on Cuba from which 2000-mile range missiles could be launched. He warned Russian cargo ships then approaching the island not to deliver more such weapons.

Now, as an extreme sense of danger engulfed the nation, Leigh was only one of many

352

planning to build shelters.

Within days, work was begun in the deep storage basement beneath the recently completed new wing at Hannah's Gate. The walls were double lined with concrete. The windows were bricked in. The door was reinforced with steel. Leigh had bunks installed, and an emergency electrical dynamo. He filled the place with canned foods, water jugs and medical supplies.

When it was finished, he proudly showed the family what he had done, leading Gordon and David down the steps. He impressed on them the need to lock the entry door behind them and to keep it locked after an attack, no matter who tried to get in. With Dora and Claire trailing after, he described what they must do when they heard the long wail of the air raid siren.

It was much safer here than at school, Elianne told him. There, the teacher had said, if they heard the warning, they were to hide under their desks and cover their heads.

Leigh ignored her comment.

That night Elianne came to her parents as they lay in bed. She clutched her doll, and whispered, "When will the bombs fall?"

Leigh heard but didn't answer.

Claire took her back to her own room. "We don't know for sure that they will."

"Could I bring my doll with me?"

"Of course. But I don't believe anything'll happen," Claire answered.

Still, there were many who thought as Leigh did. Air raid practices were conducted across the country. Bomb shelters were built in public buildings and in some private homes. How to deal with those who hadn't prepared themselves to survive was discussed at dinner tables and in pulpits, in television debates and town meetings.

The crisis passed. The bomb shelters remained, forgotten, abandoned. By August of the next year, Washington was talking about what was called the March on Washington, led by Martin Luther King, Jr. Two hundred thousand people, both black and white, demonstrated their belief in racial equality.

It was a calm and happy and hopeful day, filled with singing and prayers and speeches.

Two weeks later, four black children died when a church was bombed in Birmingham, Alabama.

That same week, as Claire read about the activities of a newly revitalized Klu Klux Klan in the South, Elianne came home from school and went to her room to change her clothes.

The shades were drawn. The corners of the room were filled with dark shadows. She hesitated on the threshold before going in. It was as if she had come upon a strange place. Unfamiliar. Frightening. It reminded her of that scary place called the bomb shelter. She drew a deep breath, made herself go in. She told herself not to be a baby. She was ten years old. There was nothing to be afraid of.

Still, she walked gingerly across the braided carpet. Midway to the closet, she froze. Something was lying on her bed, crumpled into the pillows. A ruffle of blue . . . a tangle of lace.

It was her favourite doll, the one Uncle Brett had given her. She forced herself to pick it up. It came apart in her hands. Arms, legs, small round head with real hair, rolled in all directions. Screaming, she stumbled out of the room.

Claire met her on the stairs. Elianne was white-faced, shivering. "My doll," she gasped. "My baby . . . broken, Mama!"

Later, after Elianne had cried herself into restless sleep, Claire looked at the remains of the doll. What had happened? She questioned Gordon and David. But Gordon shook his head, eyes wide and guileless. David stood behind his brother, peering around his shoulder, his small face expressionless. At last, Claire gave up. She put the pieces of the doll away, and bought Elianne another one. But Elianne accepted it without a smile. She set it on the window sill in her room, and never took it up again.

Claire was tired that grey November day in 1963. The evening before had been difficult. Gordon had refused to go to school that morning, and Leigh had allowed him to remain at home. David had broken his cat's leg, so that it had to be destroyed, and immediately the boy begged for another one. Leigh had agreed, saying it must have been an accident. But Claire insisted that they not get a replacement because David was too rough. Then Leigh had angrily accused her of favouring Elianne over the boys. Claire ended the argument by leaving the house.

Tired or not, it was good to get out. Dora had needed some things at People's Drug Store, so she went along.

The two women had almost finished shopping when there was a sudden bustle at the other end of the store. Groups formed, pressing together. Someone came in from the street, shouting, "It's true! I heard it on the car radio. The president has been shot in Dallas!"

Claire suddenly felt lost in emptiness. She remembered the day President Roosevelt had died. She had felt that she had lost a friend. She felt the same now, but more. Young, vital

Jack Kennedy had been murdered! "We'd better get home," she told her mother.

They made their way through clusters of weeping clerks and customers. There was an aura of fear in the place. What had happened? Who killed the president? Why?

And then a woman said, mouth twisted with ugly joy, "I hope he dies, God damn him!"

Dora swayed against Claire. Now she wept too.

Leigh was waiting when they arrived home. "Have you heard?"

They didn't have to answer. He could tell by their faces.

Claire heard voices from the television set in the study. "Have they . . . have they found out who did it?"

Leigh shook his head. "If they have, they're not saying. Not yet."

Later that afternoon the death of the president was announced in Dallas. Soon thereafter, Lyndon Johnson, the vice-president, took the oath of office, with Jacqueline Kennedy wearing a bloodstained suit looking on.

Washington seemed hushed as Claire and Leigh walked in dreary twilight on Wisconsin Avenue that evening.

They saw flashing lights. A long cortege of

357

cars drove before and behind a long grey ambulance surrounded by ranks of motorcycle policemen.

"It must be him," Leigh said softly. "They're probably going to Bethesda Naval Hospital." His arm went around Claire's shoulder.

It was a scene from a dream. The cortege rolled quickly up the empty avenue, lights blinking, soundless. Soon it disappeared from sight.

Leigh held her close. She felt a oneness between them, a sense of the real Leigh. It was as if the bad times had melted away. There were only the good days left. The days when they loved each other.

But, too soon, those moments were gone as if they had never existed.

Over the next five years the gulf between Claire and Leigh widened. Although he still went on occasional drinking bouts, their disagreements were now generally over the children. Leigh considered Elianne to be untrustworthy, temperamental, growing more like Rea with every birthday. To him, Gordon and David were all that they should be. They were boys, he said. Boys had to have freedom, to sow their wild oats. That's how it was, how Leigh wanted it to be.

Claire knew her sons to be spoiled, way-ward. She felt that Leigh's attitude was turn-ing Elianne into a rebellious teenager. But, seeing their faults, she loved all her three children equally, and did her best to counter Leigh's influence.

When Elianne was fifteen, she was tall and slim. She let her hair grow long. It fell loose, waving, to her waist. She wore black jeans that hugged her slender hips, and a black knit shirt that clung to her small breasts.

Leigh harangued her about her hair and clothes. He refused to allow her to go out with boys, saying he didn't trust her. He spoke to her only to criticize or ridicule her.

Claire protected Elianne, knowing how deeply the girl was hurt by her father's attitude. When Leigh took Gordon and David to football games, Claire took Elianne to mu-seums. When Leigh bought the boys expen-sive outfits, she did the same for Elianne, even though the girl refused to wear them, except on those few occasions when she went, with Dora, to visit Anna Taylor or a few others of their friends. By the time she was fifteen though, she refused to participate in those out-ings. Leigh shrugged. He didn't care if she went or stayed.

He seemed to care nothing at all about her. Actually he was obsessed by her. She had the same quality that Rea had had. He understood that much. But he didn't understand how deeply Rea had attracted him. How deeply Elianne attracted him now. He hid from his feelings in dislike and distrust. Even in his mind and heart.

Then, one afternoon in January of 1968, when Dora and Claire were out, Leigh heard Elianne come home from school. Soon the sound of music filled the house. He listened, hating the words and rhythms of the Bob Dylan song. Then he pounded on her door, yelling, "Elianne, stop that crap! I don't want to hear it any more."

The music was cut off abruptly. He stood outside the door, steaming. Finally he banged again. "Let me in. I want to talk to you."

The door opened slowly. The light was behind her, showing her slender silhouette, the narrow hips and high breasts.

"How can you stand that disgusting stuff?" he demanded. "It's immoral. It's rotten. It's corrupt."

"I like it," she said simply. She wished she could explain what the words meant to her, but she knew it was no use. Even if she could tell him, he wouldn't listen to her. He wouldn't understand.

"You would!" he yelled.

She started to close the door, but he kicked

it back. "I'm talking to you, damn it!"

"Sorry," she said.

"You're going to have to shape up, Elianne. You look like . . . like some bum off the street. I won't have it in my house. As long as you live here, you've got to do as I say."

She glared at him. What did he want? Why couldn't he leave her alone?

Her silence, her expression, enraged him even more. "Get your hair cut," he said. "Go down to the avenue and get a decent job done. I want you to look like a lady. Not like some tramp."

"No," she said. "No, I won't. I like it this way. All the girls wear it long now. Why should I be different?"

"Because I say so."

"I don't want to," she said.

He didn't answer. He stalked to his room, found a big pair of shears, and returned. He thrust the shears at her. "Okay. Do it now. While I'm watching. Don't argue with me."

When she refused the shears, he grabbed her by the shoulder, forced her down on the edge of the bed. Quickly, methodically, remembering the shaven heads of the collaborators he had seen in France when he was on his way home at the end of the war, he cut the hair from Elianne's head. He hacked away great clumps of it, close to her scalp, and let it fall from his fingers like silken rain.

When he finally stopped, Elianne's head was shorn except for a two inch brush, through which the scalp shone. He let her go, and she sagged, weeping, to the pillows.

Later, Claire found her that way. The girl's eyes were swollen, her face dead white.

Claire held her tightly. "I'm sorry. He shouldn't have done it, Elianne. But it'll grow back. In a few weeks, you won't even remember it happened."

"I'll remember," Elianne said.

She already knew that she was going to do. Her eyes went to the window, to the sky. She wasn't going to be like a caged bird forever. There was freedom out there. And she was going to it.

At dawn, carrying a small suitcase, she silently closed the iron gate in the wall around Hannah's Gate, and walked down Honey Locust Lane.

Chapter 21

The Missouri sky hung low, thick with clouds. A cold March wind whipped sheets of rain against the diner's windows.

Inside the air was hot, steamy with the odour of frying onions and beef patties.

Elianne hunched at the counter, sipping slowly at her coffee. A black cloth cap covered what short ends were left of her hacked-away hair. The bare nape of her neck looked very young. But her face seemed all angles and hollows, deep shadow beneath her eyes and below her too-prominent cheekbones. She was hungry, but her money was gone. She didn't even know how she would pay for the coffee she was drinking. She imagined herself pretending to go the bathroom, then slipping away when no one was looking.

But a man at the end of the counter was staring at her. He was big, his face windburned. He wore a star on his brown leather jacket, a big hat, dusty high boots. Some kind of policeman, she was sure. She tried to ignore his stubborn glare, to tell herself that it didn't mean anything. Wherever she'd been, always, people had looked hard at her. She guessed it was her clothes, her being alone. But why? What bothered them? There were many kids on the road. Elianne had seen lots of them, had linked up briefly with a few. How come nobody got used to them? How come nobody understood?

Now she slid another glance at the policeman. A big man, beefy. Yes, he was still staring at her.

What should she do? A quick shiver raced through her. She'd hoped to find someone here, a truck driver maybe, who was going on, further west. She'd come this far mostly with truck drivers. She couldn't wait here, though. Not with the policeman watching her. Any minute he'd get up and come over to her.

She slid off the counter stool, settling her jacket around her. Inside the bathroom, she leaned against the door. She counted to twenty, took a deep breath, and went out.

The policeman's big body closed off the narrow corridor. He didn't move when she approached him.

She finally managed a dry-throated, "Excuse me."

He grinned at her, his calloused fingers closing around her hand. "Where you going, girl?"

She couldn't answer, didn't try. Her mind had gone blank.

He set his lips, and breathed loudly through his nose. Suddenly there was something terrifying in his eyes. "You weren't going to pay, were you?"

"I only had a cup of coffee. I'd pay if I had money. I can wash dishes, if you want me to."

"*I* don't want you to wash dishes." His grin widened. He dragged her down the short corridor, across the diner, and through the steam-marked doors.

Rain and wind burned her cheeks. His fingers clenching into her arm burned her flesh. Headlights swept them as a dark van pulled in. A door slammed. A man — big, stooped and bearded — peered at them momentarily from beneath a wide-brimmed black hat.

The policeman showed his teeth in a grimace of disgust. "Looks like a whole tribe of you freaks coming through."

The man shrugged and went inside. But within moments he was back. In a slow deep voice, he said, "The lady in there, she says to tell you the coffee's paid for. So it's okay. And she doesn't want any trouble." As he spoke, his dark eyes seemed to shine out of the grooved shadows of his face. White teeth glimmered in the forest of his black beard.

The policeman spat. He turned away, saying over his shoulder, "Get your asses out of this town. Your kind isn't welcome here."

"Nor any place else much," the bearded man said to Elianne. And then: "Come on. I'll give you a ride." He didn't wait for an answer. He boosted her up to the front seat of the van, and pulled out quickly. He'd had experience with that stripe of cop. The less he had to do with them the better. There was an unpleasant squeezing in his gut.

She was saying, "Thank you. I don't know what would have happened if you hadn't come along when you did."

"It was meant to be," he told her, his voice soft and deep. "The time, the place . . . chosen." And slowly, "Listen to my mantra, you'll understand. 'Through love I serve all life . . . human, animal, the earth itself.' "

The words flowed around her, warm, gentle, a cloak engulfing her. He went on, "I have other mantras. I'll tell them to you and you can chose whichever one you want." His smile flashed. "But before that, I'll tell you my name. I'm Jake Babbitt. Who are you?"

She murmured, "Elianne."

He pushed back his hat. "You better come along with me. You're too young, aren't you, to be travelling all alone?"

"Come along where?" she asked.

"I'm going back to New Mexico. Taos. A place you've never heard of, I'm sure."

"New Mexico," she repeated. "Oh, but I have heard of it." And now, suddenly, she was excited. He was right. This meeting must have been meant to be. For New Mexico was where her Uncle Ian had lived. The uncle who had died before she was born. Her mother had spoken of him. How he had worked at a place called Los Alamos during the war, and was killed by a hit and run driver in Santa Fe.

Jake Babbitt listened as she explained. Then: "Kill City. That's what we call Los Alamos," he said sourly. "That's not like our place. Ours is Love City."

"Love City." She tried out the words. They were sweet on her tongue.

"Through love I serve all life . . . human, animal, and the earth itself," Jake said. And: "Now you say it."

She repeated his words. Tears stung her eyes. It was meant to be. She had sought freedom to find Jake Babbitt. To find love. She was certain of it. She said softly, "Yes, Jake. I'll go with you."

Suddenly the van swerved to the side of the road, slowed to a stop. He got out and went around to her side. He said, "Come on. Let's go in the back," and without waiting for her to answer, he pushed her ahead of him into the van. Her single quick glance took in a black sheen, a brilliant yellow rising sun at the top right of one long side. Golden rays spilled from it. Below them, in letters that seemed to drip like melted candles, Jake had printed 'Love Is Divine'.

Inside it was dark, the windows curtained, the floor covered with rugs. Boxes were stacked in the corners.

He said, "You know there's no free rides in this life, don't you? You pay for what you get?"

She nodded, rigid with sudden fright. She saw in his eyes what she had seen in the policeman's eyes back at the diner.

But then Jake said, "You're scared, aren't you? Don't be. I'm not going to hurt you. Don't you know that much?" She didn't believe him. But it was true.

He slid the cap off her head. She ducked down, flushing.

"No, no. Don't be ashamed," he said. He fingered her hair, and uneven bristles, some short and standing up straight, some matted and shaggy, but even so, silky to the touch. "How did it happen?"

She understood. It was so plainly an act of violence, not of vanity. This hadn't been done in a shop redolent of soaps and conditioners.

She hadn't sat before a mirror in which she would watch the neat shaping snips that would create a new Elianne. But there *had* been created a new Elianne. She whispered hoarsely, "My father."

"Ah," Jake said. "I see." His fingers spread wide to cup her head, to stroke and warm the chilled scalp beneath the uneven fuzz. Then his hand went to her pants and opened them, and slid down between her thighs to the silken curls that covered her mound. He twisted them around his fingers. He gathered them into small peaks, then smoothed them. He fluffed and flattened them. Soon he opened her shirt wide. Her breasts were small, but very round. He put his lips to each tiny nipple, his beard falling like a cashmere scarf along her shoulders as he pressed his face against her throat for a moment before sliding it down and into her armpit to kiss the short bristles there. He kissed them and licked them, and then, laughing so hard that his belly shook against her, he said, "You've got plenty of hair. Just let it grow. Let it grow again, and you'll be okay."

With that he was over her, and into her, pumping hard with his hips, and burrowing deeper with every thrust. She felt pain for only a moment. Then she was lifted, floating. She thought she would explode and blow up into death.

Suddenly he reared away, arching, his body a bow around its shaft, and her sense of having encased and held him, of having drawn him deep into her core, faded into the feeling that she was impaled on him. Impaled. Riven. She would explode and shatter into death, and be no more.

"Wait," he cried. "Wait. Don't move! Tell me again, quick. Remind me of your name. I can't fuck you if I don't remember your name."

Her breath broken on her lips, she gasped her name.

He misheard her. "Ella," he said. "Ella em."

Then his bowed body straightened. They were belly to belly, mouth to mouth, hip to hip, bodies pumping. Finally the world shattered. They fluttered together in empty space before slowly drifting into sleep.

Later, when she awakened, she remembered. She thought it was only right that she should have a new name. She had exploded, not into death, but into a new life. Ella Em. She liked the sound of it then, and for some time thereafter.

Lying beside him, wanting him to touch her again, she thought that she must love him because how else could she know such pleasure in him if she didn't. With time she learned that what she felt with him wasn't love, but that she could know the same joy with other men, men Jake gave her to.

But now he whispered, "My love opens the gates to life."

Those seemed to her, then, the truest words she'd ever heard.

She didn't know that Jake had invented that phrase, and all the other ones he offered to her along the way, just as he had invented himself.

For him, it began in June of 1964. He was twenty-six years old, an off again on again graduate student. He had volunteered to be part of a voter registration drive in Mississippi. He had been trained in Oxford, Ohio, and then, along with several hundred others, had been sent to Jackson, Mississippi.

He could remember a special day. Sunny. Warm. The hum of locusts in the hot damp air. The light achingly bright. He'd been assigned to a group. The three others were Chaney, Schwerner, and Goodman. Chaney, a young Negro from Mississippi. Schwerner and Goodman, both Jews, and from New York. They were going to look at a burned out church. Jake dragged himself to where they were waiting for him beside the Ford station wagon. He told them he couldn't go, not that day. He was having a bad belly ache, the kind that wouldn't let him get in a car for a long trip. They understood. They grinned, commiserated, waved goodbye, and got into the station wagon. They drove into Neshoba County, and vanished from the face of the earth.

When Jake heard that they had disappeared, he knew. They were dead. They'd been killed. He kept seeing their faces before him. The dark one. The two white ones. All grinning. He kept thinking that he should have been with them. Whatever had happened to them, should have happened to him.

In August the three bodies were found. They had been shot. Their joint memorial stone had been only six miles from Philadelphia, Mississippi, the freshly built earthen dam in which their bodies had been hidden.

Before the disappearance of the three, Jake had known who he was. With their going, he was lost. His past, the man he had been then, was dead too. He no longer knew hope or faith. By the time the three bodies were found, Jake had given up his work in voter registration. He drifted away from the few friends he had made, and went on the road.

By December, when twenty-one Neshoba County men were arrested for involvement in the deaths of the three, Jake had already begun to invent himself, and to invent a new language in which he could express what he felt, and to search out a new life where he could forget the cruelty of the one he had turned from.

He found the place on a small plot of land outside Taos, in the hills of northeastern New Mexico. He settled there in a leanto he built himself. Slowly he gathered to him a small group of wanderers. He taught them in his new language. They called the place Love City. They called their language the words of love. When he sat on the wooden platform he had them built for him, on what looked like a throne, although he called it a chair, he felt like the father of them all. They were his children. They loved him. He loved them.

Now, four years later, the new Jake got behind the wheel of the van. He looked sideways at Elianne. "Okay, Ella Em. We're on our way."

It was two weeks since they had met. It was 4th April, 1968. They were in a small cafe on Cerillos Road. The Beatles were singing. The music suddenly stopped. A voice shouted that Martin Luther King, Jr. had been shot a few moments before in Memphis, Tennessee.

There was a buzz of conversation. People stared at each other. But Jake pushed back his chair. "Come on, Ella Em. Let's get out of here." His face was sagging, pale. His hair, beard, both looked wild. He caught her hand, dragged her outside, ignoring her anxious, "What's wrong, Jake. What happened?"

He climbed into the van as if pursued. He drove blindly, heading for Love City, heading for sanctuary. In his mind he saw the three smiling faces . . . the Ford station wagon . . . "I love," he whispered. "I love, I love, therefore I am divine."

The van chugged and coughed, always climbing, as the road snaked through the snow-covered hills.

Elianne leaned against Jake, watching the glimmer of red rock flash and fade, the squat pinion trees, their green limbs sheathed in glittering ice coats. With every mile they left turmoil behind. They left their pasts behind.

As they slowly climbed the long narrow looping horseshoe curve toward the pass at the top of Pilar Hill, a pickup truck came up behind them. Its horn blared once, twice, raucous and commanding. Jake smiled within his beard. The van coughed and rattled and backfired.

The pickup truck spun to the dusty shoulder and flashed by on the right. A Greyhound bus passed, heading south. Up ahead, within their view across the gulf of a ravine, the truck made a u-turn. Within moments it was abreast of them.

Its windows were open. Three young men leaned towards them shouting obscenities. A hail of beer cans beat a sudden tattoo on the van.

Then the pickup was gone. But the relief was short-lived. Again it came up behind them. But that time it didn't swing out and go by. It rode right on the van's tail. Then it worked close. It bumped the van. There was a jolt, another, one more. Three times it hit the back of the van. Then it swung out, passed by.

Jake gave it the peace sign.

The driver gave him the finger, yelling, "Fucking hippies!"

"Welcome to Taos Valley," Jake said, laughing.

It was like a nightmare. Suddenly real. Just as suddenly gone. Elianne let her breath out slowly. They were in the pass. The valley spread out below them. Small houses, chimneys breathing blue puffs of smoke were scattered across it. The gorge of the Rio Grande River looked, from that angle, like a jagged black scar gouged into the earth.

By then, she had begun to think of herself

as Ella Em. A new name for a new life. She had come so far that the memory of home had already begun to fade. She had become Ella Em, who chewed the magic mushroom, and smoked pot, and dropped acid. Ella Em, who wanted to follow Jake wherever he led, and to believe in him, and who thought that peyote and marijuana and LSD would carry her, as a mother carries her child, at his side.

Jake said softly, "Say the words, Ella Em."

Her eyes still searching the valley, she said, "I see the Divine in every person. I am in tune with destiny and with myself, because I love."

"And now we're almost at Love City," he told her.

He rolled a cigarette, lit up and took a deep drag, exhaling slowly.

She watched him patiently. She already knew the rules. First it was his turn. Always. Then, maybe it would be her turn. She couldn't be sure. She could only hope.

Finally he grinned, and allowed her to take one deep lungful of smoke before he took the butt back. Sucking on it, he let the van drift down the long hill that led into the valley, to Ranchos de Taos, then Taos itself, and beyond it to the ancient pueblo, and beyond all three to the place he called Love City.

Elianne savoured the languor that spread through her, breathing deeply of the sweetish air in the van. Soon she smiled. The valley, the sky, were aglow.

Chapter 22

Late that same April day the killer of Martin Luther King, Jr. was identified as an escaped convict named James Earl Ray.

That night, and for several days thereafter, the Negro citizens of 168 towns and cities across the country exploded in anguish and anger. King's voice had been silenced; their own voices had been silenced. They took to the streets.

Television screens were filled with scenes of destruction in Harlem, Detroit, Chicago and Los Angeles.

Smoke hung over the trees of Washington. Fires blazed along 14th Street, along H Street, along 7th Street. Shattered store windows flung dangerous spikes into the roads. Mobs raced from shop to shop, screaming. Looting began in the liquor stores, which, when emptied, were put to the torch. It spread to food stores, radio and television shops, cleaners and clothing stores. White-owned, Negro-owned businesses went down together, as police sirens wailed and ambulances snaked through the boisterous crowds, and fire engines whooped through half-blocked intersections.

A curfew had been established from seven P.M. to seven A.M. No traffic passed along Honey Locust Lane. At the end of the block, but visible from Hannah's Gate, there were two National Guard jeeps filled with armed soldiers.

Claire supposed they were there in case of trouble on Connecticut Avenue. It pained her to see them. She had lived in Washington all her life. She had never expected anything like this to happen.

Perhaps she had been blind, and hadn't known it.

Leigh said he was going out. When she reminded him about the curfew, he said he wasn't worried about it.

His hair was flecked with grey now, his eyes permanently bloodshot. There were deep frown lines across his forehead, and wide furrows grooved his cheeks. His jawline sagged, the scar faded to a crooked ropey grey thread. At fifty-one, he seemed older than his age.

He saw concern in her eyes, and thought, God, she's a pretty woman still. He liked the way she did her hair. It was long, and she wore it rolled into a French twist. Her face was thinner than it had been when she was in her twenties. It made her eyes seem even larger, deeper, darker.

But it no longer mattered how desirable a woman she was. She had always wanted too much from him, and had ended up wanting nothing at all. He returned the compliment.

He was restless. He had to escape her reproachful look. Ever since Elianne had run away, proving that she was another Rea, as he'd thought all along, Claire had treated him as if he were a leper. He wasn't. He'd been right. Now he wanted to get drunk, to have a good time. He wanted to forget. A rest from his memories. A good long rest. Oblivion.

Before leaving the house, he went to say goodnight to Gordon and David. Gordon was twelve now, a full-faced stocky boy, his hair a mixture of auburn and brown. His eyes were deep-set, brooding. David was ten, skinny, quiet, with sandy hair and eyes. Gordon was out-going, stubborn about having his own way. He bullied David. David gave in easily, but had a sticking point. When he was pushed to it, he exploded into violent tantrums.

Leigh didn't see that Gordon was a bully, nor that David's tantrums were not normal. He idolized both boys, and gave them whatever they asked for so they were surfeited with toys, games, and clothes.

The cottage at the pool had become their

play room, and Leigh's. In it there were pin-
ball machines, a pool table, a gym with ropes
and rings and chinning bars, as well as a bas-
ketball hoop. Now, only months after having
everything installed, the boys rarely went
there. They had short attention spans, tried
everything briefly, remained interested in
nothing for very long. Leigh didn't see that
either.

In fact, he used the play room more than
the boys did. He had found an old 1950s
Wurlitzer juke box, and scores of records, and
kept them in the cottage. He liked to play
'Praise the Lord and Pass the Ammunition',
and 'Pistol Packin' Mama' and 'The White
Cliffs of Dover', the volume on high, so that
the property echoed with the sound of World
War II songs.

Now, as he went into the early April dusk,
he hummed another of those songs, 'I'll Walk
Alone', but he was thinking about his sons.
They belonged in Hannah's Gate. And it
would be theirs. He'd see to it somehow, and
later it would belong to *their* sons.

He drove down Connecticut Avenue. The
street was quiet, but there were sirens in
the distance. Some smoke still rose over the
eastern part of the city.

He stopped at a bar he knew. Although it
was closed, the owner was inside and let Leigh

in, locking the door behind him. Later, in a half-empty hotel lounge, the television set blaring news about looting on H Street, he continued to drink. After a while he noticed that a young girl was sitting nearby. He liked her slim ankles, the curve of her throat. He offered to buy her a drink.

"Sorry, Pops," she said. "I'm waiting for my boyfriend."

He sent her one anyway, and she nodded her thanks.

But then he wasn't looking at her. He didn't even notice when she left with a young man. He was staring into his glass, remembering Jeri.

Claire read the page twice, realized that she wasn't absorbing the words, and let the book fall to her lap.

It was near midnight. Somehow, in spite of the city curfew, Leigh had found a place where he could drink, and by the time he returned home, he would be drunk.

But she wouldn't have to deal with him. It had been nearly a year since he had touched her, nearly a year since she had moved back to her old bedroom, where the squirrels rustled in the wistaria vine, and she could look down the yard to where the Merrill house had once stood, when Leigh had been a young man coming to Hannah's Gate to visit with Ian.

That night, nearly a year before, Leigh had come home late too. She had lain sleepless, staring through the open window at the June sky. She'd heard him stagger on the stairs. He'd slammed the door open, banged it shut, muttering noisily.

She shut her eyes tightly, fingers clenched into the light coverlet under which she lay rigid.

"You can't be sleeping," he said. "You've been waiting for me the way you always do."

"And you're drunk, the way you sometimes are." She got up, took her robe. "I'm tired," she said. "I need my rest." She walked out, closing the door firmly behind her. She went down the hall to the room that had been hers before she and Leigh were married.

The next morning she had moved her clothes. She said nothing to Leigh about it, and he said nothing to her.

She wondered now why she hadn't done it years before. Why had she waited?

Now, with a glance at the clock, she set aside her book. He wouldn't disturb her when he came home. Sober or drunk, he wouldn't come to her room. He no longer wanted her. Just as she no longer wanted him.

Still, as dawn touched the street with pale light, and she hadn't heard him come in, she was concerned. She looked out of the window even as she reminded herself that it wouldn't be the first time he hadn't come home.

But that night was different. There were radio reports of angry youths roving the city. Sirens wailed through the dark, and smoke rose from smouldering buildings.

Suddenly she was filled with a deep fear. What had happened to him? Why hadn't he returned home yet?

The morning passed slowly. By noon, she was frantic.

At last there was a call from a downtown hotel. The night clerk told her that Leigh was there. He seemed to be ill . . .

It took her less than fifteen minutes to reach the place. Leigh's room stank of whiskey and cigarettes.

He lay full clothed on the bedspread. His face was grey, eyes half-open. His breaths were slow, rasping. She cried, "Call an ambulance. Hurry."

The man scurried from the room as she bent over Leigh, and took his hand. It was limp, cold. "Leigh," she said softly. "It's Claire. Wake up, Leigh."

He didn't acknowledge her. His breaths came slowly, with long frightening pauses between each one.

The twenty-two years of their marriage

were gone now. To her, he was once again the boy he had been before he went away, lithe and smiling in his uniform. He was the old Leigh, the Leigh she had loved with all her heart.

She spoke to him, reminding him of their good days together: the rides in Rock Creek Park, spaghetti by candlelight at the Roma. When he didn't respond, she spoke of Gordon and David, his sons who needed him. Her mind was full of Elianne too. Elianne, who had been gone now, without a trace, for just over three months. But she didn't mention Elianne, or the search for her of which he so disapproved. Instead Claire spoke of all he still wanted to do at Hannah's Gate.

It was twenty minutes before help arrived. The room was suddenly full of men, thrusting her aside, bending over Leigh. They slapped an oxygen mask on his face, bundled him in blankets, and carried him away on a stretcher.

She rode with him in the ambulance, its siren leaving a long trail of sound as it raced through the nearly empty streets.

The hospital emergency room was crowded. Burn cases. Cuts from broken glass, from knives. A few gunshot wounds.

Leigh was carried away. An hour later, she was led, trembling, into a small cubicle separated from the rest of the place by pale curtains. Two white-coated physicians leaned over the gurney on which Leigh lay.

She saw that his eyes were still half-open. His face shiny with sweat, and grey. There was an intravenous needle in his arm. A tube snaked up his nose, held in place by white tape.

"You're his wife?" one of the physicians asked. And at her nod: "How long has he been drinking so much?"

"So much?" she repeated. "I don't know. Off and on. For years. But not every day. Just . . . just sometimes."

Leigh's breathing had changed now. The rasp was deeper, the pauses between them longer.

The physicians moved away from him, motioned her forward.

She bent over Leigh. "Listen to me," she said. "Leigh, listen. You'll be all right. Try to hear me. Try to talk to me. It's Claire. I'm here with you, Leigh."

A long silent moment passed. Then, slowly, Leigh's half-open eyes become fully open. "Claire," he said hoarsely.

"Yes. I'm here."

A small smile touched his pale lips. He muttered, "It wasn't the way you'd thought it would be, was it?"

"It will be all right," she said.

He didn't answer. His eyes closed.

She looked fearfully at the doctors. One drew her to the doorway, and told her Leigh was suffering from alcohol poisoning. There were signs that his kidneys were failing. It was impossible to predict what would happen.

For three days, Leigh lay like that, unmoving, unknowing, while his face slowly swelled until the grooves and wrinkles in his flesh were gone, and the scar stretched thick and dark along his jaw.

Then, one sunny afternoon, while Claire sat beside him, he drew a long rasping breath, and the pause that came after it never ended, but went on forever, for him.

A nurse slowly drew a sheet over his face.

Claire mourned for Leigh, for the life they might have had together, the life that they hadn't had. She spent sleepless nights wondering what she should have done, how she could have helped him.

Perhaps if she had left him . . . She had thought of it. But she had done nothing. Suppose she had told him to leave Hannah's Gate? He would have refused. There was too much of him in Hannah's Gate now. With his reconstruction, he had made it his own. And he would never have given it up. Nor would he have given up Gordon and David. So, though she had thought of it, she had never been able to decide to divorce him.

Perhaps if they had never married . . . But he had needed her. What would have happened to him if she hadn't married him? How would he have lived these past twenty-two years?

She never knew the answer. But with time she realized that she must turn her back on the past, look forward to the future.

She had Gordon and David to raise to manhood, and she had to find Elianne.

In the days after her disappearance, Claire had gone to the police, ignoring Leigh's sour protests. The police said that for teenaged girls to run away these days was common. They soon returned home or called for money. Some way, somehow, the Merrills would hear from Elianne.

But that didn't happen. Eventually Claire traced Detective Eagan, whom she'd known from when Margo and Linda were killed. He was retired now, but he was willing to listen to her. He suggested a private investigator. The man worked on the case for several months, and came up empty-handed, except that he seemed certain that Elianne had been seen at a diner in a small Missouri town. After that, nothing.

Still, after Leigh's death, Claire persisted. She advertised widely, as the investigator suggested. Whenever she saw newspaper pictures of groups of young people, either at demonstrations — and there were many of them in those days — or at other public gatherings, she studied them with a magnifying glass, searching for someone who looked like Elianne. There were many long-haired girls, but none of them was her daughter.

Gradually, as after every crisis in Claire's life, her days began to resume a kind of normalcy. She was busy with the house, with the boys, trying to be both mother and father to them now that Leigh was gone.

Brett visited from Boston several times, bringing Keith with him. Brett had never remarried, but seemed content. He never spoke of Rea, and Claire supposed that was just as well.

At the end of the year Anna Taylor invited her to a dinner party with Dora.

They accepted the invitation, Dora atwitter with excitement at the thought of her first social outing in a long time.

Dora was sixty-seven years old now. Her hair was white, cut short and waved. She was slim and straight. She looked younger than she had in many years. She felt different too. She had been frightened when Leigh was alive. Afraid of his temper, his drinking, the scenes he made. But most of all she had been fearful because she had begun to feel that Hannah's Gate was no longer her own. With every change Leigh made, her home felt less and less hers, and more and more his. Now, freed from her long-time unspoken worry, she allowed herself to enjoy whatever she wanted to.

So she picked over her dresses, decided she needed a new one for Anna's dinner, and went to Erlbacher's. She chose a dark blue silk, with a high ruffled collar. When she brought it home she happily modelled it for the boys and Claire.

Claire too was pleased at Anna's invitation. She wore a long black skirt and a white satin blouse. When she put on the black jet bib necklace Leigh had given her years before, she remembered how much he had disliked going to Anna's house, where he would always meet friends of his uncle's. She supposed the same thing would happen at the dinner. But she would be glad to see those same people, and be happy to talk with them of Jeremiah. It was as she had expected. She saw many old friends, many who had known Leigh and Jeremiah. But there were several new faces too.

Among them was an Englishman named

Oliver Duvaney. He was formally introduced to her as Lord Creighton, but everyone called him Ollie. He was very tall and slender, with thick greying hair and bright expressive eyes. He had with him his wife, Lady Agatha. She was a small, bird-like woman, with thinning black hair, cut short, and protruding dark eyes. She clung tightly to her husband's hand.

When he was introduced to Claire, Agatha murmured to him, "Ollie, Ollie, I don't like this place. Let's go home."

Startled, Claire stepped back.

Oliver Duvaney said softly, "Forgive my wife. She's not well." And later, when Anna was sitting with Agatha, Ollie came to Claire and said, "It's why we're here in the States, you see. Something has happened to her." He gave his wife a sad sideways glance. "If you'd known her before . . ."

"Please don't apologize," Claire said quickly. "Please don't explain."

"You're very kind," Ollie said, and moved away, but later Claire saw that he was looking at her across the room.

Just before the butler announced that dinner was served, Carrie Day hurried in, breathlessly apologizing to Anna for being so late.

It had been twenty-three years, Claire realized with a shock, since she had seen Carrie, although many years before she had read one of her short stories. Carrie was in her fifties now. Her once sandy hair was blonde, a cap of tiny curls. She was bigger than ever, thick in the waist, broad in the breast. She wore black jersey, with a wide white lace collar, and low-heeled black shoes.

Claire greeted her briefly. She thought of Margo and Linda. She pictured Rea smiling at Logan Jessup.

"And how are you?" Carrie asked.

Claire said she was fine.

"I was sorry to read about your husband's death," Carrie said. "It was sudden, wasn't it?"

"Yes," Claire agreed.

"And so young," Carrie went on.

Claire nodded, moved on to speak to someone else.

Dora watched Carrie from across the room, the joy gone from her. She hadn't seen Carrie since that awful day at Hannah's Gate. She had hoped never to see her again.

She was seething when she went in to dinner and found that Carrie was seated across from her, looking at her. She and Dora exchanged long hard silent stares, and then deliberately turned their eyes elsewhere.

Later, Dora cornered Anna and asked,

"What's that woman doing here? She's not our kind of people."

Anna looked surprised. "Why, Dora, she gave me to understand that she knew you well, was related in some way. I was startled that you didn't speak to her."

"She's no relation of mine," Dora snapped.

Anna fluttered mascared lashes. "My dear, she's doing an article about Washington hostesses. And someone suggested I ought to be included. She's a well-known writer. And these days, that's how it's done."

"I think I ought to tell you that she rented a room at Hannah's Gate during the war. That's how I know her. And I don't want to know more of her."

"Dora, I *am* sorry," Anna said. "I should have consulted you."

"I swear, I don't know what the world's coming to," Dora said, but she smiled. "Well, never mind. How were you to know? The woman's an awful liar."

When she and Claire prepared to leave at the end of the evening, Oliver Duvaney came to bid them goodbye. "I hope we meet again," he said, smiling at Claire.

"Perhaps we will," she said lightly.

"If you ever come to England . . ."

His wife appeared at his side, tugged his hand. "Ollie, I'm afraid. Let's go home."

Claire said her goodbyes quickly, and she and Dora left.

"Whatever's the matter with that woman?" Dora said, as she got into the car. "And what a handsome man."

"Is he?" Claire asked.

"Don't tell me you didn't notice," Dora retorted.

Claire shrugged. "Oh, what does it matter? I'll never see him again."

Two months later, in a magazine called the *District Liner*, there was a long article by Carrie Day. It described the dinner party at Anna Taylor's Georgetown house, mentioned Lord and Lady Creighton, who were the guests of honour, and also mentioned Dora Loving, the daughter of Big Jack Gowan, the one-time congressman who had had to resign his office because of a barely-hushed-up scandal. It also mentioned her daughter, Claire Loving Merrill, the widow of Leigh Merrill, who had died less than a year ago of an unidentified illness. Leigh Merrill, Carrie wrote, had been well-known for restoring Hannah's Gate, the Cleveland Park site of two mysterious deaths more than twenty years before.

Chapter 23

Though Claire was certain that she would never see Oliver Duvaney again, the thought of him and his wife lingered in her mind. She imagined his smile, the lines fanning out from his eyes. She pictured his carriage, so straight, yet relaxed. She remembered small, grey-skinned Agatha, hanging on his arm, flinching when spoken to, and murmuring, "Ollie, I don't like this place. I want to go home."

On a bright sunny day at the end of March, two months after Richard Nixon was inaugurated as president, Anna Taylor came to Hannah's Gate for tea. The wind was cold that afternoon, but the forsythia that Leigh had had planted made brilliant yellow torches on the back terraces.

The three women sat at a table near the window in the study. The room was much the same as it had been in Big Jack's day. The bookcases still held his old books. His desk remained there too, but had been moved to a corner. His chair had been recovered. New upholstery encased the original sofa. The drapes were pale green linen now instead of brown velvet.

Dora poured tea for Anna and Claire, and then sat back, prepared to hear what gossip was presently making the rounds in Georgetown. With the Nixons in the White House the social scene in Washington would change. Every president brought his own style to the city.

But Anna didn't begin with Georgetown gossip. She sipped her tea, and sighed, and said, "It's such a pity about Agatha Duvaney." Her eyes slid sideways to study Claire. "You do remember her, don't you? Ollie Duvaney's wife. You met them both at my house last winter."

Claire nodded. Yes, she remembered.

"At least Carrie Day didn't mention that in her damnable article," Anna said.

"Didn't mention what?" Dora asked. "She wrote about just about everything, I thought."

"About Agatha's odd behaviour. Perhaps Carrie didn't notice, but I've heard from friends in London . . . Poor Agatha's losing her mind. Some sort of premature senility. And there's no treatment. Just a constant deterioration," Anna went on. "I can't imagine what Ollie will do." And, sighing, "You know, she's only forty-nine."

Claire glanced at herself in a nearby mirror.

She had only recently turned forty-nine herself. Thinking of Agatha Duvaney, she shuddered. The woman's sing-song voice still echoed in her mind.

Agatha's skin had been sallow, wrinkled as a crumpled handkerchief. Her hair, a dark brown, had hung limp around her cheeks. Her fashionable clothing had drooped on her inadequate frame.

Forty-nine. Claire stole a second glance at herself. Her hair was thick, a rich deep auburn, with only a few strands of silver. Her skin was smooth and unlined. Her eyes were the same dark unfaded brown of her youth. But who knew how long that would last? What had happened to Agatha Duvaney could happen to anyone.

Still, for now, Claire knew that she was a very good-looking woman. Men were drawn to her, and showed it. It was nearly a year since Leigh's death. She received frequent invitations. But she was wary of accepting them. She didn't want to lead anyone on, only to reject him later. She found the idea of a close relationship, of marriage, frightening. She wasn't sure she was a good chooser of men, and she never forgot that falling in love meant risking hurt. So she offered no encouragement to those who tried to express an interest in her.

Anna Taylor went on to speak of other people. After she had gone, Dora said thoughtfully, "I wonder if Oliver Duvaney will be coming for another visit? It would be nice if he did." Dora rose, gathered the tea cups. "Nice if you were to see him again."

"It's not likely," Claire told her.

Yet she thought of him often, and wasn't surprised when she received a long-delayed brief note from him, expressing pleasure at having met her, and asking her to contact him if she were ever in London. She read his words twice, then tore the note to shreds. She didn't intend to seek him out, even if she were in London, which she didn't expect to be, in any event.

Still, when she decided that she must take Gordon away for a few months, the first place she thought of was England.

It began on a grey morning at the end of the month. A call came from Sidwell Friends, the school that Gordon and David attended. Gordon was then thirteen, David eleven. The call alerted Claire that there was trouble. Gordon wasn't in school that day, and he had had three absences in the past two weeks. Was he ill? she was asked. Was he at home?

Gordon wasn't ill. He wasn't at home. If he wasn't at school, Claire didn't know where he was. He had left at the usual time that morning.

A car was missing from the school parking lot, she was told. Gordon and three other boys had been seen there, but none of them had shown up in their classrooms. If Mrs Merrill heard from Gordon, would she call at once?

She was trembling when she put down the phone. What could have happened? Where was Gordon? What had he done?

Claire wished that Leigh had never taught the boy to drive. She had protested when he did. Gordon was too young, she had told Leigh. His judgment wasn't good, not even for a twelve year old, as he was at the time. But Gordon had begged Leigh, promising he'd never drive without a licence, except in the driveway at Hannah's Gate. And, as always, Leigh had given in.

Pacing the floor, Claire waited. When David came home, she questioned him. But he knew nothing. They had gone to Sidwell Friends together that morning, as usual. Gordon had said nothing about leaving. He wasn't speaking to his brother, David admitted. Gordon was mad at him. When Claire asked why, David said he didn't want to talk about it. His gaze was wide, guileless. Claire knew that meant nothing. Over the years David had learned to conceal his feelings.

In the late afternoon Claire had a call from the school. The police had recovered the car. The four boys in it were safe, although there had been an accident on the George Washington Parkway in Maryland. She was asked to come to the school immediately.

When she turned into the parking lot off Wisconsin Avenue, she saw two police cars. They reminded her of the cars converging on a snowy afternoon near the Potomac near where Logan Jessup had fallen to his death. Hurrying now through bright spring sunlight, she went inside to the headmaster's office.

Gordon was there, with three other boys. His dark hair was tousled, his eyes sullen.

The headmaster greeted her, then said, "The boys took a car from the lot and went joyriding. Gordon was driving." He paused. Then: "There'll be no charges preferred. But we feel that Gordon, and the others, must be suspended for a year."

On the way home, she asked, "What made you do it, Gordon? You know better. You're too young to have a driver's licence. The law applies to you as well as everyone else."

He said defiantly, "The boys were teasing. Saying I was a liar. Saying I didn't know how to drive. So I decided to show them."

"You stole a car, wrecked it."

"I borrowed it for a little while. And I didn't wreck it. If that goddam fool Amers hadn't grabbed the wheel . . ."

"Why did he?"

"He was scared," Gordon sneered.

If only Gordon were sorry, she thought. If only he realized how wrong he'd been. All the seeds Leigh had sown, that she'd allowed him to sow, seemed to be flowering now. Or was this not uncommon behaviour for a thirteen year old? Was she making too much of it, feeling this sinking in her heart? Why was her intuition telling her that today was only the beginning?

Was it because of Elianne? For so many years she had tried to make up to her for her father's dislike. In the end, she had been unsuccessful, and had lost her daughter. Was that why she was so fearful for Gordon? Because she had learned that if the beginning were bad, so the ending would be?

It had been a difficult year for David and Gordon. Before they'd had Leigh, the three of them a club, with Claire excluded. Now they must feel frighteningly alone.

Still, after some thought, she decided that the best thing to do was to take Gordon away for a while. Take him out of the environment of Sidwell Friends, the neighbourhood, the boys he knew.

That was when she thought of England. She felt better immediately. The three of them would go on a trip. They would tour England, go sightseeing in London. They would learn something by travelling, and perhaps the change, being away from Hannah's Gate, would help them.

On the first day of June, 1969, they sailed for England on the *America*. Five days later, they landed at Southampton and went by boat train to London.

By then, Claire was beginning to wonder if she'd made a mistake. The boys had been difficult during the crossing. David was withdrawn as always, Gordon sullen, rebuffing every effort she made to establish warmth between them.

Although they rarely spoke of Leigh, she knew that the boys had both been intensely affected by his death.

They travelled through England and Scotland, an uneasy trio. The boys were rarely enthusiastic. Gordon came alive only when stuffing himself on scones and clotted cream, David when viewing the prisoners' quarters at the Tower of London. She considered cutting the trip short and returning home.

After a month's sightseeing the country, they settled in London at the Cavendish Hotel in Jermyn Street. It was old, but beautifully kept, and had been recommended to her as quieter and less fashionable than either the Savoy or Dorchester, which was why she had chosen it. For, although she had inherited Jeremiah's fortune on Leigh's death, she still didn't think of herself as a wealthy woman. She wore jewels and furs, but within her there remained the girl who remembered the depression, remembered too the time when rooms were rented at Hannah's Gate because money was in short supply.

She and the boys had a pleasant two-bedroom suite, with a small sitting room between, and shared an enormous bathroom, with a tub larger than any she had seen before.

Gordon began taking an interest. He and David ambled around the city, exploring Carnaby Street and all of Soho, walking along the Thames Embankment, watching the changing of the guard at Buckingham Palace. Sometime the three of them made excursions together, and Claire saw that the boys were at last beginning to enjoy themselves. David too began to show a new enthusiasm. He suggested repeated trips to Hyde Park Corner to listen to the political harangues, and led them from one soap box speaker to another, saying nothing but plainly dividing his attention equally between the speakers and the hecklers. Claire began to feel better about the trip.

One day, when Gordon and David were at the British Museum, she decided to go for a walk by herself. By then it was mid-July, a bright beautiful day. Window boxes were filled with purple and red and white impatiens, and splashed colour along the grey stone facades of the buildings. Buskers, playing guitars and flutes, gathered at one corner. On another there was a flower stall almost buried in a blanket of yellow and white roses.

A newspaper flyer caught Claire's eyes as she waited to cross the busy roadway. Tragedy at *Chappaquidick*. She didn't know where Chappaquidick was. But the name Kennedy in smaller print caught her eye. She bought a paper and stood there, reading the long front page article about Ted Kennedy, and the speculation about what had happened on Martha's Vineyard.

Sighing, she folded the paper and tucked it under her arm. She turned to cross the street, but found her way blocked.

Oliver Duvaney stood there, smiling down at her, eyes shining, his face aglow with obvious delight. She knew that she was seeing him as he had been when young . . . young and unmarked by sophistication and disappointment. She was seeing the boy who had remained within the shell of the man.

At last he said, "Claire, how happy I am

to see you. I told you we'd meet again. And how long have you been in London?"

"About a month," she said. She remembered tearing up the note she had had from him. The shreds had fallen like snowflakes from her fingers. She had decided she wouldn't call him. That she'd never see him again. Chance had decreed otherwise. And she was glad.

"You didn't telephone me," he said reproachfully. Then: "Come on. We can't talk here. The pubs are closed, so let's go back to your hotel."

She was too pleased to see him to refuse.

They returned to the Cavendish, and settled in the residents' lounge. She was relieved that he took an easy chair across the small table from her. She needed that distance between them. The urge she felt to touch him, to take his hand, unnerved her.

He sat back, smiling at her still. She saw that he was taking in every detail of her appearance, and plainly he approved of what he saw.

She felt the same about him. He had such a clean, well-turned-out look. His hair was perfectly cut. He was closely shaven. His casual jacket sat exactly right on his shoulders.

When their sherry was before them, he said, "Now, tell me. What has happened to you since we last met?"

She thought of the repeated short notes she had had, reporting no success in the search for Elianne. But she said nothing of that. Instead she spoke of Gordon's escapade, about their travels, and their time in London.

"And how long will you stay?" he asked.

She said she didn't know. Perhaps for another few weeks.

He leaned toward her. "Make it longer, Claire. For my sake. Give me a chance."

"Ollie," she said, "you've told me nothing about your wife."

"She's not well." He paused. Then: "Oh, Christ, I might as well say it. She's much worse. I must have constant help to keep her at home. She can't be left alone."

"I'm sorry," Claire said softly. He looked so lost now, woebegone, suddenly old and tired.

"I know you are. And she was a wonderful woman. But she's no longer Agatha Duvaney. That woman, my wife, is dead, Claire." His eyes suddenly shone with suppressed tears.

"There's no hope?" Claire asked.

"The only hope, now, is . . . is escape for her, for what's left of her. Escape."

Claire knew that he meant escape into death.

He said, "We can't change that. So we must make do with what we have. I want to see you. We'll have dinner together soon. All right?"

"Oh, Ollie, I don't know. I'm so busy with the boys . . ." She heard herself say the words, and knew she didn't mean them.

"Make time for me," he said. He dropped some money on the table next to their untouched sherries. "I must go now. But I'm very happy to see you, Claire." He strode away, giving her no time to respond.

Later, back in her suite, she decided that it might be better if they didn't meet again. He was still a married man. His wife had a terrible illness. And Claire had suddenly felt, as she sat across from him, a quickening in her body that she hadn't experienced for years. Even now she sensed a tingling within.

She tried to divert herself by watching television. The screen was grey, flickering. It showed a scene out of science fiction. But it was real, true. A replay of what had happened only hours before. Neil Armstrong had stepped from the lunar module called Eagle, and walked on the surface of the moon, saying, "That's one small step for man, one giant leap for mankind."

Though excited by what was happening, she couldn't keep her mind on it. She kept thinking about Ollie, telling herself that she mustn't see him again.

Still, when he called the following day to invite her to dinner, she couldn't refuse him. She was as eager to be with him as he was eager to be with her.

And, only hours after she agreed, a box of long-stemmed tea roses, their petals dewy and fragrant, were delivered to her.

That night they went to the Gay Hussar on Greek Street. The restaurant was a long narrow place, its candle-lit tables creating an aura of intimacy. Soft gypsy music filled the air, a background to their conversation.

When she thanked him for the roses, he said, "Thank you for seeing me." His eyes were on hers. "I was afraid you'd refuse." She didn't speak. He went on, "I understand how you feel, Claire. But I . . . I've thought of you so often. And I'm lonely. I'll never do anything to hurt Agatha. Still, my life goes on. It goes on," he said again. "As it must."

It was as if Agatha were dead, the wife that he'd known and loved, Claire thought. He needed someone. What was the harm if they spent a little while together?

She'd felt the same many times, hadn't she? She still felt the same. Needing someone to be close to, to care about, to love.

He touched her hand. "I'll never ask of you more than you want to give."

She smiled, and then, leading the conversation away from the personal to the general, she asked him what he was doing these days. He seemed relieved. He told her he spent most of his time in London, looking after his investments. He wanted to know more about her trip, about Gordon and David.

Later that week he took her and the boys to Brown's Hotel for tea. The lounge in which they were served was a Victorian period piece. They sat at a low round table covered with pale yellow linen. Gordon ate liberally from the three-tiered server. David had little, spoke not at all.

Ollie suggested activities that the boys might enjoy. A steamer ride on the Thames to Hampton Court's garden. Madame Tussaud's Waxworks on Marylebone Road. Without much enthusiasm, they accepted his offer to be their guide.

Ollie and Claire had their own time together alone, he pursuing her with ardour and kindness. There were flowers every week. Often he sent strawberries, huge ripe ones, that scented the small fridge in her room. Champagne arrived several times. And her most favourite of his gifts was a beautifully bound copy of *Sonnets from the Portuguese* by Elizabeth Barrett Browning.

Not long after he had given her those wonderful love poems, Ollie said, "There's a flat available on Weymouth Street. Just one block from Wimpole Street where Elizabeth Barrett lived when she first met Robert Browning. I'd like you to take it, Claire. To stay here."

"The boys . . ." she said.

"Put them in school. It'll do them good. I know of several close by London. I'll look into them for you, if you like."

She promised she would think about it, knowing that she wanted to stay, but uncertain if she should.

He held her hands tightly. "You can't go now, Claire. Not now, when I've just found you. You must give me, give yourself, a little more time."

In the end, she decided to stay. She moved into the two-bedroom flat on Weymouth Street, and Gordon and David were enrolled in Pattlewick Public School at Ascot, some twenty miles from London.

September that year was cold, the city gulfed in a grey drizzle that seemed to go on and on. The sidewalks were black and shiny with rain, and the grey stone buildings were speckled with it, but their window boxes were brilliant with colourful masses of asters.

Claire's flat looked down on Marylebone High Street, where limousines parked in front of the shops, and crowds of people walked by day. By night it was quiet, only the three pubs, and several coffee bars, open to customers.

Several weeks after she moved into the flat, Claire prepared a dinner at home for Ollie. Afterwards, as they sat drinking brandy together, he said, "I've been happier these last months than I can ever remember."

By then they were friends, able to talk about anything. He had told her about his life with Agatha. Claire had told him about her life with Leigh.

The exchange had freed them to know a closeness they had never known before. And that closeness inevitably led to that moment when they sat drinking brandy.

They belonged together, Claire thought. He needed her as much as she needed him.

She set aside her glass, and rose. She was wearing a loose fitting burgundy sheath that rippled and flowed around her. The glow of the chandelier seemed to be reflected in her eyes. She took him by both hands and drew him to his feet. As he smiled quizzically, she put her arms around him and drew him close.

There was no need for words. Their kiss was long and deep, both their bodies suddenly afire. That night they became lovers.

When she lay against Ollie, his arms enfolding her, she felt that she was part of him.

Autumn passed into winter. They were

together nearly every night. When they weren't making love, they went to dinner at Rule's, or the Grill Room at the Savoy. Often they returned to the Gay Hussar. Other evenings they went to Ollie's favourite gambling club, the Clermont. They attended concerts at the Royal Festival Hall and the Royal Albert Hall, and rode for fun on top of the red double-decker buses that clogged London's streets. Together they shopped for him in Jermyn Street, and for her on Brompton Road. Some days they visited the Victoria and Albert Museum and Tate's Gallery. Others they walked hand in hand on Charing Cross Road, visiting Foyle's and Zwemmer's. Sometimes they picked up Gordon and David at Pattlewick and took them to dinner in Ascot. Twice they flew to Paris for shopping and shows.

They had been together for three months by mid-November of 1969. One evening they watched television news reports of a massive anti-Vietnam War demonstration in Washington. Thousands had participated. Rank after rank passed before the camera. There were groups with long hair and jeans and jackets, the costume of the rebellious young. There were groups with conservative hair cuts and clothes. Women marched pushing babies in carriages. College professors walked arm in arm, carrying lighted candles. Vietnam War veterans, some in wheelchairs, were there.

Ollie and Claire were silent, absorbed in the spectacle. She was intent, staring hard at the crowds on the screen. Was that Elianne . . . the girl with waist-length hair? Or the one behind her . . . ? Ollie had his arm around Claire's shoulders. She leaned against him. The telephone rang. He sighed, and rose to answer it.

As he left her side, she felt a sudden chill. It was as if a cold wind had blown through the room.

He spoke softly, listened. Then he put down the phone. He turned to her. "I must go, Claire. Agatha has just died."

She said, "Ollie! Oh, Ollie!" and went to hug him.

A week after the funeral, he asked Claire to marry him the following year.

They were in the Weymouth Street flat. He had brought a small bunch of violets wrapped in a ruffle of Dutch lace. He'd put it into her hands, and then he'd placed a velvet box on top of it. Smiling, he said, "Open it, Claire."

She gave him a swift searching look, her heart suddenly beating quickly. She knew what he would say next. Joy and doubt swept her at the same time. She opened the box and saw the simple gold band set with fiery diamonds. She managed to whisper his name.

His arms closed around her. She burrowed close, holding him too.

"Marry me," he said, "I need you, Claire. I love you. And I know you love me."

She was close to saying, "Yes, yes, I will. I want to." And yet, as she tried to form the words, something held her back. She clung to him. "I must think, Ollie. Give me a little while . . ."

Weeks passed, and it remained impossible for her to come to a decision. She wanted to be Ollie's wife, yet she was afraid. Leigh had taught her to be afraid of love, and marriage, and now she didn't know how to find the courage to try once again.

Finally, thinking it would be easier to come to a decision away from Ollie's compelling presence, she made plans to return to Washington.

The boys protested as vehemently as they had originally protested against remaining in London. They were settling in at school, Gordon yelled. What did she think she was doing? he demanded. And when she tried to explain that it was time to go back to Hannah's Gate, to see how Dora was doing, he sneered, "It's Oliver Duvaney, isn't it? He's dumped you, hasn't he?"

"My relationship with Ollie is no concern of yours," she told him.

"I think it is. So does David."

David's thin face flushed as red as Gordon's full one, but he didn't speak.

She went ahead with her plans.

They sailed on the *United States*, and arrived home in January of 1970.

The newspapers were full of reports on the war in Viet Nam, and talk-ins on college campuses protesting against the war.

Claire and the boys had been away for a full seven months, but soon it was as if they'd never gone.

Dora was busy with her many social activities.

Claire found a private school that would accept Gordon and David in mid-term.

Brett Devlin came down from Boston to see her. He looked much older now, his colour poor, his hair greying. His limp was more noticeable than it had been. His son Keith was at Kent State now, eighteen years old and doing well. "He looks so much like Rea," Brett said. "He didn't when he was younger, did he?"

"A little." Claire smiled at Brett. "I'll write and invite him to come here for spring break. And you too, Brett. You come down then, if you possibly can."

"I'll make sure that I can," he promised.

Ollie called weekly from London. They didn't speak of the big question that lay between them. He was giving her time, she knew. But it was good to hear his voice and exchange pleasantries with him, to know that he thought of her, missed her. As for herself, she missed him. More and more she realized how much she needed him. The copy he had given her of the love poems by Elizabeth Barrett Browning was on the night table near her bed. She read it often, and thought of him.

At the end of April, American and South Vietnamese soldiers invaded Cambodia to keep North Vietnamese soldiers from using a Cambodian route to bring arms into South Viet Nam. Protests exploded on college campuses.

By then, Claire had decided that she would marry Ollie. She was planning the letter that would tell him, that would explain her long hesitation and how her need for him had wiped away all reservations.

She was planning the words she would use, when in May she heard of the shootings at Kent State and learned that Keith had been injured when the National Guard opened fire on demonstrating students.

She called Brett at once. He said, "It's bad, Claire. I'm leaving within moments."

"I'll meet you there," she told him.

As she made her preparations, she tried to believe that nothing could happen to Keith. He was too young. It would destroy Brett. Losing Rea had been terrible for him. To lose Keith now . . .

She met Brett at the hospital the following evening. Keith, she learned, would live. But he'd never walk again. "And yet," Brett said, "I'm so grateful that he's alive. Think of the other parents who've lost their sons and daughters."

Within weeks, Keith was at home in Boston with Brett.

Claire spoke to them often. They were managing well, Brett reported, but Claire thought he sounded tired. Keith was already adept with his wheel chair, and cheerful. He'd soon be working with a tutor, hoping to continue his education.

Once again Claire began to plan her letter to Ollie, and once again, she didn't write it.

In late summer, she had a call from Keith. "It's bad news, Aunt Claire," he said softly. "My father's dead."

On the plane to Boston Claire remembered the day Brett had rescued Rea and herself. She thought of him as she'd first seen him, when he came to enquire about Margo

417

Desales. His concern for Angelo Niro and his wife passed through her mind. After she arrived, she learned that Brett had risen at the usual time, and gone, as was usual also, into Keith's room, to say good morning. Then he'd started down the stairs. Keith had heard a pause in his footsteps, and a wordless cry. Then there had been a thud . . . Keith had wheeled himself to the head of the stairs. Brett lay motionless on the landing below. Later, when the ambulance came, it was decided that he'd had a cerebral haemorrhage.

Claire held tightly to Keith's hands as he told her about it. She wept with him at Brett's graveside.

A few days later, she returned to Hannah's Gate, bringing Keith with her.

Chapter 24

Washington's October sun laid shining bars on the carpet at Hannah's Gate. The sound of leaves wind-dancing along the terrace drifted in through the open window.

It was ten months since Claire had seen Ollie Duvaney. It would be three years in April, six months hence, since Leigh had died. Three years less three months since Elianne had gone away.

Claire thought of that as she held the letter she had received from Ollie that morning. 'Will you come to London soon?' he asked. 'Or shall I come to you in Washington? Say the word and I'll be there.'

She imagined the warmth of his arms around her. Suddenly her breasts seemed to swell against the blue cashmere of her sweater. Her body and heart yearned to love, to give love. Yet she was still unsure. She had needed love before, and been led into misery and pain. Did she want to risk that again? Did she dare to?

The sound of nearby laughter broke into her musings. Keith, Gordon and David were watching Saturday afternoon football, a ritual since the season began.

It was good to have Keith at Hannah's Gate. In spite of his disability, he'd made a place for himself. He was forward-looking, optimistic and remarkably mature for the twenty year old, it seemed to Claire. He had begun to exert a good influence on Gordon, and on David too.

Claire's concern for David had increased with time. At twelve he was tall, and exceedingly thin. He remained quiet, but sometimes, suddenly, his temper would flare. On most occasions, he would restrain himself. But once in a while he would explode into a violence that was shocking because it was impossible to predict what would provoke him.

On the other hand, Gordon was only too predictable. He wanted his own way. Always and forever, he was determined to do exactly what he pleased, when he pleased. He accepted discipline from no one, not even himself. He was too heavy for a boy of fourteen, his cheeks rounded, his shoulders and thighs full. His manners could be charming, as long as he wasn't contradicted or crossed. When he was, he became ugly. Before Leigh's death, he and David and Gordon had been a small club of three. The men against the women in the house. Then Gordon and David had a small club of two.

But Keith made a difference somehow. Perhaps it was because he has Rea's quick warm emotions. Perhaps because he had Brett's constant kindness. Rea and Brett's son . . . Claire's eyes suddenly stung with tears.

Why had he been deprived of a normal young manhood? Yet he wasn't bitter. He showed only a wondering acceptance as he spoke of what had happened to him at Kent State.

He was, he said, in the wrong place at the wrong time. He knew that was hard to believe, but that was how it was. He had been studying at the library that morning, and he had books in his arms, taking them back to his dorm. He saw the commotion . . . the kids yelling . . . the milling around . . . stones flying . . . the curses . . . the Commons bell ringing . . . There was a group of National Guardsmen chasing some students . . . The kids throwing rocks, shouting filth at them.

Keith stopped then to swallow, shake his head. There was a faraway look in his eyes as he went on, reminding her that the president had said back in April that 150,000 troops would be pulled out of Viet Nam by 1971. Instead there was the invasion of Cambodia. That's what the kids were yelling about, he said. And not all of them were. Not all were demonstrating. A bunch of them were onlookers, laughing . . . The sun was so bright. It was as if a cloud came up when the tear gas was fired. And afterward, he said, it was so strange that even with the bitter air, you could smell the sweetness of the grass. Then some guardsmen backed up a hill. The next thing Keith knew, they were kneeling, their guns up. Everyone started running. Keith did too. He couldn't believe it when he heard the shots. He felt as if he'd been kicked in the back. The next thing he knew, he was on the ground. He heard a girl screaming . . .

His voice faded. He said no more. He never spoke of it to her again.

With all her heart, Claire wanted to make up to him, as much as she could, what he had lost by being crippled. As long as he needed it, he would have a home and proper care. She would never turn her back on him.

She smoothed Ollie's letter on her knee. She would tell him she wasn't sure yet. She would say that he mustn't expect her to come to London now, nor should he come to Washington. But soon though, soon, she would let him know what she had decided.

Now again, she heard Keith's laughter mingling with David's and Gordon's. All three of them needed her. And what of Elianne? She must be here to continue the search for her lost daughter.

It was while she was still sitting there, beneath the portrait of Big Jack Gowan, thinking of the boys, of Elianne, and of Ollie, that she heard the ringing of the telephone. A moment later, Dora came to the door.

The older woman's face was white. She said in a whisper, "It's for you, Claire. I think . . . it may be . . ."

Claire's heart beat quickly. Who? What? She hurried to the phone in the hall. "Yes? This is Claire Merrill."

There was a moment of silence. The wires hummed. From somewhere far away there were garbled words.

Then, suddenly, a familiar voice said, "Mama, Mama, it's me. It's Elianne. May I come home? Is it all right?" And then, before Claire could respond, "Oh, Mama, I need so badly to come home."

A gush of hot burning tears filled Claire's eyes, and blurred her voice into a choked whisper, "Yes, Elianne . . . oh, yes. I'm waiting for you."

It was three years since she'd seen her only daughter. Three years of tears and prayers, of frequent dreams. Now . . .

"I'll be there as soon as I can," Elianne was saying. "It'll take a little while."

"Wait," Claire cried. "Tell me . . ."

"I'll be home," Elianne said. Again the hum of wires. But now there were no voices whispering distant words.

Claire slowly put down the phone. She turned to Dora. "You were right, Mom. It was Elianne. She's coming home."

Dora held Claire tightly in her arms. There was no need for words between them now.

Later that same evening Claire sat at her desk. It was time to write to Ollie Duvaney. It had been hard to come to her decision, and it was hard to write it. But, finally, after many false starts and fresh beginnings, she wept and sealed the envelope. She loved Ollie, and knew she always would. But she couldn't ask him to give up his life in London, to come to Washington and take on the burdens that were hers. No matter how she felt, she was needed here, and here she must stay. For the boys, for Keith, and for Elianne.

At the start of the following week she came down in the morning to find the kitchen empty, although there were used dishes and glasses on the table. She was surprised because her mother always rose early, set up breakfast for the boys, and saw Gordon and David off to school, and made sure that Keith was well started on his day. After that she ordinarily sat down to have a second cup of coffee while she read the newspaper. But today Dora wasn't there.

Now Claire heard the squeak of Keith's wheelchair, heard the outer door close. He appeared on the threshold. "Aunt Claire, is everything all right?"

"I think so," she said, but she was alarmed. Where was Dora?

"Gordon and David brought me down, and got themselves breakfast, and left for school. They haven't seen Grandma. I went out to the porch. The newspaper's still there." His young face was anxious.

It was a mirror of how she felt as she hurried upstairs to her mother's room. The door was closed. She opened it carefully. If her mother was sleeping, Claire didn't want to frighten her. Perhaps she'd had a bad night . . . she was sometimes bothered by insomnia. The room was dark and still.

Claire parted the curtains. A ray of light fell across the bed. Claire saw that her mother was asleep, head nestled against the pillow. She looked as small as a child in the big bed.

Claire backed slowly towards the door. She thought of the past week. She and her mother had spoken of nothing but Elianne's call. Together they had listened for her knock at the door, for the sound of her voice in greeting. Her mother had waited as hopefully, as hungrily as she herself had. The heartfelt expectation must have tired her. It would do her good to rest.

But then the hushed quality of the silence touched Claire. The room was totally soundless. She listened. There was nothing. Nothing.

She returned swiftly to the bed, touched her mother's cheek. It was cool. Now she saw that Dora's eyes were slightly open.

Claire understood. "Oh, Mama," she whispered. "Mama, I'm sorry."

With tears stinging her eyes, she left the room.

Dora Loving was buried on Sunday. It was a chilly but bright day. Huge chrysanthemums banked her grave.

Claire stood with Gordon and David and Keith in his chair, listening to the service.

On the far side, with the small group of mourners, including Anna Taylor and several other friends of Dora's, Carrie Day listened too.

She felt a surge of triumph. There went Dora Gowan Loving, mistress of Hannah's Gate, to her maker. And here remained Carrie Day, mistress of nothing and nobody. Oh, yes, here she remained. Hale and hearty, with at least twenty good years before her, and perhaps even more. It was a pity about her half-sister, Carrie supposed. Sixty-nine wasn't really old. Not in 1970. Still, it could be adjudged something of a miracle that Dora had lasted that long, considering the strange aura that hung over Hannah's Gate.

Some time later, in her studio apartment on Connecticut Avenue, Carrie sat at her old portable typewriter, once again thinking about the aura that hung over Hannah's Gate. Big Jack Gowan. Margo Desales. Linda Grant. Leigh Merrill. Rea Loving. All of them dead. Now Dora too. And Keith Devlin, a cripple at twenty.

Carrie's fingers picked slowly at the keys. Surely there was another story here. She closed her eyes briefly, imagining the funeral. The golden light. The flowers around the grave. The coffin covered with large wreaths. Claire and her two sons.

And what, Carrie asked herself, had happened to Claire's daughter? Carrie counted on her fingers. The girl would be about seventeen now. Shouldn't she have been there? Carrie made a brief note on a scrap of paper. She would find out.

Now she pushed herself away from the small desk, and went to the kitchen. It was only a few steps away.

The studio apartment was pleasant, a single

large room, with several good pieces of furniture. Fergie's grandmother's tea cart, a breakfront of light oak was filled with sugar pots and creamers and small serving dishes of Spode, Limoges and Haviland, all these left by Fergie, who had collected china.

Carrie took a big chocolate doughnut from the refrigerator. As she bit into it, her large frame expanded with delight. Oh, it was good, the taste of the doughnut and the comfort of the place she had made her home. True, it was nothing like Hannah's Gate, which, if luck had been on her side, could have been hers.

On the other hand, and here Carrie smiled, if she'd been Dora Gowan, instead of Carrie Day, she'd just have been buried this cold Sunday afternoon.

That reminded her of the aura that hung over Hannah's Gate. Still eating the doughnut, she went back to her desk.

Chapter 25

Early that morning there had been a four-inch snowfall, unusual for the first week of November. By noon, the temperature had fallen by five degrees and Honey Locust Lane glistened with a frozen white crust.

At the crunch of tyres pulling slowly up the hill, Claire looked out of the window. A taxi passed by, disappeared, then rolled back to nose into the driveway.

Not a moment had passed since Elianne's telephone call that Claire didn't think of her words. "Mama, can I come home? Is it all right?" And: "It'll take a little while. But I'll be there."

It was a month since she had heard Elianne's voice. A month, in which so much had happened. Her mother had died and been buried. She had written her goodbyes to Ollie. Now, having waited so long, she watched the taxi pull into the driveway.

Oh, please, please, she thought. Let it be Elianne. Let her come home now.

The door opened. A tall, straight-backed figure emerged.

Ollie! Here!

He leaned in at the taxi window to speak to the driver.

Claire suddenly found herself on the front porch. Ollie! He was here!

He stood at the foot of the steps, looking up at her. "I want to be with you," he said. "With you, and the boys. I want to help you with Elianne. We belong together. Whatever needs to be done, we'll do it together."

She had been afraid to trust love before, but that fear was gone now. Her love was here, with her.

"Oh, Ollie, yes," she said, and went into his open arms.